Three Bullets

A Novel By

Jeff Lightly

FejjMo Publishing, LLC

Published by FejjMo Publishing, LLC, Des Moines, Iowa

Published 2025

Cover design and photography by Jeff Lightly

ISBN: 979-8-9918743-0-4 (pb)

ISBN: 979-8-9918743-1-1 (epub)

For my mom, Ruth Lightly, who never stopped believing in me.

It is mine to avenge; I will repay. In due time their foot will slip; their day of disaster is near and their doom rushes upon them.

Deuteronomy 32:35

In The Beginning There Is An End

May 19, 1977, Thursday night, 9:14

TWO EXPLOSIONS TORE THROUGH the night air. The shock waves left the vehicle's occupants' ears ringing. The man felt such pain, more intense than any he'd ever experienced as it gripped his upper body. His breath faltered. He gasped for air, smelling the powerful odor of burnt gunpowder. His left arm was now a numb, lifeless appendage. Strange, other-worldly, and muffled sounds ebbed and flowed around him, breath-like and pulsing.

He trembled, a dread enveloping his entire being, far more profound than mere fear. He sensed the darkness behind him. This pang grabbed his soul and crushed his spirit. He shuddered, sensing the end rushing his way.

His eyes opened; two narrow slits. Everything was blurry as his eyelids fluttered open and closed multiple times, trying to focus. Regaining a sense of clarity was a struggle. The right side of his balding head, with close-cropped graying hair along the sides, bounced off the passenger window. A fuzzy glow from the orange-tinted sodium street lights flickered and faded across the dashboard. The lights washed across his face as the car rolled down the freeway; destination, unknown. His ears rang with a confusing mix of sounds. The tires created a steady hum, and an occasional clap-clump, clap-clump as the tires slapped the pavement when they traveled over a bridge. He heard two men yelling at each other.

Blood trickled down the white leather interior. It soaked the doorsill as it descended; it flowed down to the crack in the door. There, the wind caught the red gore, fanning it out along the side of the automobile.

His eyes widened. His body tensed as he ignored the pain. Who's blood is that? My god, is that mine? It is! What is happening to me? Why am I here? And just where is here?

Those thoughts raced through his mind, one on top of another. The pain in his shoulder was relentless, and the man wondered if he'd ever catch his breath. An odd, wet-sounding wheeze rattled with every exhale. The fear surged forward again. Heart pounding, the memories flooded back.

Two strangers, one stood just outside the garage door as he pulled up to the townhouse complex. One man brandished a gun, tapping it against his thigh. The other man, quite diminutive in stature, snuck up behind him. He made a slow, sweeping motion with his hand, and without speaking a word, he ordered him to pull the Cadillac forward, out of the light, and into his garage. Once out of public view, both men raised their arms. He stopped his car.

He snapped back to the present. That crushing dread surrounded him again. He shifted his attention as he thought of his daughter, wishing to be near her again. How to get out of this mess? He tried to shift to the left, but the agony in his shoulder and the sticky, metallic taste of blood in his mouth made him stop. Weakness overpowered him, and the fear screamed at him. His thoughts drifted in and out of focus.

Sounding as if underwater, a muffled voice said, " ... like a mob hit. It'll throw the cops off the trail." That's not possible. Did he understand that correctly? He wanted to tell them, let them know they were mistaken. He was no mobster. Why did they say this? It just made no sense. Maybe he misheard. His mind and heart raced at a frantic pace.

The two strangers yelled at each other again, but the muffled words rendered them unintelligible. It reminded the man of times that, as a very young boy, he would rest in his mother's arms, drifting off to sleep. He could almost hear her talking to other adults as they sat around the kitchen table, voices deep, soft, and comforting. Despite all the agony, a smile crossed his face. Inner peace chased the terror.

The yelling continued, and the peace he felt evaporated. As he shifted his focus to the present, he knew he had to make a move, and he had to do it now.

Make eye contact with them and talk to them, he told himself, believing words could get him out of this trouble. He'd always been an excellent negotiator. Tell them he would get them money, they could have his car, his watch, whatever they wanted.

Could he escape this nightmare? He turned his head towards the driver. Through half-opened eyes, he saw the gun barrel and felt the weapon's hard steel end as it pressed against his temple. His bloodshot eyes bulged wide with fear. He tilted his body to the right, pushing his head into the soft padding of the passenger door. The gun barrel followed him, pressed firm and uncomfortable against his bare skin. What else was there to say? How could he save himself? His mouth opened to speak.

In an instant, a bright flash of light filled the interior of the car. He never heard another sound; never uttered another word.

Anthony Warren Werner never thought of anything else ever again.

The Victim - Minding His Business

Eleven days earlier ... May 8, 1977, Sunday morning, 6:30

A MOMENT OF SORROW caught Anthony Werner off guard as he dried and stacked the few dishes he used for breakfast. It had been a decade since his wife had died of cancer and he often mourned her. Kathy was his true love. These simple moments in life gave him pause. Melancholy would wash over him. Sadness would grab at him, as it regularly happened while doing those unremarkable chores; vacuuming, dusting, or cleaning a window. He knew he had to visit her whenever this heartache would burn.

He would gaze towards the sky and talk to her. "What fun is it, having all these nice things, these beautiful trinkets and objects when you are not here? There is our daughter, she has enjoyed them. It's not the same without you, Kathy. And don't even give me any guff concerning my dating life. It occupies my time. Doing something with someone, nothing more. Without you, trips to the market, movies, restaurants, and all of life's joys are torture. It's as simple as that. I wish you had never left us, that the doctors could have helped more. And I can hear you now, 'Tony, don't mope. And don't be so sad!' See you soon, Kathy."

He dried off his hands, grabbed his keys, and crossed the parking lot to his garage. Anthony breathed in the cool dawn air and unlocked the side door of his garage. A thin film of dust danced in the early morning sunlight that burned through the windows as he climbed into his car. As a lifelong Cadillac owner, this 1977 Coupe de Ville caught his eye on the dealer's lot. The white exterior with a white interior was something he'd not seen before, and he loved it. The dealer mentioned that the man who ordered the fine automobile filed for bankruptcy. That stopped the deal in its tracks. Tony bought the car the first day he saw it, three short weeks ago.

Before leaving, he popped the trunk open and made sure he had his cleaning supplies he kept in a small box. "This trip will do me good," he said as he shut the trunk.

Kathy's gravesite was a thirty-minute drive out in the country near the farm where she was raised. The dark green fields of grain, rolling hills, and stretches of flatland were beautiful, peaceful, and timeless.

"Oh, I love how tranquil it is out here," he once said to her.

"Me too. What a wonderful space to spend eternity together," whispered her voice in his memory as the cityscape turned to farmland.

Anthony felt the fresh country air the second he stepped out of his car and onto the cemetery grounds. "Let's get your stone tidied up. What do you say, Kathy?" he asked as he reached for the box inside the trunk.

He kneeled next to their shared headstone, crossed himself, and hung his head in silence for several minutes. Small tears formed in the corners of his eyes. He read the lettering etched in the stone, as he'd done countless times. 'Katharine Louise Werner 1918-1967' and next to that, 'Anthony Warren Werner 1916-'. His eyes stopped at the blank space after his year of birth and he wondered when the engraver would carve the numbers. What would it say?

"Alright, Tony, snap out of it. Let's get after it! Hmm, looks like a country crow left you a present, Kathy. Gosh, those crows always scared you." He didn't hide his laughter. "Sorry for laughing, dear, but I can remember the time there was a mother bird that would not leave you alone. You spent half the summer walking across the yard instead of the sidewalk to avoid that bird and her nest! Oh, how you would scream!" He took a deep breath and sprayed water on the stone with an extra squirt for the bird's business. His hands made slow, sweeping circles, swirling a damp rag across the granite face. A sad smile crossed his face as he pictured her last days of suffering. When he was done, the stone was shining, and he had clipped the grass along the edges, as expert as any gardener. He was careful to scoop up the cut blades and disperse them in the gravel drive next to his vehicle. He walked back to collect his box of supplies, kissed the palm of his hand, and placed it against her name.

"You've been gone for ten years. I just can't believe that. Sometimes I'm afraid I might not remember the sound of your voice. I would rather die than forget anything about you. Until next time, my love."

Anthony always enjoyed the drive back into the city. It allowed him a chance to reflect. Behind his car, a slow-motion rooster tail of gravel dust gave way to the muted sound of tires on the blacktop. The countryside changed to cityscape. His mind shifted from the past to the present. He was always aware of this transformation. It never failed to refresh his soul.

Once back in town, he stopped off at the gas station to have his tank refilled.

"Mr. Werner. Great to see you!" said the attendant.

"Hi Tommy. Just fill it up, please. I'll get a car wash later. Need to get back home in a hurry."

"You got it."

With the car fueled up, Anthony took a side trip to the home of his daughter, Kaylie. He often dropped by unannounced, and she was always glad to see him.

"There's my little girl," he said to himself, "getting her flower bed ready." He pulled into her driveway and rolled down the passenger window. "Hey, you! Prepping your plants for summer, are you?"

"Daddy!" She pulled herself up, brushed the dirt off of her jeans, and ran over to the open window. "Hi! What a surprise. What are you doing out this beautiful morning?"

"I was out visiting your mom's grave and heading home."

"Oh, Daddy, how nice! I'm going to place some flowers there soon. Does everything look OK out there today?"

"Yes, fine, fine. Everything there is looking good. I just did some cleanup."

"Hey, your eyes look a little red. Are you OK?"

"Yes, the visit made me sad today, realizing that it's been ten years since ... well."

"I know. Would you like to come in? Adam was planning on stopping over around noon for lunch. Please join us."

"Thanks, but I'm going to head home, maybe stay away from work today. I just wanted to see you and to tell you I love you."

She ran around the back of his car and pulled his door open. "I love you very much!" she said as she planted a kiss on his forehead. "Not working tonight, you say? I don't believe that for an instant!"

"I don't believe it either," he winked at her, "but I am going to go home. Call me later this week."

"I will call you soon. Love you, Daddy."

"Love you too, little girl."

Anthony pulled out of her drive and was back in his townhouse fifteen minutes later. Hunkered down at the desk in his home office, he laughed, "You know me too well, Kaylie." He opened his briefcase and started reviewing his next project, another home remodel.

The phone rang, breaking his concentration. He picked up the receiver. "Hello, this is Anthony."

"Hi Dad! It's Kaylie. I wanted to make sure you're OK. I've been thinking about her a lot, too."

"I'm doing fine, honest."

"You're working right now, aren't you?"

He let out a deep-from-the-gut belly laugh.

"I knew it! I just knew it. Daddy, go to bed early."

"Yes ma'am. We'll talk soon, Kaylie."

"Bye-bye, Daddy." And after he hung up, she added, "I'd do anything for that man!"

The Killer - Needs A Score

May 8, 1977, Sunday morning, 11:52

DALE BOWERS WAS DEAD broke and looking to make some cash. He had no problem getting money any way he could, legal or not. Having no steady income was typical for Dale. Convicted felons with bad tempers make prospective employers look elsewhere.

The interior of the convenience store was bustling with customers paying for gas, making their way to the self-serve coffee machine, or just hanging out to pass the time. He was about to have a chance encounter that would be a life changer, and not just his.

Dale pushed the door open with the middle of his back and stepped out into the midday air. He held an unopened pack of cigarettes in one hand and an overcooked, greasy hot dog in the other. As the door shut behind him, a rusty, oil-burning Volkswagen clanked and clamored into the parking lot.

"Hey you old son of a bitch!" the man yelled and cackled through the open front passenger window.

Dale, somewhat startled, shot his eyes toward the voice, his body tensing. His fight instinct subsided once he recognized the man.

These two men first met three years earlier in, what never seemed to them to be an odd meeting place, the county jail. He had spent the night in lockup on a drunk and disorderly charge after getting into a fight in a bar. His new friend was finishing up a six-month stint for burglary.

"Well, shit! How the hell are ya, Big Man?" said Dale as he opened the passenger door, uninvited.

Dale slapped the man on his shoulder and he flopped down on the front passenger seat as if he owned the place. He took several bites of the hot dog, smacking his lips with each bite.

"Again with the 'Big Man'? You know I hate that name, dude."

"Gordo, don't be so sensitive, man. I only call you that, so I don't confuse you with all the other Gordons I know. There's a lot of guys named Gordon in this world!"

"Bullshit, even I don't know any other guys named Gordon!"

"Plus, I just like busting your balls when I see you. Damn, good to see you."

The old cellmate, Gordon Thompson, had the ironic street name, 'Big Man', because of his short stature. The running joke among his felonious friends was that he was five foot-one when he had blisters on his feet and weighed almost 110 pounds soaking wet with a full stomach. Everyone who knew him would laugh at his nickname, but he despised the moniker. Out of desperation, he dealt with it — he had to belong *somewhere*.

"What have you been up to, Dale? Staying out of lockup, I hope."

"Yeah, mostly, I've avoided county. I've been looking to earn some money," he said, pulling an empty jean pocket inside out.

"It's tough out there. I have a buddy in construction. Want a construction job?"

"No, I do not. They wouldn't want me either, if they checked my record."

"What are you wanting to do?"

"Nobody is going to want to hire this old convict. Doesn't leave me with too many choices."

"So, jobs that are less than legit? Got it." Gordon was someone who kept his eyes open for opportunities, both for himself and his friends, legal or otherwise. "Well, I know a guy who might have something for you. I've been trying to keep my nose clean, so I try to avoid him. Now, he mentioned this one side job the other day."

"Who've you been talking to and what's the job?"

"This guy's name is Steve. Does construction — same guy who might know of construction jobs — but he talked about a guy he knows that would be easy to roll. Like I said, I'm trying to avoid that line of work. I didn't pay much attention to details."

"Can you talk to him? Maybe set up a meeting between him and me? I'm about out of money, man."

"Let me try to talk to this guy and I'll get something set up. How do I get back to ya?"

"Meet me down the street at that car lot," he said, pointing over Big Man's right shoulder, "tonight at five o'clock. If anybody gets nosy, we're just looking at the used cars. Bring this piece of shit to make that story believable."

Big Man laughed, but Dale stared him down with a deadly serious look.

"Five will work. I have to meet my parole officer at three thirty," said Big Man, holding up an official-looking letter. "But don't worry, I'll be there. It's just that, damn, you're kind of rushing me on this."

"I'm kinda fucking broke, so I need this, OK? I suppose you need a cut, too."

"Damn, take it easy Dale, take it easy. I don't want nothing, alright? Not a fucking thing, man. Consider it a favor as old cell mates, OK? Maybe down the line something big comes up. Keep me in mind."

Dale let out a long, slow exhale and climbed out of the car.

"Listen, man, I'll get the scoop on this for you tonight. Promise. And I don't want a cut, really." Big Man smiled at Dale as he stuffed the letter in his back pocket. By now, he just wanted to get out of there as soon as he could. He was already sorry he stopped at that convenience store.

"Yeah, don't be late," said Dale, slapping his hand on the roof of the car. And as he walked away from Big Man, he said, out of earshot, "Bullshit, everyone wants something."

Big Man, forgetting why he stopped at the store, drove away. His car still making noises and puffing smoke. "Just do him this favor and walk away Gordon, easy money is too tempting," he said, feeling sick to his stomach.

After walking off to the side of the store and up a small hill, Dale sat himself on the ground against a large maple tree. He had nowhere to go and no one else to see the rest of the day. He'd just wait until 5:00 p.m. and walk over to the car lot. The steady hum of traffic and the wind rustling the leaves above his head relaxed him.

"Ah, this is the life," he said. Even he didn't believe that as he drifted off to sleep.

Dale woke up with the sun in his eyes, the big maple tree no longer shading him. "Shit! What time is it?" he asked, but he was alone. He looked at his left wrist but only saw the pale outline of a watch he used to own, having pawned it five days earlier. The pawn shop owner gave him eight bucks for the watch, out of pity. It only provided enough for a couple of small meals and the hot dog and pack of cigarettes he had today. Dale ran down the hill to the convenience store. A young woman with short blonde hair was getting out of a silver Datsun. "Excuse me, pretty lady. Can you tell me what time it is?" he asked her.

She stopped, looked at him from head to toe, and shook her head. "No, I don't have my watch with me."

She entered the store as Dale kept asking people for the time. "That guy bugs me," she said to the cashier. "I don't like his looks."

"That guy is bad news. Stay away from that one," replied the cashier.

"Four forty-five, young man," said a passing customer.

"Thank you sir," said Dale, "you made my day." Dale turned and walked down the street to the car lot. He leaned against a concrete pillar that held the large signpost of the dealer. The sign's sharp red and blue letters on a field of white plastic proclaimed, '*Wheeler Motors — Buy and Sell — Wheel 'er In Or Wheel 'er Out*'.

Dale opened up his new pack of cigarettes and lit one up, slowly exhaling the smoke.

"Hey buddy, we can't have you loitering. You need to move along," said a man dressed in slacks, a short-sleeve shirt, and a very short tie.

"Yeah, well, I'm a customer. More like a buddy of mine is. He should pull in soon, driving an old smoking shit box. I told him I'd meet him here and I'd help find a new car. My friend doesn't know cars very well."

"My mistake. Do you know what your friend is looking for or how much he wants to spend?"

"No, I don't. I figured him and I could just walk around by ourselves first and then come in and deal."

"Sure, if you want to do that. We're open until seven," said the salesman. He headed back inside, but kept a close eye on Dale.

At precisely five o'clock, Big Man pulled into the lot and parked behind a row of used cars.

Dale walked up to the driver's side window. "Well, give me some good news."

"Steve will meet you tomorrow. He figured he'll get off work around five-thirty so you two can talk then. There's a guy he has in mind. Same guy as I mentioned to you earlier."

"So where do I meet him?"

"He's doing construction on the west side. He'll be on a new road called, get this, Peaceful Valley Lane. Who names these streets anyway? To get to this new street, go three or four blocks west of 56th Street off of Lincoln. Do you have a car or need a ride?"

"I have a car, just conserving the gas. I'll handle it from here. Thanks buddy, I owe you one."

"Forget it Dale," said Big Man, "you know I got your back."

Dale spied the car dealer stepping outside, and he was heading their way. "Crap, let's get out of here. That guy thinks you're going to buy a car."

"I can't afford a car, Dale!" said Big Man as he fired up his car. Dale climbed in the front. Chugging and smoking, they rolled off down the street and out of sight.

"Yeah, your buddy's going to buy a car. Bullshit, he didn't even get out. You bum!" yelled the car dealer.

The Killer - You've Got My Attention

DALE HOPPED OUT OF his car and walked toward a nearby construction site; one of many popping up all over the western edge of the city as more and more families began fleeing the inner city. It appealed to many who traded cracked concrete and crime for lush, green lawns and a perceived sense of safety. A steady breeze carried the sounds of screaming circular saws, heavy equipment clattering and belching diesel smoke, and unending dust. But he didn't care about any construction job. He wouldn't work that hard for scraps. He would never consider joining suburbia.

Dale had rushed over to this side of town after meeting with Big Man about this new contact, Steve. He was assured that Steve would talk to him. Sweat beaded on his brow as he looked around the construction site for this lead. Framed houses stood in various states of construction, stretching up a sloping hill and out of sight. Most saw construction projects such as this as advancing society, a hope for tomorrow. Dale could only see what he could steal. Table saws, toolboxes full of expensive tools, and machinery. He wasn't much for ideals, just dollar signs.

He was told that Steve was a big, hulk of a man, standing around six foot three and at least 250 pounds. Dale spotted him right away and raised his arm up, waist-high, to catch his attention. He smirked a bit, thinking how odd Big Man must look next to this mountain. Steve half-jogged over, a pleasant smile on his face which was smudged with dirt; sawdust stuck in his curly brown hair.

"Dale?" he asked.

"Yeah, you Steve?"

"Sure am. How's it going, bud?"

"I'm all right. Hey, cool shirt. I've been to that bar a few times," he said, pointing at Steve's worn shirt that read Doc Andrews' Riverside Lounge.

"Yeah, me too. In fact, I helped Doc pour the concrete for the patio that runs along the river. He was a great guy, but the cancer got him not long after we finished that concrete job."

"Hey, sorry, I hadn't heard that. Look man, I'm going to get right to this; who is this dude you told Big Man about, and how do you know all this shit about him?" He had to shout above the high-pitched scream of a nearby table saw.

"Whoa, slow down, slow down. Come on, hop into my office, buddy. Let's keep this between just you and me."

Steve, still smiling, motioned him towards his pickup as he scanned the surrounding area. Though he kept that smile on his face, he took this activity seriously and kept track of his environment. He was not one to take reckless chances.

The two men climbed into an old rusty truck, the dust from their workday clothes puffing up in the air as they sat down.

"Whew, it is a hot one today," Steve sighed as he pulled a Coke can out of a small cooler that sat between the two men. "Want one?"

"Yeah, thanks," said Dale. Beads of water rolled down the cold can. Small chunks of ice were still on top. He deftly popped the can open and drank half the can in no time.

"So anyway," Steve continued, "this guy is one fucking rich guy. He always, and I mean always, carries around a huge wad of cash in his pocket. He'll sit there and peel off the twenties to hand out to the guys, right there in front of God and everyone at the job site. And fancy cars too. The man loves Caddies. You won't see him without a flashy watch. Oh, and diamond rings! It's like he collects 'em or something. He's usually got two or three on at one time, big ones. One of them is always on his pinky finger, like he's some fucking mobster or something."

"Mobster, huh?" Dale laughed nervously.

"Man, he's not connected, nuh-uh, don't worry about that," assured Steve. "In fact, if a person were to do this right, they'd just have to wave a gun in his face and he'd just give it all up. Probably head right back to the bank and refill his money clip, then have his insurance dude buy him some new jewelry. He'd be fine. Wouldn't change his life a bit. Not. One. Bit."

"So you say he carries a stash of money on him, huh?"

"He sure does. Like two or three thousand bucks at a time!"

"You mean two or three hundred, right?"

"No man, thousand! Two or three thousand!"

"Holy shit, dude! I'm liking this more and more," Dale fidgeted as his mind began to race. "That's cash-money that would make a difference. My god! That money might not matter to that rich bastard as much but, shit, that'd change my damn life!"

"I'm sure it will man, I'm sure it will," said Steve. "Dang, that sun is bearing down on me. It's like a kid aiming a magnifying glass at an ant. You ever do that as a kid?"

Dale looked off into the distance, squinting as the late afternoon sun hung just above the tree line that marked the end of the housing development. He was both dreaming of that money and scheming how to make it happen. Such was his life, dreaming and scheming. But he also didn't know this guy at all and that put him on his guard. The magnifying glass question didn't merit a response.

Dale's body tensed up, startling Steve. A serious, menacing look on his face seemed to transform him; it exposed the evil within.

"And how do you know all this?" Dale asked slowly, almost pausing between words as he turned his dark gaze towards Steve.

"Uh, me and some buddies have done some work for him off and on. Dug some footings, and poured a sidewalk or two. Did some shit work for some remodeling job. Grunt work, like hauling out old flooring or drywall, whatever he needed to be done. He always pays in cash for those jobs, leaving Uncle Sam out of the picture, ya see?" Steve laughed a bit at the thought that he was putting one over on the government.

"Dude carries that much cash. He must be packing, right? So tell me, Steve, how do I find this guy? Where does this guy live?"

"Never saw him with a gun, but he'd be smart to have one. I don't know where the dude lives. West side of town, I'd guess. I've got some friends that might know where he's gonna be, act like I'm looking for some work. I can check around and let you - oh shit, look at the time, man! Five till six! Sorry man, but, damn, I gotta get outta here. Little woman's dumb-ass kid has a baseball game I have to go to or else my ass *will* be in a sling. What are you doing tomorrow? We can meet up here and I may be able to show you where he lives. Deal? I should be done working by five."

"You got it, man. I'll be here. And hey, this is just between us, understand?"

"Sure man, sure. Don't worry about me."

Dale gave him a quick head nod as he opened the pickup's squeaky door and hopped out onto the dusty ground. Dale caught the truck's door before it shut and tucked his head inside the cab.

"One more thing — what's in this for you?"

"Me? Maybe I need a favor from you down the road. Sometimes people get in my way and they need some encouragement to move along. I'd expect you to come through for me when I ask," Steve replied in a rare moment of seriousness.

"I like your style, man. You come through for me and I'll be there for you when you need it," Dale said as he slammed the door and slowly began walking to his car. He had purposely left it parked almost two blocks away.

Steve started up his old pickup and smiled. "Lordy, I fuckin' hate baseball!"

He put the truck in gear, drove over the curb and onto the paved street. Tools and lumber in the bed of his truck, hopping up and down, banged as he drove away. The dust swirled behind his truck as he headed to a Little League ballgame that he didn't want to watch.

As Dale approached his car, he was planning out this score, wanting to expand on it. For that, he'd need a partner or two. He was going to have to talk to Big Man again. Maybe his former cellmate would get something out of this after all.

Dale leaned against his car, a beat-up white Dodge Dart he got by trading a week's worth of hard labor tearing down a farmer's old barn. The car was tucked away in a corner of the doomed barn, blanketed in dust. Dale, in dire need of transportation, had asked about the car and the barter was complete.

A dirty gray shirt hung from his thin but muscular frame, a body built by hard, back-breaking work. He usually had little money for food beyond the basics; which also helped to keep him lean. Reaching into his front pocket, he pulled out a pack of cigarettes and his lighter. He deftly pulled a single cigarette out of the pack with his front teeth and, as was his habit, began flipping the lid of his lighter ... open ... shut ... open ... shut.

He stopped to light up and looked at the old lighter he held in his hand. It was a Zippo given to him by his father on Dale's sixteenth birthday. The well-worn lighter still proudly advertised '*Zippo. The Name in Flame*' on one side and '*New Mexico, Land of Enchantment*' on the other. He thought of his parents, Pa and Mama as he called them, and half-grimaced, half-smiled.

"Wonder what bullshit you two up to tonight?" he mumbled as he put the cigarette pack and lighter back into his pocket. The blue-gray smoke escaped from his mouth as he spoke, drifting up into nothingness.

He opened the driver's side door and slid behind the wheel, pushing away empty paper cups, burger wrappers, and other accumulated odds and ends that littered the front bench seat. Aside from flopping at a friend's house or taking some bar fly back to her place, Dale had spent most of the past four months living out of this car.

"Gotta get moving," he said to no one as he turned the key.

The starter gave a weak click-click-click and then fell silent.

He gave the key another turn. Complete silence.

Dale's eyes turned blood-red with anger and rage. The fury was always just *there*, just under the surface, ready to leap out of him. It began churning over and over in his brain, a hateful flow. He knew that he would have to take this out on someone, sometime. Soon.

The Accomplices - You're Driving

May 10, 1977, Tuesday afternoon, 1:43

"Met with your buddy Steve yesterday and he's going to get me the lowdown on where to find this rich dude. He sounds legit and this guy he knows — Werner's his name — he's loaded and an easy mark. Your friend has some more information for me. Then we'll be ready to move on our mark," said Dale.

"Good to hear that Dale!" said Big Man, "See, I told you this guy would come through, didn't I?"

"Yep, you were right. Now listen up Gordo." Big Man smiled. He almost never got called anything close to his actual name. "I need a favor," continued Dale. "You gotta drive this guy's car."

Big Man squirmed.

"And we're gonna need a truck. We need to run over to JB's and convince him to join us."

"John? You want John in on this too? I don't trust that shifty little bastard. He'll screw us over if it suits him, Dale, I'm telling you. Plus, the plan is for me to drive this dude's car? Why is this thing getting bigger and bigger, Dale? Damn, I don't know. That old Dodge of JB's? I don't trust that old thing either."

Dale laughed, "Trust? Who fucking trusts anyone or anything anymore, huh? We all need some damn money and you know it. This is how we usually get it. This one is solid! Plus, it's JB, man. He'll be cool when he's a part of it. Besides, that pickup truck will hold a ton of power tools we can fence later on. Driving a car ain't a big deal. It's a good score for all of us."

Big Man turned pale. "Why me? Why not John? Couldn't everyone be in John's truck? Why not have the old man drive? We could just leave him tied up at a construction site when we're done. How about that? Wouldn't something like that work?"

"I can't hardly hold a gun on the guy and drive myself. I doubt the old man will drive me around town, showing me all the sights. A lot can go wrong. Having all four of us in JB's truck? Now you're just being stupid."

"Do you want to go to prison? You're not just going to rob him? That was the original plan. Where are you taking him?"

"Where *we* are taking him will make it easy to bump this score up. Steve mentioned the guy could have two or three grand on him. What if he doesn't? That big company of his keeps busy. Gonna have him show us some job sites and grab some high-dollar tools. You and John will look over the job sites we go to and grab the good stuff. We move on to the next one until the truck is full. It'll just look like workers coming to grab the tools they need. If anybody questions what we're doing, I'll just tell this fool to yell out the window that it's OK, that he's the boss man, and that you guys work for him. We can sell that if needed. Later on, we go on some road trips and pawn the stuff. That'll be the fun part, Big Man; money, women, drinking, and partying. Doesn't that sound good to you? It does to me!"

"I figured this would be a quick, two-minute job. Grab his money and jewelry and get out. Now you want to drive this sucker all over town?" said Big Man.

"If you wanna act like a little bitch, then you can leave now, no hard feelings. Of course, I'll be done with your chicken-shit ass, but it's up to you."

Big Man shoved his hands in his pockets and looked down at his feet, thinking before saying, "Fine, I'm in. It'll be fine. I'm in, OK?"

"That's a good boy. Don't look so sad, little buddy. Think of all that money."

"Good boy? Good boy? I ain't no fucking boy," thought Big Man. He didn't dare say it out loud, but he was getting tired of hearing it from Dale.

The Killer - Specifics

May 11, 1977, Wednesday afternoon, 4:58

"RIGHT ON TIME, DALE! How's it hanging, man?" asked Steve. He was still dust-covered and the work site was still noisy.

"I'm all right. Let's hop in your truck so we can talk."

The two men once again climbed into Steve's truck, the sun beating down on them through the dusty windshield.

"Sorry, I don't have any Coke for you. I ran out of them at lunch."

"Well, all I care about is tracking down this guy. What do you have for me?"

"I got some decent info you can use. Ran into a buddy at the bar last night; we've both done work for this Werner guy. So I asked him if he's heard of any work. Well, he wasn't sure if the guy had any work right now, so I asked him how to get ahold of this dude because I need some coin, you know?"

Dale only stared at him, waiting for him to get to the point as sweat trickled down the side of his face.

"The guy has an office on the west side of town called Werner Custom Builders. Something like that. I guess it's on West Scott Avenue, right around 66th Street. It's a dark brown brick building. One of those setups that has five or six other businesses next door to each other."

"You expect me to just drop by the office and say hello, give me some money? What the hell, man?"

"That supposed to be fucking funny? No man, I figure you could follow him from there and maybe find out where he lives. He should be easy to spot, too. My friend said he just bought a brand new white Cadillac, two-door. Might be a de Ville. So, if you see that car, you can bet that he's there. Another guy I know says he goes to a nearby Italian place every Thursday night. He has a lady friend he takes there like clockwork. That's another lead for you. Those are the choices I have for you today. I can ask around some more but I don't want to look too eager, so it might take two or three weeks; I'm going to lie low about this guy."

"No, I don't want to wait that long. I can't wait. I'm flat broke. This should work. I'll go scope the place out after I leave here. You want to go grab a beer?"

"Thought you said you were broke? I'm kidding, man, but I can't tonight."

"Another ballgame to see?"

"No, her mom is coming over and I'm grilling out tonight. Ha! You know what? That was the worst ballgame I've ever seen. My old lady's kid is a terrible ballplayer. I'm telling you, he couldn't catch a cold. Poor kid is ugly too! The old lady is kind of cute, so whoever pa is must be a sight! "

"I think I can make this work. I owe you one."

"Damn straight you do, buddy. Just be cool."

"Yeah, you too."

With that, Dale began his walk back across town, passing his broken-down car on the way. It became a reminder of the pathetic life he led; damaged, alone, no one caring about him.

And there came the rage again.

Dale walked almost four miles to get back to what he considered his side of town. He walked past the used car lot where Big Man met up with him. "Damn, the Camaro is still there. Hey you big beautiful blue Chevy, I hope to make a score big enough to scoop you right off the lot. That's my kind of car."

As he stood there, he could sense that eyes were on him. He kneeled down, pretending to tie his worn work boots. He peered between his thigh and forearm and sure enough, he was right. "Damn cop. Just looking at cars, and he's gotta get nosy." He looked back at his boots and gave them a quick dusting. The squad car pulled away, the breeze from the passing car blew dust in Dale's face. "Control yourself Dale, don't be stupid. He's leaving."

"Hey buddy, can I interest you in a car?" asked the sales attendant.

Dale stood up and tugged on his shirt. "Maybe in a week. I sure love the blue Camaro you have. She's a beaut!"

"Isn't she? I'll bet she won't last that long. I'm just saying, it'll be a quick sell. Hell, my friend, I might sell it yet today."

"Yeah, I know. Money is tight today. I am aiming to make some soon."

"If you got any money to put down, I'd love to hold it for you."

"Look, I don't have any money. Not a fucking cent! I need you to back off, man!"

"Hey, no sense of swearing and getting all upset. I was just trying to help you out."

"Well, I don't need any help." Dale, shoulders pulled back, walked across the street to the convenience store. "You prick!"

He yelled back, "Well, now, I wouldn't sell you this car for a million bucks, you jerk!"

Without turning, Dale raised his middle finger high in the air.

Eyes bore down on him again. He pushed his back up against the brick wall of the convenience store. "Please don't be the police again." He pulled out a cigarette, lit it, and took a long pull. "I can't afford to get arrested today." The cigarette smoke wafted out of his mouth as he spoke.

"Dale! Dale? You OK, man?" Big Man tapped Dale on the shoulder.

This startled Dale, not aware that anyone was standing next to him.

"Jesus, you scared the shit out of me! Where'd you come from?" asked Dale.

"Just stopped for a soda and saw you over at the car lot, arguing."

"He just rubbed me the wrong way. Acting like I can't own a car like that Camaro. We do that job and that car is mine."

"You think we're going to score that big?" asked Big Man.

"I don't see how we can miss. The guy's loaded. If we can land some of his equipment, that's just gravy."

"I'm going to get that soda. You want anything?"

"I'll do a soda too. Some scouting needs done. Hurry up!"

"Right now?"

"Your buddy Steve told me where his office is, what his car looks like, where he eats. Gotta know this stuff inside out. It's not like I'm going to follow him with my feet. Come on, Big Man. This is the big time. This is James Bond spy shit, dude."

"You're right, Dale. I'll be right back." Big Man's jaw tensed up as he went inside the store.

May 11, 1977, Wednesday afternoon, 6:10

"Right there, that white Caddie. Just like Steve said," said Dale.

"Oh yeah, you want me to pull in there?" asked Big Man.

"What are you, nuts? No! Drive around the block first! Then park across the street. We can sit and wait for him to leave."

"Then what? We're not going to follow him, are we?"

"Why do you think we're here? Of course, we're going to follow him."

"Do you hear sirens, Dale?"

"Yeah, I do. Just hold tight. Coming down the street, it's just an ambulance, no big deal."

"And a damn cop behind the ambulance, Dale. No reason the cops should follow the ambulance. Maybe something illegal is going on. If there's something illegal, you can bet there'll be more cops. I don't like this."

"Settle down. They'll be gone in a minute. Don't get all weird on me, OK?"

"Dale, why are they pulling into our guy's parking lot?"

"Shit, I don't know. Start the car up, but stay here a second."

Big Man fired up the engine, his hands squeezing the wheel. His eyes darted back and forth between the ambulance, the police car, and Dale.

"See that? They have some woman on the stretcher. Maybe a heart attack or something. It's not our guy."

"I don't enjoy sitting here with the cops just across the street, Dale."

"Nah, let's give this Werner guy another half hour. That cop just cares about the sick lady."

Fifteen minutes later, the ambulance and police car left. Soon, Anthony Werner stepped out of his office, briefcase in hand. He opened up his trunk and tucked the briefcase away.

"There he is, Big Man! Get ready to follow him. Just stay back some."

With a deep exhale, Big Man pulled the car away from the curb.

"Turn down this alley!" said Dale.

"What's the matter, man?" asked Big Man.

"That cop is back, dammit! Let's get out of here. We'll come back another time."

"I told you, Dale, it just looked wrong. You gotta trust me once in a while. Yeah, I'm not risking it, that was close!" said Big Man, who turned the car south as Anthony Werner and his Cadillac went north.

"You still living in those apartments on the east side? What's the name of the place?" asked Dale.

Big Man hesitated, "Um, Longmore? Yeah, I still live there."

"Cool. Can I crash there tonight? My car broke down again. I'm not spending another night sleeping in the backseat."

"Yeah, you can use the couch," said Big Man.

"Got an extra pillow and blanket?" asked Dale.

"I have another blanket, sure."

"And an extra pillow?"

"I just have two and I need them both."

"Bullshit. Both. Why?"

"I have a neck thing, so I have to prop it up. It takes two pillows."

"You can go one night without your little pillow. I'm a friend, ain't I?"

"Fine, you can use one of my pillows," said Big Man, fuming.

The Victim- Surveilled

DALE AND BIG MAN once again set up in front of Anthony Werner's office.

"No cops and ambulances this time. That'd be a good sign," said Dale.

Within minutes, Anthony walked out of his office, briefcase in hand. After unlocking his car, he pushed the front seat back forward and set his briefcase on the back seat.

"Nice Caddie! What is that, an El Dorado? He looks like he has money," said Big Man.

"Shut up and just watch. And no, it's a Coupe de Ville, like that matters."

Big Man knew enough to keep his mouth shut. Plus, he needed the money too, and didn't want to jeopardize that.

"Get ready to follow this guy, but stay back."

Anthony swung his car into traffic and headed east.

"Isn't his townhouse west of here?" asked Big Man.

"That's what Steve said. Let's see where he goes," said Dale.

The two thieves followed Anthony, hanging back three to four car lengths.

After driving a short way, Anthony slowed his pace. "Now what's he doing?" asked Dale.

"Gas station stop."

"Pull into this parking lot. I just want to keep an eye on him."

They watched as a young station attendant came out and put gas in Anthony's car.

"Tommy, thanks son, you're the best! C'mere." He waved him over to the driver's side window. Tommy trotted over to see what he needed, but he just smiled and held out a five-dollar bill.

"Oh, Mr. Werner, you don't need to —"

"Take it, take it. And for the love of god Tommy, it's Tony, not Mr. Werner. Mr. Werner was my dad, OK?"

"Well, it's very nice of you, Mr. Wern — Tony."

"You're welcome, young man. I always leave your dad's gas station knowing I'm in good hands. Are you planning on carrying on the family tradition here?"

"I don't think so, Tony. I'm going to college. See the world. Maybe do something good for people."

"Terrific! That's terrific Tom. You're an amazing kid. I think you're going to do big things in this world. Study hard, but have plenty of fun along the way. What I wouldn't give to be your age again, kid. Tommy, seriously, I see how your dad pushes you, maybe too hard sometimes. Don't let that get to you, OK? You're a smart young man. You'll figure out what path you want to take. It's what I have always done and I have no regrets. Do good in college. I hope to see you graduate!"

"Dad is who he is. I know, I know. But thanks for saying that. I'm looking forward to college, sir."

"It's Tony goddammit!" Laughing, he pulled his car away from the gas station, waving as he drove away. Tommy waved back and smiled.

Everything in life ends. As Tony's car sped down the road, neither one of them knew that this was their final encounter.

"He just gave the kid a tip! For pumping gas! What the hell? Yeah, he's loaded. I mean, who does that?" said Dale.

"I ain't never tipped a grease monkey for that." said Big Man.

Eager to get back home, Anthony hit the gas to squeak through several yellow lights. Making good time, he pulled into the townhouse complex's parking lot. The two-story structures stood in three neat rows with the resident's personal garage across the pavement from their front door. The buildings were completed six months earlier and, even though he did not win a sub-contractor bid on the drywall, he still loved the place. He was glad he lost out on the contract, knowing that he'd hear of any and every blemish in the finish. "Let that be someone else's problem," he once joked to Kaylie.

He pulled in front of his garage, hit the automatic garage door opener, and pulled in to his single-car garage. After shutting off his car, he reached into the back seat and grabbed his briefcase. Business was good, and he enjoyed having his hands in all of it. He was either working or thinking about work to be done. Details mattered to him.

He stopped to set down the briefcase on the massive trunk of his car. With a quick click-click, the case was opened, and he began to sift through folders. Reaching the file he was interested in, he leafed through the documentation, periodically licking his thumb to make the page turning easier. Soon he found the paper he was looking for, rapidly scanned the page, and just as quickly, tossed it back in the case and snapped it closed. When Anthony had questions, he sought out the answers. Staying in the know had kept him ahead of the game. Had he not been so preoccupied — his daughter would comment on his laser focus — he might have noticed the old orange and primer gray car sitting in the parking lot thirty feet from him, shaded by a large oak tree. A pair of scruffy and dirty men were sitting in front, watching. Neither one looked like they had any business in this neighborhood.

The two shadowy figures watched as their target walked over to the side entrance. Anthony pushed the garage door button as he exited. The large door silently swung down, shutting as he made his way across the lot to his townhouse's back entrance, locking the door behind him.

"This looks like an easy score, Dale. Grab him in the garage and take all his money and rings."

"You're thinking too small. Way too small. That's why JB is going to be with us." Dale sighed, holding back his temper. "Remember, this guy owns a construction business. Construction man! So there must be some high-dollar tools this guy owns. We just drive him around to his job sites, load up the tools and whatnot, and sell 'em. I know a guy. We *just* talked about this yesterday. Do you seriously not remember?"

"I guess I do. Maybe my mind was thinking I imagined it."

"Well, it's true and is happening. Soon. Get your shit together, Big Man. Don't embarrass me. No screw ups."

"I won't embarrass you, Dale, I promise." Big Man looked at the blue sky. "Sure is nice out, ya know?"

"Who fucking cares, Big Man? Who fucking cares about that?"

The Accomplices - We Need A Truck

May 14, 1977, Saturday evening, 7:30

JOHN BRODIGAN WAS ASLEEP in his recliner. Being more precise, he was passed out, an empty bottle of Jack Daniel's tipped over across his thigh. The smell of stale cigarettes permeated the room. Not that many years ago, his hair was dark blond, close-cropped, and clean per Marine regulations. That all changed when he'd had enough mouth from a bunkmate. He sucker punched the guy while they were eating in the mess hall. The price of this poor judgment was six months in the stockade, followed by a dishonorable discharge. His dress uniform still hung in his bedroom closet, gathering dust.

By the time this particular evening rolled around, his appearance was much different; long dirty hair, tied up in a small ponytail in the back, four days' growth of beard making him both scruffy and mean looking, and his unkempt clothes rumpled and stained.

There was a muted rap on the door. Tap-tap, tap-tap-tap. John slept right through it.

"Open up, you jackass!" yelled Dale Bowers, now laughing and banging on the door of the dilapidated house John rented from his dad, making his presence known.

Startled, he half jumped out of the recliner, almost turning his ankle and jumping away from the leg rest. "Just a, ahh goddammit that hurt! Just a damn minute, I'm coming!"

He limped over to the door, muttering to himself, "This better be worth it."

When he swung open the door, his body slowly slumped when he saw Dale and Big Man standing on the porch. Big Man smiling that simple man smile of his, Dale with his usual pissed-off face.

"You look like shit," said Dale, pushing his way past John. "Matches your house, though. God, it stinks in here!"

"Yeah, fucking great to see you too, sweetheart. What you got there Dale, a little puppy? Oh, wait, it's Big Man! Hey little buddy!" John tugged on Big Man's cheek.

"So funny JB," Big Man spoke softly, head down, and followed in behind Dale.

"We need your truck, man," said Dale.

"As always, Dale, right to the point. What for now, moving home to mommy, I hope?"

"I'm going to do you a favor and ignore that mommy comment. I've got a nice score to make. A sure thing. Well, actually JB, we need the truck AND you driving."

"What trouble is up your sleeve now?"

"I know of a guy who carries lots of dough and loves wearing expensive jewelry. Figured we could roll him pretty damn easy. He's an older guy and would never expect this."

"And you need a truck to rob a guy? What's in it for me?"

"I'm getting half of the take … ."

"Half? What the hell?"

"Yep, half … I planned all this, did all the leg work on it." He looked straight through Brodigan and repeated slowly, "Half."

John put his hands behind his head. He noticed Big Man's empty expression, then looked back at Dale.

"You two split the other half. Look, it's going to be thousands of bucks. We're all going to walk away with thousands of dollars. When was the last time you had five thousand bucks to your name? Even five hundred? You only need to help load up equipment. OK, John?"

John sat down on his recliner with a thud, blowing out cigarette smoke as he did. "Five thousand would be nice. When?"

"Probably this Thursday. The guy always takes his woman out to eat on Thursday night and comes home hauling a briefcase. Stays up for hours, probably doing work."

"Wait, there's somebody else we gotta deal with?" asked Big Man.

"Only if he brings her back to his place. They're just dating. I have enough rope for both."

"If there's a woman involved, count me out. I will not scare or rough up some woman, nope. I'm a lot of things, Dale, but I ain't hurting a woman."

"Hah! So the old soldier boy is afraid of some old woman?" blurted Big Man.

"It's not fear, asshole," said John. "Think for one second. Two people to deal with. Two people to tie up. Two people who are witnesses! Literally, it doubles the trouble, and for what? Does it double our take, Dale?"

"Doubt it."

"So, no, I'm out. Oh, and fuck you too, Big Man, leave my Corps out of this! And while I'm talking about the Corps, we ain't soldiers, we're Marines. Soldiers are those pussies in the Army. Get it straight."

"OK, listen John, take it easy Marine," Dale lowered his voice and slowed down his speech. "If, and only if, he brings anybody else with him, we call it off and try another night. Does that sound reasonable to you?"

John fidgeted in his chair and took a drag on his cigarette. He slowly exhaled a cloud of blue smoke that drifted in front of his face. "Sure. OK, fine. Anybody else shows up, and I mean anybody, and I am out."

"I hear ya. We'll walk away and do it another time. You in now?"

"Yeah, I'm in." John stood up and walked towards the kitchen. "Beer?"

"No thanks," said Dale. "I'll tell you one thing though, no woman gets in my way, ever! So just remember this favor I'm doing you, John."

"Some favor."

"Sure! I'll have one of those beers," blurted Big Man, smiling at Dale.

"You're not old enough. Where's this guy live?"

"West side, behind that strip mall. What's it called? Monroe Corner, yeah," said Dale.

"Ahh, I know the area. Nice houses, big townhouses too," said JB.

"Big Man and I have already scouted out the area."

"We sure did!" said Big Man.

"Are there any weak points we need to plan for?" asked John.

"Weak points, like what?"

"How well-lit is his place? Are neighbors usually out grilling or going for walks? What about cops? You know those rich types have more pull with them, so they probably patrol the area more than, say, my neighborhood."

Big Man looked at Dale.

"I see those hound dog eyes. We don't have to worry about that shit. You see, John, you can be our lookout. And the neighbors? We'll work fast and be in and out. If the neighbors are all outside having some fancy soiree, we wait a night. For the money we're going to get, it'll be worth waiting. And remember, these folks are too busy counting their money to give a shit about their neighbors' visitors. Everybody cool with the plan then?"

"Sure thing Dale," said Big Man.

"I'm fine with this plan. But if this shit goes off the rails, man ... " said John.

"Trust me, this will make an enormous difference in all our lives. Huge!" said Dale.

The Daughter - How About Brunch?

May 19, 1977, Thursday morning, 8:10

KAYLIE WERNER, CHEWING ON the tip of her fingernail, knew she needed to chat with her father. Her boyfriend of two years, Adam, had been dropping several hints about taking their relationship to the next level — marriage. She loved Adam and could see spending her life with him. She knew he would stand with her in all of life's ups and downs, no matter how serious the issue. She still needed to talk things through with her father. Her mother had passed when Kaylie was just fourteen, leaving her dad to raise their only child. Their relationship became close over the years. Even as an adult, she would talk to her dad several times a week, in person or on the phone.

"Werner Custom Builders, this is Patricia. How may I help you?"

"Hi Patti, this is Kaylie. Is dad busy?"

"Kaylie, sweetie! Hi!" answered Patricia Jordan, long-time receptionist, bookkeeper, and general 'Jill of All Trades' for Anthony Werner and his business. Patricia, Patti as most called her, had worked for Mr. Werner for fifteen years and had seen Kaylie grow up from a young girl through college and into early adulthood. Patti often attended Kaylie's school plays, fundraisers, and too many softball games to count. Many people assumed she might be Kaylie's mother and were surprised when they learned she was working for her dad. "Oh hon, I'm sorry, but he's meeting with a couple of gentlemen right now, going over a new project. They've been in there for more than an hour and, knowing your dad, he'll be taking the clients out for lunch soon."

"Well, darn it, I was hoping to get him to take *me* to lunch this week. I have something important to talk to him about."

"Let me slip him a note, see what his plans are. Just hold on for a sec, OK?"

"Sure." Kaylie rested her free hand on her forehead while she held the phone close to her ear, listening and waiting.

After a couple of minutes, Patti returned to the phone. "Kaylie? I'm sorry dear, but he has already promised these two guys lunch. But he jotted down a note for you. Want to hear it?"

"Of course, if you have the time."

Patti read the hand-written note, "'Please tell my beautiful daughter' ... Oh, how sweet, he underlined beautiful!" Patti commented, a small, happy tear weighing down her eyelid.

She continued reading, "'that I would just love to do brunch with her tomorrow morning. Around ten, Hamilton Club.'"

"Is brunch OK, dear?"

Kaylie laughed and said, "Yes, you tell my daddy I'll be there. I just hope he recognizes me!"

"Why do you say that?"

"I went to the hairdresser yesterday and made a risky move!"

"What did you do? Please, not a mohawk!"

Laughing, Kaylie responded, "No, nothing like that, just a color change."

"I wish I could color my hair, get rid of this gray, you know. But with my thin hair and my luck, I'd end up bald! What color did you go with?"

"It's a beautiful auburn color. So I'm a redhead now!"

"You'll have to let me know what your father thinks. God, I hope it doesn't kill him!"

In unison, they both laughed.

"Other than that, what's the big news, anyway? Good news, I hope!"

"Nothing bad, that's for sure. Some Adam questions to hash out."

"Ooh, sounds serious."

"Patti, you know Adam and I have been seeing each other for quite a while now and I'm just positive he's getting ready to ask me to marry him. Things are just fantastic between us and his financial consulting business is taking off. Now don't get me wrong, I feel I'd be so happy with him. He's wonderful. I just wanted to run a few questions past Dad. It's just to ensure he doesn't have any issues to discuss."

"So, as you know, he thinks the world of Adam and admires how he's built his own business. No doubt he'd give his blessing. Just you talking to him will mean so much to him."

"Oh, I hope so. Thanks for talking with me and for getting that note to him too! I'll call you next week. Let's have lunch soon! I hope you have a terrific weekend, Patti!"

"You too, my dear. Bye-bye."

Patti was glad the call had ended. At least she didn't ruin the surprise. She knew it would be hard to keep the secret she held to herself. Exhaling, she smiled as she glanced at the office appointment schedule. The 8:30 a.m. entry caught her eye. Earlier in the week, Adam called to schedule a meeting with Anthony. Two thick pencil lines highlighted the words, "Important Matter". When Adam called to set up a time, he confided in her. He explained how much he loved Kaylie and wanted to marry her. He mentioned he had this old-fashioned streak in him, so he just had to ask her father for permission. Patti found it sweet and heart-warming; reminding her of the beautiful story her father had told when he asked for permission.

"Adam is way ahead of you, dear!" Patti whispered to the empty office, wiping away that little tear. "Way ahead."

The Killer - Deadly Night

May 19, 1977, Thursday evening, 8:12

THE THREE MEN SAT along the bench seat of the pickup as they headed down a side street toward their target. The lowering sun was shining in the passenger's eyes, but the driver, John Brodigan, had dropped his visor, shielding him from the blinding light. Dale reached to pull down his visor. "Don't touch that!" John yelled, but it was too late. The visor dropped out of its broken bracket, smacked Dale on the knee, and fell on the floorboard.

"Piece of shit truck you got here, bud."

"I'll turn it around if you got a problem using it tonight."

"I'm just joking, just joking," Dale said as he rubbed his knee, glaring at Big Man.

No one spoke for several minutes after that. Dale's eyes darted from side street to side street, constantly looking behind him. "You know where the place is, right?"

"Yeah, I told you. I drove by last night and could see the guy's garage. It's cool, man. Fucking relax. We'll grab the guy, take his money, and then haul his ass around to some job sites. Should be lots of tools to sell, right Dale?"

"Uh-huh. Hand me that duffel bag."

Big Man eased his grip on the dusty gray bag and set it on Dale's lap. He unzipped it and checked out its contents; duct tape, rope, empty paper bags to hold any money and jewelry they score, and, ominously, a gun. The silver Smith & Wesson felt solid in his hand. He ejected the magazine. "Full magazine." He rotated his wrist, examining the firearm as he held it low to the floor, taking care to keep it out of sight. A half-empty box of cartridges lay on the bottom of the duffel bag.

"Dang, this gun is huge. That'll scare the old man, don't ya think, Dale?" asked a smiling Big Man.

"Let's get off this empty street. We can't stick out like this. Turn here, John," Dale said as he nodded to the left, ignoring Big Man's question.

The truck creaked around the corner, the force of the turn pushed Big Man into Dale.

"Get off me, man. You stink. Do you ever bathe?"

"Sorry. Sorry, Dale." Big Man looked down at the floorboard as the truck rumbled down the road.

"And put that gun back in the bag. Why you gotta play with shit all the time?"

———◦◦◦———

May 19, 1977, Thursday evening, 8:25

"Oh, that was just a lovely dinner, Anthony. I hope you enjoyed it too," said Joanie.

"Yes, I did. Did I or did I not tell you they have, bar none, the best bistecca?" replied Tony as the pair walked arm-in-arm across the parking lot.

"Simply delicious, and I'm not a huge steak eater, as you know. And the bruschetta. And the wine. And the tiramisu! All unforgettable! Can you make the evening even better? Please spend the night at my place tonight. Please say yes!"

"I'm sorry, I just can't. Several bids coming up and I have to be ready. Believe me, I'd love nothing more than to spend this perfect night with you and wake up next to you."

"I understand. I don't like it," she laughed, "but I understand. What a beautiful evening, don't you think, Anthony?"

"It is dear and you make it more so."

"You're so sweet."

The happy and full couple walked over to Anthony's Cadillac. He opened the door for her. Sitting down in the passenger seat, she purred, "Ooh, I just love these leather seats. And that new car smell! Anthony, you've outdone yourself with this car of yours!"

"I love it too! I've always been partial to these wonderful Cadillacs," he said as he shut her door.

Joanie's house was a quick ten-minute drive from the restaurant. As they pulled into the driveway, Joanie insisted that he just drop her off there. "I know you are busy. The sooner you start, the sooner you get done." She leaned over and kissed him on the cheek. He placed his hand over hers.

"I will call you in the morning when I get into the office."

"You'll *call* me when you get home," she said, winking and smiling.

"Of course. We'll talk soon."

Tony stayed in the driveway, watching her unlock the door to her house. Once she was safely inside, he backed out of the drive and headed for home.

***

May 19, 1977, Thursday evening, 8:28

The light blue pickup truck rumbled down the freeway, its driver taking care to stay at or below the speed limit. Inside, three career criminals prepared to do what they knew best; steal from another person.

"There, turn there. We can access his garage from the back. I want you to let me out for a quick look," said Dale, his tone hushed.

"Got it," replied John.

"Yeah, this is it. Pull into that drive there. It'll curve a bit to the right and lead us right there."

John did as asked and slowly pulled up to garage number six. A small light centered over the garage door faintly illuminated the area. The glow of the day faded away.

"Stay here a sec. Big Man, if it's clear, I'll wave you over. Then grab the duffel bag and bring it with you. We can hide out of sight. I'll be behind the garage. Big Man, hide across the drive behind a tree. John, pull up to that street," he pointed to the north, "and wait for our guy. When he gets here, give us one quick honk on the horn, got it?"

"No problem, a quick beep."

Dale jumped out of the truck, gently pushing the door but not quite closing it. He ran to the side of the garage and peered inside a window. No car. Big Man, his head cocked far to the left so he could see Dale out the rear window, felt his stomach leap with excitement as he saw Dale motion to him.

"Here we go, Johnny." Big Man hopped out of the truck and quietly shut the door. In a flash, he was over to the garage, standing next to Dale.

"Big Man, shit, leave the bag here! Other side of the driveway! Sit your ass down against that big tree. I want you coming in from behind him after I show my gun. Come on, man, don't you remember?"

"Sorry Dale, I remember. I'm thinking about the money." He scampered over to the tree and sat down, pulling the ball cap down to hide his face, feigning sleep. Dale stood next to the side door. His eyes looked skyward as he exhaled a deep breath.

Moments later, a resident of the complex came down the sidewalk, parallel to the parking lot, walking his dog. The little Yorkie noticed Big Man first and started barking; an excited, high-pitched bark. "Quiet Dolly," he said to his pet as he gently tugged the leash. Then, to the stranger, he asked, "Can I help you with anything? This is private property. You can't just hang out here."

Big Man kept his head down, chin against his chest. "I'm just waiting for my ride. She should be here any minute."

"Well, I hope so. I don't like people I don't know hanging about."

"I'll be gone soon, sir, thanks."

The dog snarled at this strange man, showing his tiny teeth. The pair walked away, around the corner. Neither one noticed Dale crouched down behind a garbage can next to the garage. His gun was in his hand at the ready.

———◆———

May 19, 1977, Thursday evening, 8:32

They both heard it; the short, quick honk from the truck. Dale held his left hand up, palm out, indicating to Big Man to stay put. Dale peered around the corner of the garage, the silver gun pressed against his thigh. There it was, slowly coming towards the two men, a white Cadillac. Dale noticed there was a single occupant and held up one finger for Big Man to see. Big Man gave Dale a thumbs-up and once again hung his head down.

As Anthony Werner pulled his car up towards his garage, he reached up to the visor and pressed a large button to open the garage door. Dale stepped out from his hiding place. "Who the hell are you fella?" asked

Anthony as he brought the car to a stop. Dale deliberately walked towards the Cadillac, then stopped. He swung the .45 in front of him, then down to his right. Tapping it against his thigh and motioning with his left arm, he directed the driver to pull into the garage. Anthony froze, then noticed motion in his rear-view mirror and saw a second man. Anthony felt the trap close. Dale banged his hand against the hood of the car, causing the driver to jump. A wide-eyed Anthony pulled the car into the garage and came to a stop, not knowing his fate.

"Shut the garage door," demanded Dale.

"What?" said Anthony as he rolled down his window.

"I said, shut the fucking door! Press the button! Press it!" hissed Dale through his clenched teeth.

"All right, all right," said Anthony. With a jerk, the single-car garage door slowly swung down, closing the three men inside the garage.

"Hey, Big Man, check that glove box over there for a gun. We don't need that kind of surprise."

Big Man trotted over to the passenger side.

"Dale? Door's locked, man."

"Unlock the door for him," demanded Dale.

Anthony did as he was told. Big Man got inside the glove box. "Nothing but papers, Dale."

Dale opened the driver's door and pointed the gun in Anthony's face. "Slide your ass over to the passenger side, Anthony," barked Dale.

Anthony started to slide over, but stopped suddenly. "How do you know my name? Do I know you?"

"Just move it over, old man." Anthony complied.

"Big Man, search him for a gun while you're there."

"Nothing there either," said Big Man after doing what he was told.

"Good. Get over here and drive."

"Ah, come on, you sure about this? Let's just roll him and leave," said Big Man.

"No way. There's more to do. You are not backing out now. We talked about this!"

"Look guys, I've got plenty of cash on me," said Anthony, reaching into his wallet. "You can have the car. Just let me go, OK?"

"Give me that wallet," said Dale, "and move your ass over!"

Quietly, and with his head down, Anthony handed over his wallet. He slid the rest of the way across the bench seat and began planning.

"What is this? There's only a couple hundred bucks here. There should be thousands! Where's the rest, old man?"

"I don't carry thousands on me. Why would you think that? What kind of idiot would do that? We can't do that anymore because of idiots like you!"

Dale leaned back. "These seats are nice. Bet this car costs thousands. I know you have money and we're going to get it." Motioning towards the driver's seat, Dale looked at Big Man. "Now we go to those other places. Two hundred fucking bucks! Drive!"

With slumped shoulders, Big Man sat down behind the wheel.

"You'll need to move your seat closer. The adjustments are on the left. They're electric," said Anthony.

"Ha! See Big Man, even he notices!"

"Just shut up old man," yelled Big Man. He took an awkward swing at Anthony, who easily blocked it with his left hand.

"Big Man, just stop making a fool out of yourself and drive. Adjust your seat first," said Dale.

Dale climbed into the back seat, sitting in the middle, between Big Man and Anthony. "Look, Anthony, I'm not afraid to use this gun if I need to; don't be stupid." Anthony stared back at Dale without saying a word.

"Ready Dale?" asked Big Man.

"Just a second. Now, Anthony, we're making a few stops. We're going to need some of your construction tools. I'm looking for the good stuff, understand? Where do we go first, hmmmm?"

"You're making a huge mistake. You can't get much stuff in this car," replied Anthony.

"Let me worry about that. We have a friend with a truck. So I'll ask again. Where do we go first?"

Anthony exhaled and said, "Third and Seventh Avenue, a light blue house on the corner."

"Just be cool and you don't get hurt. We get what we want. You go back to your life, your girlfriend. Let's go!"

"You've been following me, haven't you? You leave her out of this!" demanded Anthony.

"Hey, she'll be all right, don't worry," piped in Big Man.

"You seem like a nice kid. Don't be a part of this. Such a mistake. Just let me go," pleaded Anthony.

"I ain't that nice, but I am broke. So shut up, mister."

Big Man hit the garage door opener and slowly backed out onto the driveway.

"Mr. Werner, you pissed Big Man off. I'm impressed!" Dale smiled for a brief second. "Don't ever do that to me! I'll tear you apart!"

Big Man's hands were shaking on the wheel.

"Looks like you scared your little buddy. You didn't piss yourself, did you, little man?" asked Anthony.

The butt of the gun crashed down on Anthony's left ear, cutting the lobe almost in half. Anthony winced, but kept quiet.

"I'll use the other end next time."

Anthony only stared back at Dale.

The white Cadillac idled down the parking lot and turned left onto the street, passing JB and his truck.

With an eye on the side-view mirror, Anthony saw a pickup following them. "Hey, looks like your friend's truck has a headlight burned out. You want to risk him getting pulled over for that? You really ought to do better planning."

Dale glanced back. "Not your concern, old man." He silently mouthed, 'fuck.' "Big Man, let's get to the freeway and head east. We'll go to that Third and Seventh house first."

"First?" piped up Anthony. "How many houses do you think I'm going to lead you to?"

"As many as we want, so start thinking of our second stop. Just do it quietly. My gun is always pointed your way."

"Look guys, I have money on me and I can get you some more. There's no need to steal our equipment, too. What do you say?"

"That was our first plan, wasn't it, Dale? Just get some money. And his rings?" asked Big Man.

"Yes, my wallet and my rings. Here, take them," Anthony said. He handed over his wallet and pulled off his rings. "Here is one. Has lots of diamonds, you can get some nice cash for it."

Dale reached over the seat and held out his hand. Anthony placed the first ring in the palm of Dale's hand.

"This second ring," he said, "was a gift. I'm afraid the sentimental value is greater than the monetary value. But take it too."

Anthony had the ring between his fingers. As he handed it over, the car went over a bridge. The car bounced abruptly, knocking the ring out of his hand. The small ring bounced off Anthony's knee, hit the door to the glove box, and fell at his feet.

"Dammit. Sorry."

"We'll get it later. I guarantee you I'm going to get those tools, too."

"About those tools. Most of them belong to my workers. Guys like you two, just trying to make ends meet, working hard. You steal their tools and you might as well put them on the unemployment line."

"Dale, that ain't right. Maybe we shouldn't," said Big Man.

"Bullshit, you got insurance, they'll be OK," said Dale.

"I'm sorry, but you are wrong. Unless they have their own policy, they're screwed because mine does not cover their equipment. It says so explicitly."

"Dale?" Big Man pressed down on the gas pedal as the car entered freeway traffic.

"You like this car, uh, Big Man, is it?" asked Anthony.

"Drives and rides like a dream."

"Why don't you guys take it, then? Stop up here. Let me go."

"Car like this is easy to spot. Shitty idea old man," said Dale.

"Guess I'm just full of bad ideas today. Maybe I'll try one more. What do you say, Dale?"

"I have no idea what you mean," said Dale.

"Your pickup driver, I mean, what's he doing now?" asked Anthony as he looked out the rear window.

"What are you talking about?" asked Dale as he turned and looked behind him.

Anthony had his chance. Leaping sideways, he grabbed the steering wheel with his right hand and jerked on it, causing the car to swerve back and force. Anthony lost his grip on the wheel and fell back into the passenger seat. Dale regained his balance in the back but swung forward too hard. The barrel of the gun pressed against the seat just behind Anthony. Dales's finger was on the trigger and the impact of the gun hitting the back seat caused him to pull the trigger.

"Why did you do that!" yelled Dale.

Without another word, he pressed the end of the gun against the seat again. He pulled the trigger again. This time, he meant it.

All three men momentarily lost hearing. Anthony's weight slammed against the door, forcing it ajar. The sound of the road grew louder. The deafened men did not notice. Big Man yelled out, "What the hell happened? Dale, you shot him!"

"Did you see what he did?" asked Dale, yelling to be heard. "He almost wrecked us!"

"What do we do?"

"Head to the house, like we planned."

Big Man hit the gas and pushed the speed to eighty miles per hour.

Anthony tried to move his left arm, but he couldn't. He could hear muffled yells, but could not understand what they were saying. He slowly reached out with his right hand and grabbed the door latch. Escape may be his only hope. He undid the latch, and the door popped open five inches. The hiss of tires on the pavement and road dust filled the interior of the car.

"No, goddammit!" Dale tossed the gun on the back seat and reached up and over Anthony's limp body, pulling the door mostly shut. He didn't see his lighter fall out of his pocket. It hit the floor and leaned against the door.

Anthony sighed deeply and passed out from the pain.

"Dale, what now, man? You shot him!" said Big Man.

"Let me think, let me think."

Anthony stirred a little and opened his eyes. He gazed at the interior of the car. His breathing got more difficult.

"This is the plan. Keep headed to the house and park on the street. Hop in the truck and leave!"

"This man does not look good. Is he dying?" asked Big Man.

"Oh, he's going to die. I'm going to finish him off, execution style. Make it look like a mob hit. It'll throw the cops off the trail. I bet this guy has mob connections, anyway."

"No, Dale, you can't do that!"

"I'm going to and right now." With that, Dale pressed the gun against Anthony's temple. He tried to move away, but Dale kept pressing the muzzle against his head. Then, without warning, he pulled the trigger.

"Jesus Christ, Dale! Oh my god, I've got his blood all over me."

"Just drive," said Dale as he looked at what he had done. "Wow, would you look at that!" He cocked his head, fascinated by the trickle of blood that dripped out of Anthony's temple.

The Killer - Leaving The Scene

May 19, 1977, Thursday evening, 9:24

BIG MAN BROUGHT THE car to a stop and got out. Dale pushed the driver's seat forward and also exited the car.

"The ring fell on the floorboard," said Dale.

John pulled up next to them. "What have you done? You shot the guy! You fucking killed him, didn't you? I want no part of this shit Dale, I'm out." John got out and paced around his truck, fingers interlaced with his hands on top of his head.

"You're not going anywhere," said Dale as he trained the gun on John.

"You son of a bitch. Don't you ever point a gun at me. After what you did to that guy? Killing me is not a bad thing. Taking me out of this world would be doing me a favor, you fucking idiot. And the gunshot would really wake the neighbors up, if we haven't already. So go ahead, Dale, shoot me and see how far you two guys get."

Dale tucked the gun in his waistband and said, "Big Man, go get that ring. It's on the floorboard somewhere."

"Dale, do you see all the blood? And there's, like, parts of the guy stuck on the window."

"Hurry it up, go get it!"

Big Man ran around the back of the car and slowly opened the door. Anthony's lifeless body sagged towards him. He didn't hear the subtle metal-on-concrete sound the lighter made as it fell out of the car.

"Dale, there's too much blood. I can't find any ring. I'm going to get sick if I look at this anymore. Forgive me, sir," said Big Man as he pushed on Anthony's body, forcing it back inside, quickly shutting the door. Big Man noticed the door was not completely shut. Frightened, he ran back to the pickup.

"We've got to leave, Dale. People are going to come outside. Then what? Shoot them too? This whole thing has gone to shit. Let's go," said John as he hopped into his truck.

"Let's grab some tools first. We can do this!" said Dale.

"Dale, there's no time. Sorry, but it's over," said Big Man, who also hopped into the truck and slid next to John, making room for Dale. "Let's get out of here!"

Without a word, Dale climbed in the passenger seat and slammed the door.

John threw the transmission in gear and stomped down on the accelerator, squealing the tires.

An outdoor light came on as an old lady's face peered out her picture window through parted drapes.

The Killer - Cover Our Tracks

May 19, 1977, Thursday evening, 9:29

As the truck lumbered through the streets, heading back to John's place, Dale reached in his front shirt pocket for his cigarettes and lighter. The pack was there, almost full. The lighter was missing. He checked his pant pockets. No luck. Now he started to worry.

"Give me a light, Big Man."

Without saying a word, the still stunned accomplice passed a yellow Bic lighter to Dale.

Dale took a long drag on his cigarette and exhaled slowly. "I think I lost my lighter."

Taking his eyes off the road, John turned his head towards the two passengers. "You what?"

"I can't find my lighter and I know I had it with me in that asshole's car."

"We gotta go back and get it. What if it's in the car? There could be prints!" Big Man's stomach sank.

"No way we go back. Ain't no way we do that," said John.

"You're right, JB. We can't go back. We just gotta hope it's not found. Son of a bitch!" Dale slammed his fist on the dash and stared blankly out the side window.

The three men sat silently as the truck continued its journey.

After a few minutes, Big Man decided to speak. "I mean, it's just a lighter, right? I see them everywhere. I bet no one notices some plain old lighter."

"You think my lighter is plain?" Dale asked. "A nice Zippo with New Mexico on it? See those every day on the street? Do ya?"

Big Man slunk down in the seat, childlike. He'd learned that it's best to be quiet when Dale got like this. He saw more than one jail house brawl happen when someone else would try to get him calmed. Dale could fight, and he was brutal when he did. He had few rules in life, none when it came to fighting.

John could feel Dale staring past Big Man and right at him, eyes boring into him. "Look at me all you want, Dale. You need to have a plan. And what about the gun? The gun that was going to scare the guy and give us what we wanted? Not the gun that ended up blowing his brains out. You gotta take care of this."

"Don't worry, man, I'll figure it out."

"I want my cut. I'm walking away from both of you. It just wasn't the plan. Why did you do it man, why?" Sweat was running down John's face.

"The guy tried to grab the wheel when we were on the freeway and I couldn't let him wreck us. He was moaning and groaning. It didn't look so good, so I just finished him off."

"That's right John," injected Big Man, "he almost grabbed the wheel from me and … "

"Shut up, Big Man!" screamed both John and Dale simultaneously.

"Pull up over here John, on Market Street. I'll walk back to my car from there."

"And this duffel bag full of crap? And the gun? You're taking the damn gun with you."

"I'll take the gun with me and dump it somewhere. You can hold the money and that ring. We'll split the money. Later on, take a trip out of town and pawn it."

"Fine by me. I'll hide that jewelry somewhere and toss the bag. You cool with this Big Man?" said Dale.

"Yeah, sure, whatever you guys think is best."

John pulled the truck onto Market Street and stopped, letting Dale out. No words were spoken.

Big Man slid over, taking Dale's place in the truck, moving the duffel bag to the floorboard at his feet.

"Big Man, this was so wrong. That man did not need to die. So help me if we get caught," said Brodigan.

"I know, JB. It all just happened so fast. Dale wasn't lying. The guy got ahold of the wheel. We were lucky we didn't crash. Then Dale shot him. Bang! Bang! I'm still deaf in my right ear. After that, the guy tried to open his door. Before I knew it, Dale just shot him again, right in the fucking head. The guy's blood sprayed on me, dude! On my face! There was blood all over the place. Thought I was going to puke."

"Like I said, I'm done working with you two. You need to get away from Dale. Split up the money and walk away. He's out of control."

"But we got, uh, what you call, history. Done jail time together and all that."

"You're fixing to do a hell of a lot of jail time. It'll be like you're an old married couple. How does that sound? Because he got greedy and he panicked, we could go away forever. Dammit!" He slammed both fists on the steering wheel.

"Now you know that's not right. We didn't shoot nobody."

"Don't matter, we're part of the crew, so it's just like we both pulled the trigger too — that's what the law says. Just my words of wisdom to you. Stay away from this guy. Take it or leave it. I don't give a fuck anymore."

The truck pulled to a stop in front of Big Man's apartment complex. Again, no words were spoken as he walked away from the pickup.

The Victim - Where Are You?

May 19, 1977, Thursday evening, 9:30

"TONY, PICK UP THE phone, pick up the phone. No, not the answering machine again," Joanie waited for the greeting to finish. "Anthony, where are you? It's the third time I've left a message. Please call me as soon as you get this. I will give Kaylie a call in case you went over there. Don't scare me like this!"

Joanie exhaled deeply and dialed Kaylie's number.

"Hello, this is Kay —."

"Kaylie, it's Joanie. Is your father over there?"

"No, he's not. Is he supposed to be?"

"I'm not sure where he is, but he was supposed to call me when he got home. That was over an hour ago. He's always called me after we've been out, but not tonight. You know how I worry about everything."

Kaylie rolled her eyes. "Yes you do, Joanie. I'm sure there's a good reason he's not answering."

"Yes, like a heart attack. What if he's in the middle of the living room and needs help? What if he got mugged? Can you go there and check on him, please? I hate to ask."

"I doubt you hate to ask," Kaylie said softly, covering the phone. Then, speaking directly to Joanie, "I doubt he got mugged, Joanie. That's a very safe neighborhood. Tell you what, I'll wait until ten o'clock and call him. If he doesn't answer, Adam and I will hurry over there. We'll see what he's up to. Will that be OK?"

"Can you just go over there now?"

"Joanie, that's just thirty minutes from now, and I'll call him. Not before. I'm not going to pester my dad every time he doesn't answer the phone. Maybe he got some groceries or ran into a neighbor and is outside talking."

"Well, that doesn't sound like your father."

"Thirty minutes." Kaylie hung up the handset, not too gently.

***

May 19, 1977, Thursday evening, 10:02

"This is Anthony Werner. I can't answer your call right now. Please leave a message at the beep. Thanks!"

"Dad, dad, are you there? Dammit!" Kaylie hung up the phone. "Adam, we should run over to Dad's. He didn't answer."

"Really? This late?" asked Adam.

"I know, but I promised Joanie I would do that. I don't like it any more than you, but the sooner we go, the sooner we're back home."

"I'll get the car keys."

The couple walked, arm-in-arm, out to the street and into her car. Adam took the driver's seat. Kaylie spent the trip biting her lip, staring out the window and hoping to see her father. Fifteen minutes later, they drove through Anthony's parking lot.

"Why is the garage door open?" asked Kaylie. Adam slowed the car to a stop. Her eyes darted between the garage and the townhouse.

"That's odd," said Adam, "and his car is gone."

"This is not like him. Adam? I'll run up to his townhouse. Where are those keys?" Kaylie rifled through her purse. "Got 'em." She climbed out of the car and ran up the sidewalk.

"Kaylie, wait," called out Adam, "Let me go with you."

Without a word, she waited for Adam to be at her side. Together, they went to the door.

"Let's just go in, Adam. He's probably not home, anyway."

"Doesn't look like it. I don't see any lights on anywhere."

The two walked into the entryway. Kaylie turned on several lights. "Dad? Dad, are you here?" The echoing sound of her voice made her feel uneasy. The ensuing silence made her fearful. "Let's take a quick peek. I'll look in his office. Can you check his bedroom and bathroom?"

"OK. Mr. Werner?" Adam disappeared down the hall and went into the bedroom, flipping on the light. "Mr. Werner? Nothing here. Nothing in the bathroom, either." He walked back towards the office where Kaylie was looking.

"I'm not seeing anything either. Nothing looks out of place; neat as a pin, just like usual. Maybe he is visiting a neighbor. But who? Why is his car gone? Well shit!"

"What now?" asked Adam.

"He's not here and I'm not going to start pounding on doors. Let's go back home."

"What are going to say to Joanie?"

"I'd like to say 'Hey, I don't like you', but I'll just tell her what we found. Actually, what we didn't find."

"Yeah, let's go home."

Adam followed Kaylie out the door, locking it behind him.

—◦—

May 19, 1977, Thursday evening, 10:52

"Joanie, this is Kaylie. No sign of Dad. His car is gone and the garage door is wide open. The house is empty. Please tell me he's gotten hold of you."

"No, dear, I haven't heard a word. What's going on? Now I'm even more concerned."

"Me too. I'll tell you what Joanie, I'll stay up tonight, as long as it takes, and call him every fifteen minutes. Let me take care of this. You should just go to bed and I'll call you tomorrow."

"Well, I am tired, my dear. I doubt I'll be able to sleep, but I'll try. Thank you for checking on him. Just let me know the instant you hear anything."

"Will do, Joanie," Kaylie said, shaking her head from side to side, "talk soon," and she hung up, not waiting for a reply from her dad's girlfriend.

"What do we do now, Adam? I'm worried."

"Come here, honey." She fell into his arms and felt the comfort of his embrace.

"Where is he?"

They wouldn't wait long for an answer.

The Police - The Investigation Begins

Larry McDermott needed his hand-held router to help his dad with some cabinets he was going to make. He knew the tool was on one of the job sites, probably the one on Third Street. He headed that way despite the late hour.

He pulled his truck into the driveway of the remodeling project. Not expecting to stay long, he left the truck door open. As he walked up the sidewalk, his breath leaving a trail in the cool night air, and passed a bundle of two by fours stacked in the yard, he saw a familiar car — a white Cadillac. It was parked, somewhat askew, on Seventh Avenue.

"That man never stops working," said Larry out loud to no one.

Reaching the front door, he quickly tried turning the doorknob. Locked. A puzzled look came over his face. He expected it to be unlocked with Anthony Werner inside somewhere going over the project. Pulling out his key ring containing the keys to all of their current projects, he began flipping through them. They jingled and clanked until he came across the one marked with a piece of masking tape and pencil, '3rd & 7th'. He quickly unlocked and opened the door.

"Tony? Hey Tony! It's me, Larry. Where you at?"

No answer.

He walked over to the stairway and climbed the stairs. He had to squeeze past a pallet of tiles on the landing. "Tony?" he called out again. And again, no answer.

"Well, where the hell are ya?"

He found the router he needed in the master bath. Grabbing it, he headed for the door. He shouted out once more for good measure, but the house remained silent.

Locking the door behind him, Larry decided to walk across the front yard to the Cadillac. Approaching the passenger side, the windows looked hazy. "Tony, you in there taking a nap?" his voice echoing down the street. He stepped towards the front passenger window and froze, his eyes widened.

"What the fu … " but the words caught in Larry's throat. The router fell to the ground. The unmistakable shape of Tony's balding head was pressed up against the window, surrounded by and covered with blood and white chunks of what was later determined to be brain matter.

Running over to the driver's door, he checked the handle. Locked. Peering inside the car, partly illuminated by a nearby streetlight, Larry saw his boss staring out the windshield. "Oh, thank god," he thought, but those hopes evaporated quickly as he noticed the dark round circle on Tony's temple. A small stream of blood, now dried and crusty, had flowed down to his shirt collar, staining the shirt a dark red.

"Son of a bitch!" he screamed as he turned and ran toward the house, frantically gaining entry again, and rushed to the phone in the kitchen.

Dialing zero, a woman came on the line, "Operator."

"Police! I need the police," he was nearly out of breath, "and an ambulance. Now! Help!"

"Sir, I'll need your location, please."

"Yeah. Yeah, um, I'm at Third Street and Seventh Avenue. Oh, my god."

"Sir, I am contacting the police. Please stay on the line." The phone clattered against the floor. A dazed Larry went back outside and walked aimlessly around the house and car.

Larry was sitting on the curb behind the Cadillac, head in his hands, and didn't notice when the patrol car with two officers, Ron Tyler, and Chris "Sonny" Ward, arrived.

"Sir? Sir! Did you call?" asked Officer Tyler.

He looked up at the cop, eyes red and tear-soaked. A shaking finger pointed at the car.

Officer Ward approached the car on the driver's side, placing his right hand on his service revolver, and the other officer stood watch on the passenger side, next to Larry.

Peering into the car's window, he assessed the situation at once.

"Sonny, this is gonna be a 10-79 here. Call it in," he shouted over to his partner, indicating that the case would be for the coroner.

His partner clicked on his radio's mic and asked for the coroner, a detective unit, additional units to assist, and his sergeant.

Within minutes, several squad cars descended, sirens screaming, on the crime scene. Two officers set up yellow crime scene tape, cordoning off the entire corner, enveloping both the house and the Cadillac. Lights in the neighborhood clicked on in virtually every house and several pajama-clad occupants gathered together to try to piece together what happened.

Twenty minutes after the call came in Detective Charles Jacobson, Jake to his co-workers, and his junior partner, Detective Jay Winston, Winnie, even to his face, pulled up in their spotless black Ford LTD. Exiting the passenger door with an air of confidence, if not superiority, Detective Jacobson buttoned his suit jacket and began surveying the area from where he stood.

"Sounds like the coroner is … " began Detective Winston, but he could not finish the sentence.

"Uh-uh-uh, let me take this in," his partner said with unabashed aloofness.

"Sorry," was all Winston could whisper as he stepped back.

Jacobson reached into his suit jacket pocket and pulled out a notepad and pen. He began to draw a map of the scene, beginning with the intersection, the car, and the house. "Corner of Third Street and Seventh Avenue, white Cadillac facing west, parked on Seventh Avenue." He was dictating to himself. "Hey Winnie," he yelled over to his partner, "what year is that Caddy, and is it still running?"

Winston had already pressed the back of his tanned hand against the hood of the victim's car, it was warm. "77 and already checked. It's not running. The hood is a little warm but not much," came his partner's reply.

"Very nice observation Winnie," he whispered, making a mental note of the solid attention to detail. Then loudly, "Let's knock on some doors! You two officers, take the north side," he said, pointing to Third Street. He shouted at two more patrolmen, "Take the south side of Third. Everyone, no detail is too small. Winnie, let's look around the vehicle. We'll let the coroner do his thing and then we'll open her up."

The two detectives walked deliberately around the vehicle, Winston following Jacobson.

"You see any keys, Winnie?"

"No sir. None in the ignition. Nothing around or under the vehicle. Maybe they're on the floorboard."

"True, but we're going to need the lockout kit. Grab that from the trunk when we're done, OK?"

"Roger that."

"I'm not seeing smudging on the doors. Have the team dust all four doors and the trunk."

"Noted," said Winston, jotting down the request.

"There is a lot of blood splatter on the dash and window, so I'd say we have at least one GSW. Look to you like he's clear over in the passenger seat, Winnie?"

"Oh yeah, he's on that side."

"Ever hear of anyone sliding over before killing himself?" Winston shook his head no. "Me neither. Suicide goes down on the list. I do not see a weapon. Let's get some more units here. One to canvass the neighborhood. The other to help us search the area. Have them look for weapons, shell casings, bullets, car keys, and the like."

"Got it, I'll call it in."

"I'm going to go talk to our caller."

The detective headed towards the victim's employee, his burnished black Oxfords clicking smartly on the pavement. Looking around, he spotted Larry McDermott and headed his way. "Mr. McDermott," he shouted across the yard, "can I speak with you sir?" An officer who had stayed with McDermott said something to him and motioned him towards the detective. They met in the middle of the side yard.

"Mr. McDermott, Detective Jacobson sir. Sorry we're meeting this way and I'm sorry we have to ask you a lot of questions."

"I understand. I want to help. I'm just stunned. Oh my god, his daughter, Kaylie; this will crush her."

"Yes, this is always tough. His daughter, does she live at home with," he glanced at his notepad, "Mr. Werner?"

"No, she's an adult on her own, not married. Lives in a house on Devan Avenue. I don't know the house number, sorry."

"That's OK, we'll figure that out. Sir, can you tell me what brought you here tonight?" He walked the detective through all that he had done and saw since he arrived.

"So you've worked with him quite a while? Did he treat you and the other employees well?"

"Nearly twelve years. He was the best to work with, my god, the best."

"Are you aware of any enemies, unhappy customers, problems at home, that sort of thing? Anyone acting strange at a job site?"

"None that come to mind. He's widowed about ten years now and he's dating, but I stay out of that part of his life. Loves his daughter. Just a great guy, generous."

"Generous? How?"

McDermott hung his head. "Whatever you needed, he'd help you get it. Any laborer needing an advance, he'd give it to the guy on the spot. Even if the guy just started working for Tony."

"He'd just have that cash on him? Normally have money on him?"

"Yeah, I'd say so. You think he's gone because of that?"

"I don't know, sir, but it happens all the time. We're not even sure he was robbed at this point. Why would he stop over here? At this house and in the evening?"

"Not unusual. He tracked all our jobs and would visit the job sites regularly. He'd make notes. The next day, he would talk to the guys about what he wanted done. That kind of thing."

"Thanks, Mr. McDermott. Go home and get some rest. If you think of anything, let me know," he said, handing him his card. "Someone will contact his daughter, probably the coroner, perhaps myself. Let us deal with that, OK? Does Mr. Werner have any other family in town?"

McDermott shook his head no and sighed as he took the business card and walked quietly away.

Jacobson noticed the coroner had just arrived and, at a quick pace, headed towards him and the Cadillac.

Dr. Robert C. Walters, nearly twenty years in his post as the county coroner had also carved out a stellar career in private practice. He was known for his amiable demeanor with law enforcement, victim's families, and the media as well as his exacting nature during court proceedings. In short, he was respected by most who knew him, including Detective Jacobson.

They exchanged greetings, and the detective filled him in on what he knew thus far as the two slowly circled the vehicle, the doctor already taking notes.

"We'll need to unlock this when you're ready Doc, our kit is right here."

"Very good," said the doctor. He crouched to see beneath the door. "Nobody has opened this door?"

"No, sir, not since the patrolmen arrived. Why?"

"This mostly dried stream of blood on the panel below the door. There's also blood ponding on the concrete. I wouldn't expect that. Did you notice that the passenger door was not fully closed?"

"No, I did not."

"Another interesting finding is that long streak of dried blood. The streak ends at the front of the rear wheel. Almost looks windblown, doesn't it, detective?"

"I believe so. How the … ?" The freeway traffic hummed across the street. The two men looked at each other.

"Probably so. And there is this," said the doctor. He pointed to a small white object resting in a small pool of blood.

"Is that bone?" asked Jacobson.

"Yes, we'll analyze it to make sure of its source. My opinion is we're looking at a shard of skull."

"You amaze me, doc! Someone did open this door." The detective hurriedly wrote in his notebook. "Winnie, get on the radio. Ask patrol if there were any reports of suspicious driving on the freeway over the past twelve hours. Maybe we can establish a solid time frame, direction of travel, or some info on the perp or perps riding along with our vic here. Also, see if they can get an address for his daughter, Kaylie. She lives somewhere on Devan Avenue. We'll need that for the notification."

"You got it," said Detective Winston, turning away from the car. He clicked on his radio and began asking questions of dispatch.

Detective Jacobson kneeled next to the passenger door, shining his small flashlight on and around the vehicle. "Well, well, what have we here?" His hands were pressed against the curb to support his weight as his eyes focused on a silvery object. "Doc, look at this!" he called out.

"What do you see Jake?" he said as he too kneeled.

"I'm seeing a lighter just under the car, which often could be a red herring, just random trash, you know. Do you see what makes this intriguing?"

"Yes, yes, I do see. It's lying on *top* of the blood pool."

"I think you're right, Doc. Sure looks like it fell there sometime after the car was parked. I'll get ident on this ASAP. Maybe we just got lucky."

"Jake, you want me to do the notification?" asked the coroner.

"You know, Doc," replied Jacobson, "that would be helpful. We can help canvas the area. Detective Winston should have the address for our vic's daughter by now. Her name is Kaylie."

"I'll get the house number and head over. That'll give the teams time to photograph and note the evidence before we remove the body."

"Sounds good, Doc."

"Excuse me, you're Detective Charles Jacobson, aren't you?"

Detective Jacobson turned around and saw a short, rather round young man. He was armed with a pen and notepad. "That's me, and you are?"

"Edward Evans, I'm with The Courier, and I was just heading home when I saw the commotion."

"How the hell did you get past the tape, Eddie?"

"It's Edward sir. The officer saw my press credentials and let me pass."

"This is my crime scene, son. A crime scene you are leaving right now."

"I understand, but can you tell me what the crime is? There's a deceased person in that car."

"Incredible observation, as usual. Leave or go to jail, Eddie."

Detective Winston walked over to the two men. "What's up, boss?"

"Nothing, detective, this reporter was just leaving."

The reporter remained silent and walked just beyond the yellow tape and stood, waiting.

The Coroner - Next Of Kin

May 19, 1977, Thursday evening, 11:21

"Did that sound like a car door?" Adam looked out the front window. "It sure was."

"Is it Daddy? Please let it be him."

"It is a Cadillac, just not white. There's a man walking up our sidewalk."

Kaylie rushed to the front door and out to the porch, wide-eyed and excited for good news. "May I help you?"

"Yes, perhaps you can. I'm Dr. Robert C. Walters. Are you Kaylie Werner?"

She looked back at Adam, standing in the doorway. The excitement she felt five seconds ago drained to nothing. "Yes, I'm Kaylie. What's going on? Is this about my father, Anthony Werner? We've been trying to contact him without any luck."

"It is about your father, yes. Can we go inside and talk?"

"Oh no, no, no. There has to be some mistake. What's wrong? Where is he? Adam, what's happening?"

"Please, let's go inside," said the doctor, looking at Adam for help.

"Honey," said Adam, "let's go sit down."

Though shaking, Kaylie made her way to the sofa with Adam next to her side. The doctor remained standing straight across from them.

"Please doctor, have a seat," said Adam, pointing to the matching love seat across from them.

"I am very sorry to intrude on your life with some terrible news," he said as he sat down. "As I mentioned, I am Dr. Walters and I am the county coroner."

Kaylie gasped. Adam placed his hand on her shoulder.

"I am sorry to tell you that your father has died and … ."

"No!" Kaylie wailed and buried her face in Adam's chest. He caressed her head with his right hand.

"What happened to him?" asked Adam.

"About an hour and a half ago, one of her father's co-workers went to an old house they had been working on. He noticed Mr. Werner's Cadillac parked out front. At first, he thought nothing of it. Upon looking into the vehicle, he saw his boss sitting in the passenger seat. It was at that point he knew your father was deceased. He immediately called the police. Which lead us here."

"I still don't understand. What happened? Was there a car accident? Did he get sick? I've been telling him he needed to take better care of himself, haven't I, Adam?"

"You certainly have, sweetheart, yes."

"I'm even sorrier to tell you two that your father did not fall ill. He was a victim of homicide."

Kaylie fell back on the sofa, numb. She tried to speak, but no words came out.

"Are there other family members we could contact?" asked the doctor.

Adam looked at Kaylie. She was still motionless, though her mind was racing. "Kaylie was an only child. Her mother passed away several years ago."

"Is there anyone else who can help during this difficult time? We can contact them as well."

Kaylie suddenly sat up on the sofa, hands on either side of her hips, giving her support. "What do I do now?" she asked. "What am I supposed to do next? Can I see him? Where is he?"

"I'm afraid you won't be able to see him tonight. His body is still in his car at the crime scene. I have the utmost confidence in the detectives who are seeking justice for your father. They will want to speak to you. I realize this is a tremendous shock and if you'd rather they wait until morning to speak with you, I will let them kn … ."

"No!" Kaylie demanded. "They can come over tonight. I have to know what happened. What are we going to do? Oh, my god … he's … oh Adam!"

"Very well Ms. Werner. I can send Detectives Jacobson and Winston over tonight. I will be returning to the scene and sending them your way. I promise I will take care of your father's body with the utmost care."

"Thank you, thank you," came her tear-soaked response.

"Are there any questions for me before I leave?"

"Who did this? Why did they do this?" asked Kaylie.

"I do not know. That will be the detective's primary mission — solving this case. They're the best at what they do. I mean that."

"Thank you, sir," said Adam.

"I want whoever did this to pay for it!" said Kaylie.

"Yes, ma'am, we all do. I'll show myself out."

With a quivering mouth and chin, Kaylie got up and ran to the bedroom. She threw herself on top of the bed, whimpering and crying as an eight-year-old child would. She wished she was eight again, and that her daddy was safe.

The Police - Crime Scene

May 19, 1977, Thursday evening, 11:29

"We all set?" asked Jacobson.

"Yeah, we've got both Third and Seventh taped off a block in each way and patrol has given us ten officers for canvassing and searching," replied Winston. "That going to be enough?"

"Should be. Looks like all the street lights are working. That is good. I see the neighbors are up now. Let's check the houses on this side. We can split up and alternate houses."

"Done," said Winston as he trotted over to the first house. Jacobson walked to the second home.

"Excuse me, do you live here?" Winston yelled over to his first interview — an elderly couple, probably in their late eighties, standing in front of a small but well-kept house.

"Yes sir, my wife Doris and I do. What's all the fuss about?" asked the man.

"Yeah, as you can see, we've had some excitement in your neighborhood. I'm Detective Winston. Did either of you notice anything suspicious tonight? Maybe some loud noise or people yelling, screeching tires, that kind of thing?"

"Well," said the older woman as she pulled her robe tightly across her nightgown, "I want to say I heard some loud voices about ten o'clock. No, just before. I was waiting for the TV news. It comes on at ten o'clock, you know, and I hate to miss it. Well, I'm waiting and waiting for it to come on." The detective shifted his feet a little and sighed. "But before it does, and I swear, I heard two men yelling. Then I heard two doors slam. Real hard slams, gosh, they were noisy. Then the fella hit the gas pretty good and they were gone."

"Did you see either man?"

"No. The door slamming happened just before I looked out the front window."

"Did you notice the vehicle that sped away?"

"Sort of, yes. It looked like one of them old, big pickups. The ones with those letters on the back."

"Big letters? Like F-O-R-D?"

"Young man, you can just say Ford. It's not a swear word around us!" The couple glanced at each other and laughed in unison. Winston just looked at her, then her husband, then back to her.

"Oh, I see. Good one. Was it a … Ford?" he asked with a bit of trepidation.

"Nope, I'm pretty sure it was a D-O-D-G-E, Dodge!" This time, they all three laughed.

"Your wife, she does stand-up comedy? That's a good one, ma'am. So it was a Dodge. Did you make out a color?"

"Not real sure about that. It was a light color, not white, but light like a pale green or blue."

"Any chance you saw part of the license plate?"

"No, I'm sorry, but I didn't."

"That's OK. Do you remember which way they went?"

"Sure, that way. North."

"That's some very good information, Doris. Sir, what about you? What did you see?"

"I'm afraid I didn't see nothing," said the elderly man. He looped his thumbs around his bib overall straps as his wife straightened out his collar. "Didn't hear nothing either. I was on the other side of the house, answering nature's call, you see, plus my hearing aids were out. I always take them out before bed."

"What about the house next door, the one getting remodeled? Anything unusual lately?"

"Just the … Doris, will you stop that!" The man softly pushed his wife's hand away from his collar. "I can groom myself! This young man doesn't need to see you groping me and all."

"I'm not groping you, you silly old man!" said the woman with a laugh.

"So, sir, back to the house. Anything odd there lately?"

"Just a lot of trucks. Always coming and going. Sometimes they park in my yard. Lot of hammering and sawing. Pisses me off. Can you do anything about that?"

"I'm afraid I can't. I appreciate your time, both of you, and you keep us laughing, ma'am, OK? I've got your address written down. Now, you are Doris. And you, sir?"

"I'm Henry, Henry Mitchell, we're married. Nearly sixty years!"

"I thought so, Henry. That's a long time; congratulations to you both. So here's my card. Give me a call if something comes to mind about tonight. You two have a good evening."

The couple struggled to read his card, the old man leaning over her shoulder. The detective was halfway to the next house when the old lady yelled out, "Take care D-E-T-E-C ... uhhh, well, however you spell it, take care detective."

With his back still turned to them, Detective Winston waved back.

Winston and Jacobson met in the middle of the street, the night air starting to chill.

"Please tell me you had better luck than I did. Four houses on this side, everybody out milling around. No one saw or heard anything. Dammit!" said Jacobson.

"I got a decent lead and may have found the next Mearer and Stilla duo."

"Stiller and Meara."

"Yeah, that's what I said. The lady, who I'll call Meara though she says her name is Doris, heard two guys yelling and slamming doors, and then she heard a truck racing off to the north. A light-colored Dodge."

"Good work, Winnie. Let's see what patrol found."

The two men walked south, passing the car with its lifeless body. The crime scene team was busy photographing the scene, marking objects of interest, and bagging other potential evidence. Detective Jacobson stopped to talk with the two members of the Identification Team, "Ann, Gerald, we have a lighter under the car. Label and photograph it, but leave it in place for now. We'll bag it later."

Ann answered, "You got it, Jake."

"Detectives, I may have something," yelled out a uniformed officer.

The detectives walked half a block south of the vehicle to where the officer was pointing.

"Hey Randy," said Winston. He recognized the officer from his time on patrol. "What do you have?"

"I thought that was you Winnie, good to see you, buddy," the officer replied. "I've got a set of keys here on a keychain. It even has a Cadillac emblem on it with the initials A. W. W."

"Jake, I don't know our vic's middle name, but I'd say we have his keys."

"Yes. Officer, get Ident down here for processing," ordered Jacobson. The officer trotted over to the identification team and spoke with them.

"You suppose our perps tossed them this way to try to throw us off their scent a bit?" asked Winston.

Jacobson looked back south, then north again. "It's certainly possible. Are they really that conniving? This is a solid piece of evidence. Let's hope we get some usable prints."

Nodding back towards the car, Winston said, "Looks like the coroner is back. I don't see how he does those notifications every single day. It'd wear me down."

"Me too. He's a special guy. I'm sure he's going to want to get that body moved soon."

Doctor Walters exited his car and walked over to a white van with dark blue stripes with the words 'CORONER'S OFFICE' stenciled in small, black letters on all four sides. Its two occupants, Terry Starmer and Glen Caldwell, stepped out to meet him.

"Doctor, are we ready to let Ident process the scene inside the vehicle?" asked Terry.

"Let me take a walk around the exterior again with Detective Jacobson. Detective Jacobson!" the doctor called out, "Can you come here, please?"

Jacobson walked up to the doctor. "Yeah doc, what can I do?"

"I'd like for us to take a walk around the car. Then we can open it up. You game?"

"Sure, let's do it."

"OK," the doctor began, "the driver's side door is locked. No noticeable blood on this side. The door is completely shut.

"Now I'm seeing something here," said Jacobson as he shined his flashlight in the driver's side window. "It looks like there is some blood spray inside the window. Maybe on the dash. Do you see that too?"

"Could be. Hey, Ident Team! Over here!"

Ann and Gerald walked over to the vehicle, each carrying a large chest that contained everything needed for an investigation; evidence bags, fingerprint kits, vials, various chemicals, film, and dozens of other tools of the trade. Each team member had a camera with a flash strapped across their shoulder.

"When we open the vehicle, go through the driver's door. I want the driver's side processed for prints and possible blood spray. I need one of you to handle that side. The other will assist me with the passenger side and our victim."

"You got it, doc," replied Gerald. "We'll process the back seat and trunk after the body has been removed. I'll get the driver's side worked. Ann can assist on the passenger side. Sound good to you, Ann?"

"Got it," replied Ann.

Dr. Walters and Detective Jacobson continued around the front of the car, flashlights in hand. "Let's just take this last pass nice and slow, Jake."

"Of course. Ann or Gerald, be sure to print the hood and the trunk lid in case they happened to lean up against it."

To which Ann replied, "Detective, we usually do that back at the impound garage. I've checked and there is no rain expected the rest of tonight."

"Very well."

They worked their way over to the passenger side. "This is key right here, Dr. Walters. I can feel it. Our vic either tried to jump out or the perps couldn't get the door shut afterwards," said Jacobson.

"Or both. Don't forget that possibility," added the doctor.

"Very true. I've never seen blood on the outside of a car like that. There's the puddle on the road. And the trail along the side."

"Stay in this business long enough and you'll see it all, trust me."

They completed the circuit around the car but found nothing else of immediate value.

"OK, listen up," said the doctor. "We're going to open up the car now. Everyone going in; fresh gloves. Jake, do you have your lockout kit?"

"Winnie does." Jake looked at Detective Winston and nodded his head towards the door.

Silently, the junior detective inserted the thin metal rod, hook end first and with a few quick turns and a pull, had the door lock knob grasped and raised. His gloved hand slowly opened the door.

Those closest to the door could smell the familiar and bitter iron odor of blood.

First to peer inside was Detective Jacobson, scanning for any clues. "I see the blood spray from our victim and back towards the driver. Enough blood to create what appears to be the outline of the driver. It's smudged, but it's there. Looks like a bloody partial print on the steering wheel. I can see two distinct holes in his suit jacket, left shoulder, an inch or two apart. Well, that's odd."

"What is it, Jake?" asked Winston.

"Looks like two corresponding holes in the seat. I think he was shot through the back of his seat."

"No shit? Isn't that rare?"

"Certainly is." Jacobson pulled back out into the fresh night air and took a deep breath. "Did you catch that, Dr. Walters? Through the seat back."

"Yes, I heard. We've seen that a few times, rare but not unheard of either. Shall we go around?"

"Let's do it," said Jacobson. "You ready for this, Winnie?"

"Of course."

"Jake," the doctor began, "have some uniforms hold up sheets on the passenger side. One near the front of the car, the other towards the back. My techs will bring the sheets over. There's too many people milling around. We'll give Mr. Werner some dignity."

Jake whistled, "Sergeant Riley, give me four uniforms to hold up some sheets once we're ready to remove the body."

"Wilson, Smith, Barbieri, and McGee; over here," barked the sergeant. "You four guys hang out over there. We will want some privacy once the coroner moves the body for transport."

"Yes sir," mumbled one of the officers.

Detective Winston brought over the lockout kit to work his magic on the passenger side.

"Try not to touch his head. I know the lock is quite close to him," said the coroner.

"Got it, doc," replied Winston.

"And before we do anything, I need to have Terry reach over the driver's seat and steady our victim's body. I want a quick look before we place him on the stretcher."

Terry double-timed it over to the driver's side and positioned himself for the task. "Ready here," he called out.

"Officers, please take your positions and raise those sheets," said the doctor

Winston worked his way through the crowd of personnel to the door. "Doc, are all these folks needed here?"

"No, they aren't. Listen up," said the coroner. "Besides the officers screening the scene, I only want myself, Detectives Winston and Jacobson and Glen, on this side of the car. Sergeant, can you handle the gurney, please?"

"You bet," the sergeant said as he took hold of one end of the stretcher, steadying it against the uneven ground.

"Let's do this," said the coroner.

The detective stepped up to the window and carefully fed the thin metal tool inside the door jamb. "It's easier getting that inside with the door ajar," observed Winston. "There got it. We're unlocked. Let me get the tool out and then I'll stand back."

He stepped back to give the others more room. Detective Jacobson, the coroner, and his technician, Glen, stepped in and filled the void.

"Charles, please take control of the door. Glen and I will slide the victim onto his back. Terry will help from the other side. We'll have you, Sarge, push the gurney on my go."

With that, Detective Jacobson slowly let the door swing open as the coroner's team manipulated the body as planned.

"Sarge, bring it!"

With that, the gurney wheels clattered as they dropped off the curb onto the street.

"OK Glen, let's lift on three. One ... two ... three," ordered the coroner, and they deftly placed Anthony Werner on the gurney. Terry had come around with a fresh sheet and placed it over the body. Glen and Terry each secured a strap, one around the chest, the other below the knees. Two techs lifted the gurney behind the car and onto the street. From there, it was a short roll to the coroner's office transport van.

"Good job everyone," congratulated the coroner. He then called out to his techs, "Ann, Gerald, secure the vehicle for transport, please. We have garage space for it at our facility."

"Will do doc," said Gerald.

"Now we solve this," said the coroner.

The Police - Next Of Kin

May 20, 1977, Friday morning, 12:43

"Is that them?" Kaylie yelled from the bedroom upon hearing the two car doors shut.

"I'm sure it is." Adam headed out the door to meet them.

"Good evening sir. I'm Detective Jacobson and this is my partner, Detective Winston. Is this Kaylie Werner's residence?"

"Yes, it is. I'm her fiancé, Adam Carlson. So this is true. Tony has been murdered?"

"I'm sorry to say that is correct, sir. You have our condolences. Is Kaylie well enough to talk? I imagine this must be a shock."

"A shock? My god man, yes, it's a shock to all of us."

"Sorry, I didn't mean it that way. Can I speak with her alone and perhaps Detective Winston can talk to you out here? That way, we can speed this up. I know it's late, and this is such a difficult time. If it becomes too much tonight, we can talk in the morning. We must speak to both of you to help us with this tragedy."

"I'm sure she will want to talk now. That's just how she is. Let me go in and make sure. I'll be right back. By the way, we went over to Anthony's place earlier tonight. The townhouse looked normal, but the garage door was wide open. Of course, the car was gone. He never leaves the door open."

"About what time was this?" asked Winston.

"Around ten."

"Did anyone close the door?" said Jacobson as Adam headed back inside the house.

Without turning back, Adam replied, "No, we did not."

"I *imagine* this must be a shock. Why did you say that, Jake? You *imagine*?" asked Winston.

"Winnie, I had to see his reaction, and he passed. Like our coroner friend, we do things in this job that are difficult. Testing someone, seeing if they slip up, is one of those things. Even when you know they are innocent."

"Well, he passed with flying collars, no less."

"Colors, flying colors."

"That's what I said."

"Why do you do that? Never mind, now I know I won't have to ask, 'Hey, Winnie, how come you're not married?'. It's because you're a fucking idiot."

"I'm a catch and you know it. Maybe you even think I'm pretty ... ."

"Pretty stupid."

"That's what *you* think."

Adam stuck his head out the front door, "You can come in now."

"Thank you, Adam," said Jacobson. "My partner can talk to you if you're ready." Turning towards his partner, he said, "Winnie, get on the radio. Get some uniforms to secure that garage."

"Take it easy on her, please," said Adam as he passed Jacobson on the sidewalk.

"Ms. Werner? May I come in ma'am?" asked Jacobson.

"Yes, I'm in here."

Jacobson turned left into the brightly lit living room. "Ms. Werner. I know Dr. Walters stopped by earlier. Myself and my partner, Detective Jay Winston, offer our deepest condolences. You need to know we will do everything we can to catch those responsible."

"I appreciate that. I really do. But I have to know what happened. The coroner wouldn't tell me anything more than my father has been murdered. I don't know where he is. Why did this happen? When can I see him? I have so many questions. I know nothing, and I hope you can help with that."

"I can answer most of those questions before we leave here. I have several questions for you. If it's all right with you, can we start there?"

She waved the back of her hand, "I suppose. Go ahead."

"Thank you, ma'am. I will tell you that dispatch received a call notifying the police that your father was found. The person calling also requested an ambulance. Two officers were the first to respond and determined that your father had passed."

"Who was it that called?"

"We can talk about that later. I need to ask you some questions first. When did you last speak to your father?"

"I called his office Thursday, but he was in a meeting. We had planned a brunch the next day … ." Her voice trailed off as she hung her head. "Sorry, we had brunch planned, but it never happened. I last talked to him sometime Monday night. I called him just to say hello. We talked for maybe ten minutes, and that was it. That was it."

"Aside from normal little family squabbles, did you get along with him OK?"

"Of course, my god! Since my mother died, we've been nothing but supportive of each other. I can't remember when we had any cross words. So, no, not at all."

"Ms. Werner, please, I … ."

"Call me Kaylie. It's OK. I understand you are just doing your job."

"I am. Thank you for the understanding. Do you know of anyone he was having problems with? Such as a neighbor, co-worker, or clients of his?"

"I can't think of anyone. He never mentioned anything like that. You should talk to his secretary. She knows everything about the business and all of Dad's clients. Patti Jordan will be in the office by seven this morning. Oh god, she can't find out from the news or a client. I will have to call her before she leaves for work."

"Had your father hinted at any financial problems with the business, any money problems at all?"

"If there were, he kept them to himself. He's always enjoyed the finer things in life. Clothes and cars. He loves … loved his Cadillac cars. Mother and daddy always had nice homes. Took vacations all over the world. They both loved jewelry. He never had money problems."

"Did your dad wear jewelry, flashy clothes, flaunt his money around?"

"Well, he always had his wedding ring on, even once he started dating again. Maybe he would wear a pinky ring, a nice watch."

"Dating? Was he seeing anyone?"

"He's been seeing one woman, Joanie Relaford, for the past year or so, unfortunately."

Detective Jacobson sat up straight. "You say unfortunately. Why is that?"

"Oh, it's nothing. Just my opinion of the woman. I'm sure she likes him a lot, maybe loves him. I feel she loves the perks his money has brought her. I don't think she is evil, she's just used my daddy for trips and clothes. Everything my mother should have enjoyed."

"Kaylie," he said, "my watch is telling me it is very late. I had promised I would answer your questions. What I can tell you is that your father was shot to death in his car. An employee of your father's, Larry McDermott, found your father in the Cadillac. Do you know Mr. McDermott?"

"Yes I do. He's a hard worker, a good man. He must be broken-hearted."

"He was taking it pretty hard, of course. The car was parked at Third Street and Seventh Avenue. He was the only occupant. By now, the coroner will be ready to remove his body from the scene and will transport your father's remains to the coroner's office for autopsy."

"Can I go there and see him?"

"That won't be possible tonight. That just can't happen. I'd like to speak with you again when you are ready. Here is my card. Call me day or night. I'll send your fiancé back in and we'll be on our way. Again, I am so sorry this happened."

Without a word, Kaylie watched the detective walk out the door. Adam came in and said something. Exactly what she didn't hear. He sat down next to her and embraced her. Car doors slammed. An engine started. The car's tires rolled away softly on the pavement and the rest of the sounds faded away. The room was silent as Kaylie slumped across Adam's lap and wept.

The Young Man - Innocence Chipped

May 20, 1977, Friday morning, 6:45

THE SUN HAD BEEN up for forty-five minutes and the young man was ready for work. This quiet seventeen-year-old looked outside through the scalloped, white-laced curtains that bracketed the family's breakfast nook window — gazing but not seeing. He always thought of the day ahead. He thought of his life ahead. His young, but already rough hands lifted a tall glass of orange juice to his mouth as he swallowed down the last few sips. He sat dressed in a light blue pinstriped shirt that was, thanks to his mom, laundered and ironed. Stitched above the left shirt pocket in dark green, cursive letters, told all who noticed that this was Tom. He stood and stretched, yawned, then continued to look out the window. An occasional car would pass in front of the house, but it was otherwise peaceful and quiet. He liked late spring mornings here in the only place he had known as home. He could slow down his mind and feel very peaceful to start his day. It was important to him to start his day that way, calm and relaxed, as his days often ended up hectic, even for a seventeen-year-old. Another day of work for him. He stepped outside, being careful to not let the screen door slam behind him for fear of waking up his parents. He reached into his jeans pocket and pulled out his set of keys. Unlocking and opening the door, he hopped into his truck. Not really his truck, but the gas station's. The All-City Service logo was emblazoned on the doors. His father, who owned the business, often warned Tom that he'd better not get in an accident with that truck. The short ten-block drive to work through the still sleepy neighborhood calmed him.

It was, in many ways, a classic American town, a small city. Not quite Norman Rockwell. No large congregations of poverty. No dilapidated city center. On its surface, it was idyllic. Beautiful shade trees lining the streets and, in keeping with the stereotype, white picket fences in what seemed like every other yard. However, the fences neither held in that idyll nor kept out the unsavory elements.

Tom pulled up to the gas station that spring day. The air smelled fresh and new and the breeze carried with it such hope and promise. For Tom — Tommy to his friends — hope meant escaping this small city. He wanted bigger things than carrying on the family's small yet prosperous enterprise. He had to strike out on his own someday. To that end, he studied hard, took extra classes, and was set to graduate high school a year early. He had applied to several universities, was accepted by most of them, and even offered generous scholarships. Now he had to decide which offer to accept, and soon. He was proud of these scholarship offers as his intent was to pay for school on his own; he wanted to prove he could be independent. Today was just another day of work.

His dad, Lou Newton, was very proud of the business he started well before Tom was born. He toiled night and day, usually seven days a week. Early on in life, he ingrained in all of his children his personal slogan, 'When you're working, work as hard as you can. When you're playing, play as hard as you can'.

On this day, Tommy was working hard pumping gas, changing oil, fixing flat tires, and washing windshields; exceptionally busy for a Friday. The work was hard. Long hours came with the place. Sweating during the long, hot, humid summers; trying and failing to stay warm while the winter's frigid air tried to take your breath away. But working with his dad could be fulfilling. He loved helping the family business thrive, as well as seeing how happy his father was with its success. The money did not define this prosperity. It also gave them pride knowing that they built this from nothing as a family.

A few hours after starting work, Tommy was busy finishing up an oil change on Mike Harrison's 1975 Buick Regal. It was a beautiful blue car with a white Landau roof, one that Mr. Harrison adored, maybe to excess.

"Tom, did you get that oil plug back on tight? Just not too tight, OK?" he asked.

Before Tommy could answer, he was asking about the oil filter. Did it get changed as asked? Was it also tight enough?

With a smile on his face, albeit a forced one, Tommy said, "You bet, sir! I sure did!"

"For heaven's sake, before you back her out, make sure your clothes are clean, OK?"

Eyeing the accumulation of dirt and grime on the kid's work shirt gave Mr. Harrison a bit of a start and a change of heart. "Scratch that. Let me back it out, then we won't have to worry. OK, young man?" He smiled, patted Tom on his shoulder, and glided past him and into his car.

Tom shrugged and watched him climb into his cherished automobile. He meticulously adjusted his tie and then the rear-view mirror, checking both before starting up the car. He backed it out, tires banging the heavy metal car lift against the concrete floor. Tom waved, and nodded with a fake, insincere smile, adding a mocking thumbs-up parting shot to Mr. Harrison.

Once out of his line of sight, the kid shook his head and muttered under his breath, "Whatever. You strange little man."

Pulling a rag out of his back pocket, he habitually began wiping his hands, wondering what else the day would bring. That question would soon be answered.

Tom could see his dad walking his way. He was a large and muscular man, standing around six feet tall. If his physical presence didn't intimidate you, his stern and often brusque demeanor would. As he got closer, the look on his father's face made Tom stop in his tracks. It was an expression he'd seen often in his seventeen years and he knew it was not good. He sighed, knowing he must have screwed up something. With shoulders slumped and mind racing, he walked towards his father.

In a mild panic, his eyes darted from the service bay, then down to the ground. He looked back at his father's face, even though Tom could rarely maintain constant eye contact with him. His eyes were red and his lips were pursed together. Tom noticed the newspaper in his father's hand, tightly rolled, his hand squeezing it slowly and rhythmically.

"Tommy," he said quietly, "heard some bad news. It's just ... I mean ... well, here."

He reached towards his son, newspaper in hand. Tom took the paper from him and unrolled it. Tom was confused, yet felt an odd sense of relief that he wasn't in trouble.

"What's the matter? What is it, Dad?"

He looked quizzically at his dad, but his expression remained the same, not giving Tommy any clue. He quickly shifted his focus back to the paper and started scanning the print. *STOCKS SOAR* screamed the main headline, obviously not the source of dismay. *Tornado Claims Five in Texas* read another, slightly smaller headline. He didn't think they knew anyone from Texas, but still pointed at the article.

"Is it this? The tornado?" he asked without much conviction.

Tommy's dad glanced down, shook his head once, and tapped his thick index finger several times on the story at the bottom right corner of the front page. There, in smaller but also bold print, the headline read, *Local Construction Company Owner Dead*. The first few words of the article caught in Tommy's throat as he read them out loud, "Anthony Werner, local homebuilder and remodeling specialist, was found dead … ."

Dumbfounded, he looked at his father. "Mr. Werner? But what happened? Why? I saw him the other day. Everything seemed … ."

His voice trailed off in silent disbelief as he walked around in a compact circle, trying to understand what he just read.

"Can I get that car wash now?" It was Mr. Harrison, interrupting. Locked in a fog, Tommy simply ignored him. He sat down in the office and stared at the newsprint; not comprehending any of the words.

As if vaguely echoing from a faraway tunnel, he heard his dad say cheerfully, "You bet, Mike, just pull it into the car wash and I'll get it started for you."

After a few minutes, Tommy caught his breath and tried to pull all of his thoughts together. He thought about this kind man, suddenly taken from this world. He was easily twenty years older than Tommy's father, and he had just seen him the day before when he stopped at the gas station. He remembered his sleek white Cadillac, how it was always clean and seemed to be freshly waxed. Always smiling, asking Tommy how he was doing. He was always in good spirits. Tommy saw him two or three times a week to fill up with gas. He put a lot of miles on that car. Tommy assumed that business must be good for Mr. Werner.

He eased back in the chair and looked up at the ceiling, slowly exhaling. Picking up the newspaper, moving quickly past the stories about the stocks and the Texas tornado, and focused on the short story about Mr. Werner. It read:

Local Construction Company Owner Dead

By Edward Evans, Staff Writer

Anthony Werner, a local homebuilder and remodeling specialist, was found dead last night near the corner of Third Street and Seventh Avenue. A police spokesman stated that Mr. Werner, owner of Werner Custom Builders, was found unresponsive inside his 1977 Cadillac Coupe de Ville by an employee of his company. The employee, Larry McDermott, was en route to a nearby building site to retrieve some tools when he recognized Mr. Werner's car parked along the roadside. Thinking it strange he would be there at that time, he walked to the car. He noticed his employer slumped in the passenger side of the front seat. Mr. McDermott tapped on the passenger window. Finding the car doors locked and getting no response, he ran to a nearby house and phoned police.

The police arrived and cordoned off the area around the vehicle. The medical examiner was summoned to the scene and declared Mr. Werner deceased.

A cause of death has not been released, pending an autopsy. The county coroner's office stated that the autopsy was expected to be completed tomorrow.

Police stated no further details will be released at this time.

"Oh my god!" was all he could say.

Soon Mr. Harrison's car wash was complete and Tommy's dad walked into the office.

"Did you read the story, son? Just terrible. He seemed like a good man. Good customer too."

Looking up from the desk, Tommy's red eyes told him the answer.

"Yes, he was very nice. What do you suppose happened?"

"I don't know. Wonder why he was in the passenger seat? Kind of odd. A heart attack and fell over there?"

"Yeah, could be. He was pretty old."

"Old to you, maybe. I think he was only around sixty."

"Guess it doesn't matter how he died. Man, I don't know what to think."

Tommy thought back to the last time Mr. Werner stopped in, maybe a week ago, and remembered that he was his typical, jovial self. He recalled his tank was nearly empty, marking down twenty-three gallons of premium as well as two quarts of windshield washer solvent on the running account the station kept for him. He needed to run his Caddy through the car wash as it was pretty dirty, probably from driving around all those construction sites. But Mr. Werner seemed too busy that day.

He remembered Mr. Werner saying, "Tommy, thanks son, you're the best!" as he held out that five-dollar bill.

The kid would never see him again.

Two cars pulled into the drive, running over the bell hose, announcing their presence by singing out *ding-ding! ding-ding!* as their tires crossed. The sound snapped Tommy out of that memory. His dad trotted out to one car, and he slowly walked to the other. The day was a blur of customers. He found his mind unsettled. He needed to know what happened. How this man he genuinely liked was now gone.

The Coroner - Autopsy

May 20, 1977, Friday morning, 9:30

Anthony Werner's body was waiting for Dr. Walters when he entered the examination theater, followed by his assistant, Dr. Marsha Fullerton. The twenty degree drop in temperature from one room to the next was noticeable. Both doctors were wearing light blue scrubs and scrub caps. As they neared the body, they pulled their face masks over their mouth and nose. They each pulled a pair of surgical gloves out of a supply box that sat on a table next to the body. A thin blue sheet covered his naked and lifeless body. Dr. Walters flicked on the room's overhead lights, replacing the dimly lit room with a flood of bright white light.

"Turn on the recorder please Marsha," the doctor said to his assistant as he glanced at the long, thin overhead microphone that hung down above the body. The light click of the button echoed in the cool, sterile room.

"Today's date is 20 May 1977. The time is 9:32 a.m. I have before me the remains of one Anthony William Werner, a white male, sixty-one years of age. I'll begin with the postmortem anatomic diagnoses. Assisting is Dr. Marsha Fullerton, who will be responsible for the accurate measurements of wounds, fluids, and organs, as well as providing oversight. Two gunshot wounds to the left shoulder are observed. Entrance wounds are located thirty-eight millimeters apart, in the middle third section of the scapula. Both wounds exhibit some minor gunpowder burns and fiber material consistent with firearm muzzle-to-clothing close contact. The stippling, while faint, surrounds each abrasion rim. Fiber material is partially embedded in each abrasion rim. The origin of the fibers is likely to be from two sources — the deceased's clothing and the vehicle's padded leather seat. I was present at the crime scene, leading to that theory. A study of fibers from this wound will be compared with the deceased's clothing and the automobile's interior fabric. The posterior wound path is skin, subcutaneous tissue, muscle of the left shoulder, and scapula. The projectile then penetrated the upper lobe of the left lung, nicking the posterior third rib, aortic artery, and esophagus. Significant blood pooling in the chest cavity is noted. The projectile was recovered in tissue adjacent to the lower right lung. The anterior wound path is skin, subcutaneous tissue, muscle of the left shoulder, and scapula. The projectile then passed through soft tissue and adjacent to the right lung. Minor hemorrhaging is observed at the approximate center of the right lung. Exit wound between posterior right fourth and fifth rib. Exit wound approximately fifty millimeters in width, jagged in appearance. Outward beveling of the margin is observed along with the expected subcutaneous hemorrhaging. Per the police report, the projectile was recovered at the scene."

He paused and asked his assistant, "Doctor, do you have any concerns before proceeding to the head wound?"

"The fresh abrasion, top of his head should be noted," she said. "I see faint bruising on the left forearm that could be a defensive wound. I note abrasions on the knuckles of the right hand. Those could be offensive wounds in nature. Hmmm, the left ear lobe is partly severed."

"Notable bruising behind the ear. The wound is consistent with a slightly curved object. Outwardly, it does not appear to be contributory to death."

"Agreed," said Dr. Fullerton

"Excellent observations," said Dr. Walters. "Perhaps my friend here put up a fight."

"There is one gunshot wound to the left temple, again exhibiting heavy gunpowder burns consistent with firearm muzzle-to-skin contact. The stippling surrounds the abrasion rim. Unlike the other two wounds, no fiber evidence in or around the wound's entry. The wound path is skin, subcutaneous tissue, upper right quadrant of the sphenoid bone. Significant fracturing of the zygomatic arch and orbital plate. Projectile passed cleanly through the prefrontal cortex. The projectile exited the right cheekbone, fifty millimeters below the eye socket causing significant damage to the bone structure on the right side of the face including complete fragmentation of the right zygomatic bones, a fractured mandible with numerous fissures radiating from the coronoid process. Multiple upper teeth are loose or fractured. The exit wound is jagged and is approximately seventy to seventy-five millimeters at its widest. A large amount of tissue and bone was found inside the victim's vehicle, samples were taken for analysis. Blood and bone tissue were also found outside of the victim's vehicle and were collected. Detectives located bullet fragments lodged in the passenger door next to where the deceased was found."

The standard 'Y' incision was made, exposing the internal organs which were removed, weighed, and measured. Blood and other fluid samples were taken and sent to the lab for analysis. The top of the skull was opened for removal and examination of the brain.

"Cause of death is the gunshot wound to the left temple. However, the posterior shoulder wound would have been fatal unto itself unless emergency medical intervention was provided in a timely manner. Preliminary toxicology reports are expected to be completed within twenty-four hours as well as organ measurements and tissue sample reports."

Dr. Walters clicked off the overhead recording device and began sewing up the 'Y' incision. He turned to Dr. Fullerton. "I played a couple of rounds of golf with Mr. Werner, a very nice man."

"What a small world. His company did some remodeling work at our lake home, maybe even our kitchen here in town. I remember him as very kind and very professional. Any leads on this?" asked Dr. Fullerton.

"As of this morning, no. Detective Jacobson is the best. I would expect whoever did this will be apprehended."

"Good. I'll get the tox screens, measurements, fiber, and tissue samples processed right away."

"Excellent. I'll give Detective Jacobson a call and get a meeting set up this afternoon."

The Coroner - Police Report

THE CORONER'S OFFICE DESIGN was simple with distinct functional sections of the building lined up in sequence. Beyond the reception area, there was an open area providing room for all the support personnel's desks, four meeting rooms, a few private offices for management, and a private observation room with large glass windows providing visitors a view of the autopsy room. Beyond the autopsy room was a refrigerated morgue. Bodies were held here prior to autopsy and before being released to the family. The final area was the receiving room.

Detectives Jacobson and Winston were led past the open office area with its steady, chattering noise and into one of the meeting rooms by the receptionist, Nicole. The room itself was plain. The walls were painted off-white color and full of framed, professional designations the employees had achieved. A mini refrigerator hummed away on a counter. Above it, a corkboard with small posters announcing the next staff picnic, a photo of a small dog below the words, 'Have You Seen Me?'.

"Gentlemen, Dr. Walters will be with you in a minute. He apologizes but he had a meeting run long. Can I get you anything? Water? Coffee?"

"No thanks Nicole, we're good," replied Jacobson.

The receptionist closed the door as she exited.

"God, I cannot get used to the smell of the chemicals here!" said Winston.

"I don't even notice it anymore, and that's kind of sad."

"Say, after this we need ... " but the doctor's entrance interrupted Winston.

"Gentlemen," said the doctor as he sat down, "good afternoon. I trust you are both well. How is the investigation going, Detective Jacobson?"

"In a word, slow," said Jacobson. "We hope you have some good leads for us."

"There was no confession, if that's what you mean," the doctor chuckled briefly. "I don't have anything pointing to a suspect. I do have my preliminary report containing all the medical information about Mr. Werner's demise." He slid a folder to each detective. "You'll also find autopsy photos in the back of the file."

Detective Jacobson started to leaf through the file. "Can we skip all the ten-dollar words and tell me what you think, doc?"

"Always direct, Jake. I like that about you! As you know, he suffered three bullet wounds. Two in the shoulder. One in the temple. The shot in the temple was the kill shot. One of the shoulder wounds could have led to his death on its own. He had a few slight wounds I can't explain. There is bruising on the left hand, perhaps he hit someone or something, indicative of a defensive wound. A minor abrasion on top of his head — a trivial injury. For some reason, part of his left earlobe was cut. There was bruising behind that ear. Something struck him there. Quite hard."

"Perhaps our vic put up a struggle. Might explain the partially open passenger door," added Detective Winston. "Doc, would there have been a lot of blood loss from the shoulder wounds? I'm trying to explain the blood we found on the outside of the vehicle to determine the order of events."

"I'm certain most of the blood on the outside was from the head wound. There was considerable blood pooling in the abdominal cavity from the shoulder wounds, though there was one exit wound in his side. Perhaps that provided some of that exterior blood. That head wound was devastating. Ballistics is running tests on the bullets from the scene and in the body. They are the same caliber — .45's. Ballistics will probably confirm they are from the same gun. Have you found a gun?"

"Nothing yet and our neighborhood canvas has not yielded much either," said Jacobson.

"The lab has some preliminary results, nothing unusual, very low blood alcohol level. He may have had a beer or a glass of wine earlier in the evening," offered the doctor.

"We're going to talk to with daughter later today," Jacobson said, pointing to his partner. "Our brief questioning last night was tough on her. She was so distraught, Winnie felt it was best to give her some extra time."

"I'm sure her fiancé, Adam, is with her now," added Winston.

"Ok, gentlemen, shall we go take a look?"

Quietly, the three men rose. The detectives followed the doctor down a short hallway and into the autopsy room. There were three tables, each holding a sheet-covered body.

"Glove up, please," said Walters. The men gathered around the body as they pulled on the latex gloves. The detectives stood on one side. The doctor stood across from them. The sheet was pulled back, giving the detectives their first glimpse of the lifeless, naked body. "The entrance wound to the temple," he said, pointing at the wound with his index finger. He tilted the head towards the men, "Obviously, this is the exit wound."

"Jesus Christ!" gasped Winston.

"Indeed," said the doctor, "as I said, a devastating wound."

"The minor injuries you mentioned, show me those," said Jacobson.

"Yes. Here is the abrasion. Just scuffing on top of the head. Nothing serious. However, the cut on the ear must have hurt. It may have knocked him out. On his left hand are the possible defensive wounds across the knuckles. Before I turn him over, notice the exit wound in his side. That shot could have been fatal. He would have bled out. Unless, that is, he received medical care within half an hour. Now let me roll him over for a second. Detective Winston, when I get him moved, please steady the body so we can get a good look at the entrance wounds on his shoulder."

"You got it, Doc."

The doctor rolled the body towards him, revealing the wounds to the two detectives. "As you can see, they are quite close to each other, and my gut tells me they were fired in rapid order."

Jacobson looked at Winston, then back at the doctor. "You're good, Doc. We noted that the back of the seat had two entrance holes. The exit holes overlapped each other somewhat. It looks like there may have been a struggle and our gunman panicked and let Mr. Werner have it. I'll bet those perp's ears are still ringing. Shooting a .45 off inside of a car would be tremendously loud! It may have even caused some hearing loss, at least temporarily. Any other injuries of note?"

Dr. Walters replied, "No, nothing else. There were no injuries below the waist. Help me lower him back on the table, Detective Winston."

"Anything of note about personal belongings?" asked Winston. "I can let the family know."

"No, there was no jewelry on his person or in his clothing. As I recall, we saw a ring on the passenger floorboard," the doctor said. "That got bagged by a tech. No wallet was found anywhere. There were three five-dollar bills folded neatly in his back left pocket. The bad guys didn't find those, but that's it."

The doctor pulled the clean blue sheet back up and over the body.

"What about these other two bodies? Anything involving us?" Winston asked the doctor.

"No, nothing suspicious about them. Unattended deaths."

The men walked towards the exit. They dropped the gloves off in a waste basket as they left the room.

"Great work, as usual. We'll be in touch if there are questions," said Jacobson.

"Of course, feel free to contact me or Doctor Fullerton. She assisted me with the autopsy and is overseeing tissue and tox reports. Good luck gentlemen."

"Until next time, doc!" said Winston as he nodded and followed his partner out.

"My god Jake, that exit wound was the worst I've seen."

"I know. They'll need a talented mortician if they want an open casket. We'll just keep that detail from the daughter. Let's head over there now." Jacobson tossed the keys to Winston. "You drive. I'm going to sift through the file again."

The Young Man - A Way To Cope

May 20, 1977, Friday afternoon, 1:25

THE WORKDAY SEEMED ENDLESS. Tommy needed to talk to someone about this. He also felt he needed a drink. Both of these needs could be met by a visit to his friend Richie.

First, he needed to ask his dad if he could take off for the rest of the day. With a deep breath, he followed his dad into the service bay. A gentle breeze flowing past the large bay doors provided a respite from the ever-present odor of oil and lubricating grease.

"Hey Tommy, good job on cleaning this bay up," said his dad with his back turned to his son.

"Yeah, yeah, no problem," Tommy paused for several seconds before continuing. "Dad, this Mr. Werner thing is hanging over me. It's bothering me."

"Yes, he was a good man. I'm sorry he has passed," said his dad while checking the inventory of alternator belts.

Tommy shuffled his feet back and forth and took a deep breath.

"What's on your mind, Tom?"

"Dad, I need the day off. I need to clear my head. Maybe talk to some friends about this."

"Talk about what? Mr. Werner? What is there to talk about? The man died, which is sad. Life goes on."

"I know, I know. This caught me off guard. I'm just stunned by it. It's weird."

"I don't understand. You've known people who have died and didn't act like this. Hell, my dad died and you just kind of went about your day. You went to school the next day. Go ahead! Hang out with some girls or fuck off with that Richie character. Go!" He walked past Tommy and into his office, slamming the door behind him.

"I was five when Grandpa died. Five … ."

After a quick stop at home to shower the grime off and change clothes, he was on his way over to his friend's house.

Richie had lived just up the street from Tommy for several years. The two hit it off right away. They shared many memories of childhood: adventures in the neighborhood creek, riding bikes throughout the town, playing just about every sport together. Despite Richie being two years older than Tommy, the two were close as brothers. People often thought they were brothers because they were inseparable. As they grew older, they would be each other's confidante and sounding board. They discussed everything from girls to pizza, parents, life, and death.

Tommy got to Richie's apartment and walked in without knocking. Knocking was not necessary for those two. As usual, the place was immaculate. Everything was in place, everything was dusted. The carpet was freshly vacuumed. Tommy had long ago stopped kidding Richie about this, and he ceased to notice the cleanliness. His friend was sitting on the couch in a bright red and white striped shirt; his thin blond hair bouncing to the blaring music. He had his arm around a girl Tommy had never met. But Richie liked to play the field, so seeing yet another attractive girl didn't phase Tommy.

"Tommy!" he shouted, jumping and accidentally whacking the back of his new friend's head with the inside of his forearm.

"Ouch, Richie! Jesus!" she yelped, quickly checking her short, blond hair and patting it back in place.

"Sorry, sorry," he said, turning to her and kneeling as if to beg forgiveness. She rolled her eyes and waved him away, giggling slightly. She also looked up at Tommy and smiled, tilting her head just a bit.

He got up off his knee and trotted over to Tommy, smiling broadly. They exchanged hand slaps and sat down. Tommy sat on an old rocking chair across from the couch. Richie sat back down next to the girl.

"Tommy, this is the lovely Rita." With dancing eyebrows, he looked over at Tommy.

Tommy smiled and nodded. Her natural beauty, complete with short blonde hair and soft, tanned skin struck him instantly. She wore a white tank top and blue jean shorts, the kind with the fringe hanging down, that accentuated her petite figure. Richie always had pretty girls in tow.

"Hey Rita, how's it going?" he nodded towards the girl, fighting the urge to stare at her.

"Doing good, doing good," she said as she snapped the gum she had in her mouth and smiled back — a certain sideways smile that caught Tommy's attention.

"Rita here is a meter maid, Tommy. How cool is that?" asked Richie.

"That's not true, Tommy," said Rita.

"You make a Beatle's reference and you go with that one? You need professional help. Maybe listen to more music too!" joked Tommy.

Tommy sat up straight in the recliner next to the sofa, which was also next to Rita.

"What's going on, man?" asked Richie.

"Bad day. Bad, bad day."

"Well, you work in a gas station so … ." Richie laughed, but Tommy stared straight ahead.

Rita swiveled her body to the left, facing Tommy, and said, "I hear your daddy owns the service station. My friend Tanya mentioned that. All-City right?"

"What? Wait … oh sorry. Yeah, my family runs the place."

"Well, I think it's a big deal. Just ignore Richie's shitty little joke."

"Hey!" shouted Richie, arms reaching out, a wide grin on his face.

"No, it's cool. I'm used to his quote,unquote humor," said Tommy, "Its just that one of the customers I knew pretty well died last night and I feel, well, I'm not sure how I feel."

"Oh yeah? Who?" asked Richie, sitting up straight now.

Rita reached over and touched Tommy's knee, pursing her lips as she tilted her head again. He tried not to notice, but he certainly did.

"Um, Mr. Werner. They found him dead last night, sitting in his car, but they didn't say what happened. He was a pretty cool guy. I'm just freaking out a bit because, other than one of my grandpas, I haven't known anyone very well who died."

"Let me treat you to a brewski man. Rita, get him a beer!"

"Of course, I'll get him a beer. And up yours Richie!"

Nimbly jumping from the sofa, she happily swooshed past Tommy. He could feel the gentle breeze created as she passed, carrying with it a sweet fragrance that also caught his attention. He wanted to ask Richie about this Rita girl, but she quickly returned from the kitchen.

"Here you are, sweetie, nice and cold." Rita cracked open the can, taking a small sip before handing it to Tommy. "Who's contributing to the delinquency of this minor? Me or you, Richie?"

"You should be able to figure that out soon enough, eh, Rita? Tommy, this fine-looking lady is going to college to become a lawyer. What do you think of that? Go ahead and get into trouble. Play your cards right and Rita will get you off. Scot free!"

"Very cool. You must be going to Sunderson." Tommy pointed at her t-shirt.

"That I am. How about you? Is college in your future?" She gave him a wink as she sat down on the sofa. This time, further away from Richie.

"Looking at a couple of places out of state, engineering, I suppose."

Richie interrupted, "More like a few schools are looking at you! Rita, this guy is a wanted man! Oh, and Tommy, I know you were looking at her boobs when you saw the name on her shirt!"

"Very nice, Tommy," she said, smiling at Tommy with her eyes as she took a sip of beer and completely ignored Richie's side comment.

"So Tom-Tom, this Werner guy, he the construction guy, big money guy ... all that? The guy you can't stop talking about?" asked Richie.

"I can stop talking about him long enough to tell you to fuck off!" Tommy glared at Richie.

Rita and Richie froze. Richie's beer can did not move from his lips. Tommy held his scowl for a few beats, then laughed out loud, easing their tension.

"Oh my god! And you're hilarious too!" said Rita, resting her chin on her palm.

"Yeah, Richie, he was the rich guy. He stopped at the station maybe a week ago and he seemed fine. His daughter stopped at the station a couple of days back, too. I hadn't even thought about her. She must be a wreck!" Tommy's voice halted as he held back the tears.

"Even though it has to happen to us all, I think it's sad when someone you know dies. I'm so sorry Tommy," said Rita.

Tommy could feel the sincerity in her voice. He half-smiled, nodded his head, and said, "Thanks. Thanks Rita. That means a lot."

"Another brewski anyone?" asked Richie.

"No thanks, Richie. Sheila should be here soon," said Rita.

"Me neither," said Tommy. "I should get home and let you two be. Sorry for being such a downer. It was very nice to meet you Rita. Hope to see you again."

"OK buddy. Talk to you later," said Richie.

Rita stood up and followed Tommy to the door. "It was very nice to meet you, Tommy. I feel bad for you and I'm sorry you lost a friend. Life can be unfair like that. Take care of yourself. I really hope to see you again, and soon!"

"Same here. Have a good night, Rita," said Tommy. He left Richie's house for his home and solitude.

Rita closed the screen door, but waited until Tommy had driven away. She turned to Richie and said, "Why have you been hiding him from me? He's such a sweetheart."

"I've known Tommy since I was this high," he said, holding his palm two feet off the floor, "and he is a good guy. I'll call him if you want. Let him know you like him. Because then we get to pretend that we're all back in high school."

"Richie, come on, I'm serious. He seems so nice."

"Because you are Sheila's friend and Sheila is ... I'm not sure what she is to me. Anyway, I'll talk to him."

"Thanks, Richie. By the way, Sheila thinks you're her boyfriend."

"Really? Nice!"

The Police - Interview The Daughter

May 20, 1977, Friday afternoon, 2:45

THE DETECTIVE'S CAR PULLED up in front of Kaylie's house just fourteen hours after their initial interview. They were still sitting in the driveway when she came out her front door. "Did you catch him? Did you catch who did this?" she yelled towards them.

Exiting the car, Detective Jacobson held up his hands, chest-high. "No, we have not. We need to talk to you so that we can nab them. But let's take this inside, please."

The detectives followed her. Dark circles under her eyes and disheveled hair were something the detectives had seen plenty of times from survivors.

"May I get either of you two something to drink? Coffee, a Coke, a bit of rum? Maybe some rum and Coke? No, sorry about that." She exhaled slowly. "I'm sorry, but I'm exhausted. I've been up all night."

"Please, you're fine, and we don't need anything to drink, but thank you," said Jacobson.

"Ms. Werner, is Adam here? We have a couple of follow-up questions from earlier," asked Winston.

"Adam went to meet with Patti, that's Daddy's secretary, first thing this morning. After he came back, I asked him to leave."

"Leave?"

"I needed to be alone. He went to his office to let staff know about ... well, Daddy. I can call him if you want to talk to him now. It's OK."

"Not to worry, ma'am, I'll catch up to him later," said Winston.

"Kaylie, I wanted you to know that your father is at the coroner's, as is his car. An autopsy was performed this morning. Afterwards, the coroner met with us and gave us some preliminary findings."

"What was found? I need to know," she asked.

"I can confirm he was shot with a large-caliber weapon. I can assure you that he did not suffer."

"I'm glad of that. Jesus, I feel heartless saying that!" She started to sob.

Handing her a handkerchief, Jacobson responded, "You have nothing to feel bad about by saying that. We take what solace we can get."

"We found several promising pieces of evidence, and at least one witness may have helped with tracking down the getaway vehicle. But we don't have enough to ID anyone. Additionally, we have no gun. Your father's wallet is missing, and we have no eyewitnesses to the actual crime at this point."

Winston spoke up, "Can you think of any other people or situations that seem suspicious?"

"Believe me, I've spent a lot of time thinking about that, in between the tears, and I just can't believe anyone would have it out for him."

"We would also like to look at your father's townhouse and garage. Without objection, we'd like to have a key to his place."

"Of course," she reached into her purse and pulled out a keychain that had a white piece of tape labeled 'Dad'. "Here you go. You're free to look around. Please don't tear it up. Daddy keeps his place immaculate. Kept his place ... ."

"We will be respectful, I promise," said Winston, taking the keychain.

"I am meeting with the funeral home later this afternoon to make arrangements. Mom's family has a large section in a cemetery out in the country. There's already a marker there for Daddy. He loved going out there to visit. He found it very peaceful. He scrubbed and polished the headstone every time he went out there. Now that duty will pass to me; I just hope I can do right by them." Tears welled up in her eyes. As she wiped them away, she asked, "Is there anything else you need from me?"

"No. Please reach out to us if needed. And thank you for the keys. I'll return them as soon as we're done."

"Thanks. Just drop them in the mailbox if we're not home."

The detectives left, headed for the townhouse.

The Police - The Townhouse And A Lead

May 20, 1977, Friday afternoon, 3:15

THE DETECTIVES DROVE OVER to Anthony Werner's townhouse. Upon arrival, they saw the requested officer's car in the parking lot, sitting between the garage and the sidewalk leading to the townhouse. Yellow tape surrounded the garage, extending from both sides of the front of the garage, enclosing the entire front yard of the residence.

"Looks like it's buttoned down now," Jacobson said. Their car came to a halt next to the garage and the crime scene tape. The officer stepped out of his cruiser and walked toward the detectives, giving a quick wave as he did.

"Detectives. Good afternoon. All has been quiet here today except for the normal lookie-loos. I've not had anyone stop by and offer any information. Any more officers needed to knock on doors?"

"No, but thanks for the offer," he glanced at the officer's name tag, "Officer Shuman. We can handle it from here. Just two buildings with ten units each. That shouldn't take long. Detective Winston, let's look over the garage."

The two men began walking across the parking lot. Jacobson stopped halfway and turned around to take in the crime scene. He needed to get a feel for the townhouses. "Several mature trees between the building and the parking lot. All deciduous trees here. Full of leaves, making it hard to see anything from a window. Might muffle the sound, too."

Winston agreed. "Yes, I see that. His garage unit is in the middle of the complex. The streets are about 150 feet away in either direction. We've got a row of privacy bushes behind all of these garages."

"Damn good place to kidnap somebody without being seen."

"It is. That may make it tougher to get any witnesses. Let's look in the garage."

"Excuse me! Excuse me, you two." In the middle of the parking lot stood a man, one arm waving. His small dog gave off a small, unending growl.

The detectives walked over to the man. Winston bent over to pet the dog. "Hey little buddy, how are you, boy?" The dog squealed and tried to run away, but was stopped suddenly when he ran out of leash.

"He's a she, not that it matters. Her name is Dolly. Barks a lot, but she won't hurt you."

Winston stood up straight as Jacobson addressed the man. "I'm Detective Jacobson. This is my sidekick, Detective Winston. How can we help you?"

"Well, gentlemen, perhaps I can help you. The scuttlebutt in the complex is that Mr. Werner was murdered."

Jacobson asked, "And your name, sir? And how can you help us?"

"Vern, Vern Danielson, and I'll tell you how I can help. Last night, Dolly and I were taking our last walk of the evening. We came down this sidewalk," he said, pointing to the sidewalk next to the police cruiser. "Where the police car is now? That tree, see?"

"Yes, I see it," replied Winston.

"There was this man just sitting there. I've never seen him before. We don't usually have bums hanging out here. Had his back against the tree. His head was down, not moving much. So I asked him if he needed something. Well, he said he didn't and I recommended he move along. Said he was waiting on a ride. I just let him be."

"About what time was this, Mr. Danielson?"

"Just before nine o'clock. Not exactly sure, but I don't think it was nine yet."

"Can you describe the man, white, black, big, tall, fat, skinny?"

"Little guy, looked short even though I never saw him stand up. Pretty skinny. White guy with shaggy hair, kind of dirty-looking, homeless guy."

"You say you've never seen him before?" asked Winston.

"Never have. After I talked to him, Dolly and I walked down around the corner there. I live in a townhouse to the east."

"In case we need to get in touch, would you write your name and phone number on my notepad?" Winston said, handing him the pad.

"Sure thing." He began to write down his information. Mr. Danielson asked, "Is it true that he was murdered?"

"I'm afraid so."

"That's just terrible about Mr. Werner. Not like I knew him real well. The residents are too busy with their careers. We don't mingle that much. Hope you catch the bastard who did this. I think I only met Werner twice, but he seemed like a nice fellow."

"That's what we keep hearing. With some luck and help from people like you, we'll catch him. Here's my card if you think of anything else. Thanks again, sir."

"OK then, take care gentlemen," he said and walked away, around the corner.

"I wonder if that's our driver or shooter that the neighbor saw. I doubt it's some random homeless guy. We need to search under that tree," Jacobson said.

The detectives walked over to the tree and began searching.

"What's this? A torn piece of paper about where the subject may have been sitting." Jacobson reached down and carefully grabbed a shred of paper. It was skewered by a piece of bark at the base of the tree. "Hmmm, it's the top of an official-looking letter. This torn piece has part of a letterhead, looks like 'The Office of Correc' … ."

"Office of Corrections! That can't be a coincidence," exclaimed Winston.

"No way it is. We've got the date of the letter, just last week, and I'll be damned," said Jacobson. He dusted off the smudged dirt and read out loud, "'RE: Parole Officer Ch'. The next line says 'Parolee: Gord', and the last line just has the number seven. Shit, this is solid! Grab me an evidence bag."

"Got it right here." Winston held open the bag as Jacobson dropped the partial letter inside. "Let me label this and then grab my briefcase. Maybe there's some evidence in his garage."

"I hope so. Let's go."

Jacobson walked into the middle of the open garage, looked around, and threw his arms in the air. "There are no evidence markers anywhere. They haven't been here to dust. Unbelievable!" Turning to the uniformed officer he called out, "Hey Shuman, can you call dispatch and have them send the Identification Team out here? They should have already processed this scene. We need them here immediately."

"You got it, detective."

"Damn, Winston. Someone dropped the ball on this."

"Oh my god," Winston turned his head to the sky. "It was me. I did, I dropped it, Jake."

"You?"

"We were at the daughter's house. You asked me to call dispatch. I didn't do it."

"Goddammit Jay!" yelled Detective Jacobson. "We can't make mistakes like that. That means this scene sat for how many hours unguarded?" Turning back to the officer, he yelled, "Shuman, how long have you been here? Who put up the tape?"

Looking at his watch, Shuman replied, "Sergeant Riley just sent me out here forty-five minutes ago. I put up the tape."

"Dammit. I'll have to let the DA's office know."

"No, it's my fault, I'll do it."

"Bullshit. I'm your partner, and I'm your boss too. Shit rolls uphill around here. I'll take care of it. Never make a mistake like that again. Ever! I hope we don't lose that paper evidence too.

"I'll take care of it. Again, I'm sorry Jake."

"Drop me off at the DA's office. I want you to get down to the corrections office with that new evidence immediately. We need a full name."

The two men climbed into their car. The silence was deafening.

The Daughter - Talk To The Coroner

May 20, 1977, Friday afternoon, 3:25

"You sure about this?" asked Adam. His hand touched the middle of Kaylie's back.

"I have to do this," said Kaylie.

Adam opened the door labeled 'Coroner's Office', with Kaylie stepping in front of him and walking to the receptionist's desk.

"Good afternoon. How may I help you?" asked the receptionist, Nicole.

"I'm Kaylie Werner and this is my fiancé, Adam. We're here to see Dr. Walters. We have a three thirty meeting."

"Of course, I see it here. I'm going to take you to Conference Room C, and the doctor will join you shortly."

"We were told we would be seeing my father, whose body is here," said Kaylie.

"That's fine. The doctor will handle that. Right this way, please."

They were led past several desks and into a side hallway. Conference Room C was clearly labeled by a sign that protruded above the door. Nicole led them inside.

"Here we are," she said. "We have coffee and water in the corner. Is there anything else I can get you before the doctor arrives?"

"No, I'm fine," answered Adam.

"I'm fine. Thank you," echoed Kaylie.

"Well, I'm Nicole. Please see me if you need anything."

"Thanks," said Adam as Nicole gently shut the door.

"That chemical smell, ugh," said Kaylie. "Do you suppose it's like that all the time? I could not stand that all day."

"It's pretty strong. Maybe they get used to it. Kaylie, before the doctor gets here, are you certain you want to do this? I've heard that the kind of wound your father received is just horrible to see. I don't want this scarring you for life."

"Thank you for looking after me, Adam, but I've thought this through. What did that monster do to him? Why? I'll always wonder if I don't see this through. I can't live the rest of my life, not knowing."

They both sat down at the table, Adam sitting to Kaylie's left, facing the door. There were no words, only silence.

The doctor tapped on the door. Before entering the room, he paused.

"Good afternoon, Kaylie, Adam. Thank you for meeting with me. I've since learned quite a lot about your father, Kaylie. Everyone tells me he was a kind and generous man. An energetic, hardworking man. Does that sound like your father, Kaylie?"

"You are correct on all counts. I'd also add that he was a family man, through and through. Nothing would come between him and his family. He would be quick to praise those who helped him. He would always return the favor. Like that kid from the gas station, Tommy, super kid. Daddy admired how Tommy was kind and upbeat. He also knew Tommy wanted to go to Stanford. Electrical engineering, I believe. Seems Tommy's dad didn't like that idea. It would take him away from home, meaning work. Well, one day Daddy got into it with Tommy's dad about Stanford and convinced him, somehow, to let the kid apply there. I don't know if he got accepted. I don't even know if the kid knows about the conversation. My point is, Daddy would get involved and do what's right. No matter the cost."

"He applied," said Adam.

"How would you know that?" asked Kaylie.

"I had a meeting with your dad the morning before he died. He happened to have a Stanford baseball hat on his desk. I asked about it and he told me that story. Plus, he somehow knew the Dean of Admissions there and called in a favor."

"What was the meeting about, Adam?"

"Us, our future. I asked him for permission to marry you."

Kaylie broke down in tears, reached over and hugged Adam.

"It certainly sounds like your father was a wonderful, caring man. Such a blessing for all of us. I do recall," continued the doctor, "having the good fortune of playing golf with him on at least two occasions and I remember how interested he was in not only our foursome, but anybody he happened to run into on the course."

"Sounds like Daddy," Kaylie smiled through a tear-stained face. She ran her hands through her red hair.

"And very competitive!"

"Which also sounds like him!"

"Now, not the best of golfers, but … ."

"Yes, you did golf with him!" Kaylie said as all three of them laughed.

Once the laughter subsided, Kaylie looked around the room, biting her lip. The government-issue wall clock ticked through the silence.

"Before we go see your father, I wanted to discuss what happened to your him. I don't know what the detectives told you. I'm also not going to get into any discussion full of medical jargon. And if you've heard enough at any point, please stop me. This is for your benefit. You don't have to see him. Understood?"

"Yes sir," responded Kaylie.

"Very well. I'll just dive right into this. Your father suffered three gunshots. Two entered his left shoulder blade. One entered the left side of his temple. Medical attention would have likely saved his life from one of the shots to the shoulder. Now, the gunshot to the temple was fatal, and it did cause instant death. It was at that point your father no longer suffered."

Kaylie flinched, then rested her head in her hands, slowly shaking it in disbelief.

"Did he put up a fight?" asked Adam.

"We believe so. He had defensive wounds on his left arm, right knuckles, and, for some reason, it appears he was struck on the head with a solid object. I'm assuming these could have been caused by a struggle. We may be able to confirm this when there is an arrest."

"I'll bet he tried to talk his way out of it first, but it didn't … " she could not finish the sentence.

"He was certainly put in a horrible position with few options," said the doctor. "Would you like a moment, Kaylie?"

She shook her head.

"We currently have a sheet over your father's body that covers him up from here," he said as he drew his hand across the top of his chest, "to his feet. Due to the severe trauma, I've covered the right side of his head. I recommend we keep it covered."

"People keep telling me that and I keep saying that I have to see what happened. I can process that, but if I don't actually see it, I'll only imagine what happened. It will torment me the rest of my life."

"Yes, but Ms. Werner, I … ."

"Sir, she won't change her mind, believe me," interjected Adam.

"Very well. When you are ready to see him, we can."

"Let's do it, Dr. Walters," said Kaylie as she rose to her feet.

The Daughter - First Viewing

May 20, 1977, Friday afternoon, 3:36

Doctor Walters led Kaylie and Adam down the well-lit hallway. Framed photographs of staff, past and present, lined both sides; several dating back over one hundred years. At the end was an overhead sign that read 'Autopsy Theater'. Kaylie wondered to herself, 'Why would they call it a theater? Seems to make death slightly trivial.'

The doctor paused before opening the door, turning to them both. "It's just your father in the room. As I said, he is mostly covered up. I'm sure you noticed the chemical smells that get into most parts of the building. It is a bit stronger inside these doors. While not the most pleasant scents, they are harmless. If you feel the need to leave the room, don't hesitate. Don't ask for permission, just go ahead. OK?"

"Yes," said Kaylie. Adam nodded his head.

"Follow me please," said the doctor as he pressed the automatic door opener with his elbow.

"I'm right here with you, Kaylie," said Adam, his arm wrapped around her waist. "We'll get through this."

"There he is," said Kaylie. The bright overhead lighting brought out the detail of every wrinkle, scratch, cut, and gunshot wound. "Oh, my god!" said Kaylie.

The doctor stood next to the body as he waited for Kaylie and Adam.

"Oh, Daddy! What have they done to you?" She rested her hand on her father's upper arm. "He's so cold. Adam, he's so cold!"

"I know, babe," replied Adam.

"My God! Daddy! Is that the wound you mentioned?" she asked.

"Yes, Ms. Werner. That is indeed the entry wound that proved fatal for your father."

"Entry wound?" She stopped talking and noticed the right side of her father's face was covered with a smaller sheet. "That side?" She pointed as she asked. "The severe trauma?"

"It is."

"Kaylie, we don't need to see everything," said Adam.

"I know. We can leave the sheets on. Doctor, will the funeral home be able to make my father look nice? Well, can they cover up his injuries?"

"Honestly, the entry wound should not be a problem. I doubt they can make this side presentable," he said, pointing at the covered part of her father's head. "I can provide them with the x-rays we've taken. Perhaps they have experience with this type of restoration. They may be able to position his head so the wound is not noticeable. I will have my staff leave that information for the mortuary transport person. I will help as much as I can, but I can't make promises."

"I know. Thank you, Doctor. I've seen enough. I need to leave. Good bye, Daddy. Is it OK if I kiss his cheek?"

"Of course," said the doctor.

Kaylie gently kissed her father's cheek, turned, and exited the room, sobbing as she went.

"Thank you again, Doctor. These are tough times and we appreciate all you are doing," said Adam.

"You're welcome. Please look after her. The first days, weeks, can be unbearable at times."

"I will. Goodbye."

The Police - Tell The D. A.

May 20, 1977, Friday afternoon, 3:41

"Kerri, I have to speak with Jennifer ASAP."

"Hello to you Jake. She should be finishing up her meeting with Mr. Sartori and back soon. Do you want to wait?"

"Yes, I'll wait, it's important."

"OK. Nice weather out there today?"

"The weather? Fine, I guess, I don't know."

"Should I just leave you alone?"

"Why do you say that?"

"Jake, I've known you for over ten years and something has got your attention. You're not the usual friendly Jake we all know and love around here. Plus, you look different. Upset? Want to get it off your chest?"

"Ahhh, I'm here to let Jennifer know that we may have compromised a piece of evidence."

"Oh, geez, say no more. I get it. But believe me, this happens pretty often. They have ways of getting evidence admissible when you'd think it is impossible."

"Winnie has some evidence to check on. Hopefully, this will give us a name involved with this murder. If we can grab the perp and put the heat on him, maybe he'll talk."

"I've heard you can get suspects to sing like a pair of skeets."

"You mean a parake ... for the love of god! Winnie told you to work that in a conversation, didn't he?"

Kerri just smiled, got up, and filed away several papers.

"Unbelievable what I put up with. Him all day and now you!"

"There's a chair in her office if you'd like to wait there."

"Why? Then I'd miss out on this stand-up routine going on here!"

"That's fine. I'll be here all day. Just thought you might be more comfortable."

Detective Jacobson stood up and walked into the Assistant District Attorney's office and said, "That was sarcasm, Kerri!" He laughed until he sat in Jennifer's guest chair.

Kerri grinned from ear to ear and looked back, watching him enter her boss's office. "He's so cute. Does Jen see that?"

Jacobson sat in a chair leafing through his notebook for the Werner homicide case. He scribbled a note reminding him to check in with the Identification Team when he got back in the office. He hoped the garage had been processed, though its admissibility was in question.

"Jake! So good to see you again! Please, don't get up," Jennifer said as he rose from the chair.

"And it's great to see you, Jennifer. Your opinion may change when I'm done talking but, I'll bask in that for a bit."

"This is about the Werner case? I'm curious now. Can we skip right to the issue? Tell me what's going on," she said as she sat down in her high-backed chair, placing her blazer across the seat back. The dark cherry stain matched the large desk. The desk was beautiful, somewhere underneath all the papers and file folders.

"Yes, of course. We may have a compromised secondary crime scene."

"So far, I'm not pleased. Go on."

"We went out to Mr. Werner's townhouse this afternoon. Everything appeared to be in order. While there, we interviewed a neighbor. He noticed a stranger sitting against a tree the night of the murder. This tree was across the parking lot from Mr. Werner's garage. Not expecting much, we proceeded to the base of a tree. We found a torn letter at the base of the tree, just where our witness placed the stranger. Detective Winston is over at the Department of Corrections office, running this down now."

"Jake, what's the issue? This all sounds good to me. Where is our compromise?"

"Sorry, just trying to give you the background on this. The scene was not secured for at least twelve hours. The officer was not told to oversee that scene until forty-five minutes before we arrived."

"Well, why was the scene left unsecured?"

"My team dropped the ball. It's on me."

"Jake, I know you better. No way was this your mistake. Your partner fucked up, didn't he?"

"Look, we're a team, so we failed. I have addressed the problem. I'm the boss, it's on me. End of subject."

"OK, OK. We may have to fight any defense team motion on this. If the piece of paper leads us to a suspect, I doubt that gets challenged. It's sitting out in the open, in public view. And it's just a lead to a name, not evidence of a crime. The unsecured garage is a different matter. Prints, for example, could get thrown out. At the very least, it could introduce some doubt in a jury's mind. But I'm getting ahead of things. It's good to know Jake, since I'm required to tell the defense team about this. I appreciate the honesty. It gives me plenty of time to consider our options."

"Of course, Jen. Again, I apologize for the mistake."

"Anything else?"

"No. I'll keep you posted on what the Identification Team finds."

"Great, thanks Jake. I received the autopsy report earlier today. I'll catch up on that this evening."

"Dr. Walters gave us the in-person walkthrough. Just prepare yourself for the head wound. It's bad."

"I'm sure I can handle it."

"Whatever you say. I gotta run. Detective Winston should be here soon."

"We'll talk soon, Jake."

Jake walked out of her office and past the receptionist's desk. "Pair of skeets, huh!"

Kerri laughed, "What's a skeet, anyway? I don't know what that means. That's the funniest part! Your partner is nuts."

When Jake got to the street, Winston was sitting behind the wheel, waiting. Jake snuck up behind his partner and whispered in his ear, "I need a pair of skeets, asshole."

"Jesus Christ!" said Winston, banging his head on the roof of the car and his knees on the steering wheel. "What the hell?"

Jacobson was already around the car, opening the door. "We may have dodged a bullet on the letterhead. Any garage evidence, may be a problem."

"I see that grin, pal. Did you enjoy that? Dang, I think I broke my kneecap."

"I enjoyed that. Did you like feeding Kerri your little birdie joke? Is it worth looking like an idiot?"

"Ahh," said a wincing Winston, "yeah, it's worth it!"

Laughing, Jacobson pointed forward and said, "Back to our office, bird boy."

The Police - Who's This Felon?

May 20, 1977, Friday afternoon, 3:52

Detective Winston strode into the solid but plain cold war era government office building. A quick glance at the directory that hung in the lobby pointed him to the third floor where the state's Department of Corrections - Parole and Probation Division was located. The drab office space was packed with dozens of desks in the main room. Each one was weighted down with folders and paperwork. Ringing the light green colored walls were the enclosed offices reserved for managers.

"May I help you, sir?" said a smiling receptionist. Her name was Marie, an attractive, nearing middle-aged woman dressed in black slacks and a light blue, frilly blouse. Matching blue reading glasses sat atop her well-kept dark brown hair.

"I hope so, ma'am," he flashed his badge. "I'm Detective Jay Winston and I'm investigating a homicide that occurred last night."

"Oh no, that's awful," said Marie.

"Yes, it is. We found this shard of paper that may have some relevance to the case." He held up the piece of paper, still in the plastic evidence bag. "I'm wondering if this looks familiar to you."

The receptionist pulled down her reading glasses and looked at the scrap of paper. "It looks like our letterhead."

"Do you have a parole officer whose name starts with the letters C and h? Like Chestnut or Chappy?"

"You think there's someone here named Chestnut? Or Chappy? How about a Charlotte?"

"Charlotte works," said a smiling Winston. "I can see that."

"Charlotte, Charlotte Goodwin. The third office on the left. Let me see if she is available."

"Oh, she's going to be available," Winston called out as he headed towards her office. Once there, he opened the door, uninvited, without knocking.

"What are you … excuse me, may I help you?" the confused parole officer said.

"I'm sorry, Ms. Goodwin. The detective here took it upon his own damn self to come down here to speak with you," said the receptionist as she caught up with the detective.

"It's OK, Marie. I'll handle this," said Charlotte.

Marie stared at Winston, shook her head and walked away saying, "Unprofessional Mr. Detective. Unprofessional."

"Excuse me for barging in, but this is urgent," said Winston.

"And you couldn't even knock? Or extend my receptionist a common courtesy? Who are you? And what the hell do you want?"

"My apologies. I'm Detective Winston. My partner and I are investigating a murder and I need to know if you have a client whose name starts with 'Gord'?"

"You just jump right into it, don't you? Have a seat and let me think."

"Thanks."

"Two come to mind, a Gordon Wicker though I may lose him as a client since he's in jail awaiting trial in Gary, Indiana."

"How long has he been there?"

"Month, maybe two."

"Can't be my guy. And the other name?"

"Gordon Thompson, released from county lockup a little while back," she turned and thumbed through a file cabinet, pulled out a folder and thumbed through it. "Looks like he's been out for two months. Low-level criminal, petty crimes, some burglary."

"Anything violent?"

"No, not this guy. I'm kind of remembering him now. He's a shy guy, a follower I'd guess since he's always getting caught with other, more serious, career offenders. Oh yeah, now I remember. He is AKA *Big Man*, an ironic nickname because he's just a little guy."

"A little guy? How little?"

"He's five-foot-two and skinny. Imagine a thirty-year-old head on a ten-year-old body. That's Big Man."

"That sounds like our guy. Can I have this file?"

"Noooo, but I can have Marie make a copy. Just apologize to her in your sweetest voice. Anything else I can help you with, detective?"

"Is his current address in there?" Winston asked, as he tapped on the folder.

"Yes it is. Follow me."

They walked up to the receptionist. "Marie," said Charlotte, "can you make a complete copy of this folder's contents for the detective and return the original to me, please? Detective, I wish you luck. I'll let you know if this guy contacts me. Goodbye."

"Goodbye, Ms. Goodwin, and thank you very much."

"Let me guess; you want this now?" asked Marie.

"I do. I hate to rush you, but I need to get this back to my boss ASAP. Listen, I'm sorry for being such a jerk earlier. I have to stay on top of this case. The information you're giving me is huge!"

"Oh, you're not a jerk."

"I appreciate that."

"Let me finish, please."

"Again, sorry," he said, straightening his back.

"Listen, you aren't a jerk. You're an asshole. Stop being an asshole. Now I feel better. I'll get this file copied for you right now."

"Well, I deserved that."

"You did deserve it. Now we're all good. That's how this woman operates. I'll be right back. Watch the front desk for me please, detective. Maybe tidy the place up a bit."

"I like your style, Marie. It's too bad I'm so much younger than you."

"Yes, it is too bad. Too bad for you, young man!"

They both laughed as she walked over to the copy machine.

Ten minutes later, he headed back to the DA's office to meet up with his partner.

May 20, 1977, Friday afternoon, 4:41

"Please tell me you have some positive news from Corrections," said Jacobson.

"I got a match on the name. Here's the file," Winston said, pointing at the file folder that lay between them. "A guy named Gordon Thompson who looks like a small-time operator. His PO, Charlotte Goodwin, told me that he's a hanger-on with a lot of small-time convictions, nothing ever violent."

"Did she give you an address for this guy?"

"It's there," Winston said, tapping the folder, "and get this. The guy is AKA 'Big Man' because he's just a little shit. Like five-foot-two. Sound familiar?"

"Got to be our tree guy. Excellent work, Winnie. Look, it's been a long couple of days. Drop this file back at the station. After that, call it a day and we'll regroup tomorrow morning."

"You got it, boss. Maybe the Yankees are on TV tonight. This is their year, I can feel it," exclaimed Winston.

"Fat chance. My Reds will destroy them again, sorry."

The Police - Looking For A Big Man

May 21, 1977, Saturday morning, 7:17

Detective Jacobson was already at his desk when his partner sat down next to him. The cramped office they shared meant that papers on one desk often slid over to the other. No phone calls were private. They shared their lives, whether they wanted to or not.

"Glad you could make it, Winnie. Alarm clock broken?"

"It's a fricken' quarter after seven. What are you, a vampire?"

"I'm just a dedicated civil servant. Catch your game last night?"

"Listened to it on the radio. Baltimore took it though, six to five."

"Say it isn't so," Jacobson said, devoid of sympathy.

"It's just one game. I still believe in them."

"I read through the file you picked up yesterday. Good information, good job. I think we both know this Thompson guy is a part of our case. Right now, it's all circumstantial. We're still missing the piece that ties him to the murder scene," said Jacobson.

"Or ties him to one of his co-conspirators," added Winston.

"Do we bring this guy in and put the screws on him, risking his buddies taking off before he breaks, or ... ."

"Or," said Winston, adding his own thoughts, "just keep a close eye on him. Maybe he leads us right to the others? The way his parole officer talked, this guy is a follower. My bet is he always gravitates to big trouble. He's usually a small-time offender and a follower. If he's involved in this murder, and I think he is, he won't be able to help himself. He'll show up at their doorstep."

"I agree. This address is for some apartments?"

"Yes, the Longmore Apartments."

"We've been there before, yes?"

"We have. I can recall a couple homicides we worked there. It's a big place."

"I say we pull surveillance on the place. Who knows what we'll see?" asked Jacobson.

"Yep, maybe lunchtime? There's a great taco stand nearby."

"Marking my calendar now. Before we go, get a plate and description of this guy's car."

"Will do, Jake."

May 21, 1977, Saturday morning, 11:30

"Tick-tock," said Jacobson, tapping on his watch.

"Right. OK. Yes, but ... " Winston pretended to bang his phone on the table, then held up his index finger, silently pleading with his partner to wait patiently.

Jacobson whispered in his ear, "I'll be in the car. Wrap it up, junior." He left Winston alone and headed to the parking lot.

"I know and I ... ."

Jacobson sat in the passenger seat, one foot pressed against the dash, absentmindedly examining his fingernails. Winston hopped into the driver's seat with a deep exhale.

"I thought the ADA was fine with my mess up with the garage?"

"I did too, why?"

"She was pissed about it and let me know."

"Probably had to let you know who's boss. Don't worry, she doesn't hold grudges. She just expects perfection."

"Thanks for standing up for me, though. She mentioned that a lot. She also told me how fortunate I am to have a partner like you."

"Go on ... ."

"I'd love to, but it's Big Man time," said Winston. "But first, tacos!"

"To go. Tacos to go. We could be sitting there all afternoon," added Jacobson.

Kate and Ken's Taco Shack stood just off the side of the road and only four blocks from the Longmore Apartments. Peeling white paint did not stop families from flocking there. It was one of the first and arguably the best Mexican food venues in the city. The detectives parked their car along the street and walked the half block to the stand. The line was twelve deep.

"Man, that food smells good. I'm getting a burrito and a taco today," said Winston.

"Yeah, I'm probably going ... Winnie, look at that car sitting at the light. The one puffing all that blue smoke."

"Holy shit, look at the driver. He can barely see over the wheel. Gotta be our guy."

"Let's go!"

The two detectives rushed over to their unmarked car just as the light changed.

"Don't lose him, don't lose him!" yelled Jacobson.

"I still see him. He's not heading back home, is he?"

"Nope. Let's see where this takes us."

"Where is all this traffic coming from? It's wall to wall cars."

"Probably all the nine-to-fivers catching up on shopping. Plus, Memorial Day is coming up. Any plans for the holiday?" asked Jacobson.

"Nothing yet, you?"

"Thought I'd grill out, have some beers. Come on over, bring friends. If you have a date, bring her along, too."

"Do you see him? I lost him," said Winston, as his head swiveled from side to side.

"I see him, one lane to your right, about a half a block ahead."

"Got him, thanks. So I'm not dating anyone right now. This job makes that difficult, but you know that."

"I do. I don't have the time. Any relationship would suffer."

"I know a good fit for you, Jake."

"Drop it right now, Winnie. I know you're just going to start joking around so ... ."

"I'm serious. ADA Jennifer Nichols."

"What? No, she's ... ."

"She's perfect for you, is what she is. Look, she's in law enforcement, you're in law enforcement. You both work long hours. She would understand that. She's really good looking. "

Detective Winston kept driving, keeping a decent gap between themselves and Big Man.

"So you stopped at 'she's really good looking'. Keep going," said Jacobson.

"Uh, no, I was done."

"I knew you'd try to be the funny man. You little prick!" They both laughed.

"Seriously though, I think she has the hots for you."

"Shut up and drive. The hots? You still in high school?"

"Looks like our boy is pulling into that little grocery store. There's other stores closer to his place, bigger too."

"Yeah, but look where he's parking. The back row," said Jacobson.

"He works here!" said Winston.

They pulled into the parking lot and found a slot near the front door and watched their subject walk right in front of them and into the store.

"What is this place?" asked Winston, as he craned his neck for a better look. "Brambilla's Grocery. Never heard of it."

"Let's give this guy a few minutes. Let him get settled into work. This is an old family Italian store. Probably used to be one of dozens of neighborhood stores that dotted the city. These old stores are pretty rare. And this one, tucked in between a car parts store and a fabric store, it's kind of hidden in plain sight."

"Good low-profile place for an ex-con."

"Who goes in?" asked Jacobson.

"You know what?" said Winston as he removed his tie. "I'll go in. Take this tie off, no suit jacket. Makes me a little more casual looking."

"You look like a junior-level car salesman.

Winston shot him a sour look.

"Don't give me that look. It's a good cover. Use it if needed."

"You've used that cover before, haven't you?"

"Of course, now go."

Winston exited the car and checked his appearance in the side-view mirror and gave himself a thumbs-up.

The store was quite small, with only ten parallel aisles plus the aisle that ran along the back edge of the store. Winston also noticed the old, musty smell that, while subtle, was everywhere. He grabbed a shopping cart and went looking for Big Man. To blend in, he'd randomly stop and pick up a grocery item. He grabbed a cantaloupe and tapped on it a few times. He wasn't sure why people tapped them, but the lady ahead of him had done so. Up and down the aisles he went, pushing the empty cart. Then he saw his target. "That is a tiny guy," he said.

Big Man walked behind the meat counter and stood at the ready. Winston paused and observed the suspect interact with an elderly female.

"So the salmon, it's fresh, yes?" the older lady asked.

"I helped unload it last night, Mrs. Rayburn," answered Big Man.

"I'd like some of that please, Gordon. How about two pounds? Two of my daughters are coming over tonight to visit Henry and me."

"Oh, that's wonderful. It sounds like you have a wonderful family." He had hand-wrapped the salmon as they talked. "Here you go. Enjoy the salmon and your evening too."

Jacobson saw Winston leave the store and walk over to the car. Hands placed on the top of the roof, he leaned into the driver's side window. "It's him, Gordon Thompson. I heard a little old lady call him by name. He's working the meat department and I have to tell you, he seems like a nice guy."

"Remember that word — seems. The guy played a part in a murder. Don't let that one interaction jade your judgment, OK?" said Jacobson.

"Yeah, I know that Jake. I'd like to just add this to our intel on the guy, and if we need somebody to flip, he's my leading candidate."

"Agreed. Let's go home."

Winston climbed into the driver's seat and set a small bag between them. "Cannoli?"

The Young Man - The Girl

May 21, 1977, Saturday morning, 10:14

"Hello?"

"Tommy, Tommy, Tommy! What have you done?"

Tommy's confusion disappeared when he realized it was his friend. "Richie, Richie, Richie! What do you mean? How are ya?"

Laughing, Richie replied, "Doing good, just not as good as you, it seems. You made quite the impression last night, young man."

"OK, I'm not in the mood for riddles. Out with it."

"Do you remember that girl you met at my place?"

"Oh sure, what was her name again?" Tommy was lying. He knew full well her name and just the thought of her made his heart race. He found himself daydreaming about her ever since he left Richie's house. But he needed to play it cool since she was with Richie that day.

"It's Rita. You don't remember her name, eh? She sure remembers yours!"

"OK. What about, uh, Rita?" he said, still being coy.

"Well, my friend, she's into you and would like to see you again."

"I don't understand. I thought for sure she was with you?" Tommy was trying to hold back his feelings but couldn't help fist-pumping the air. "She wants to see me," he silently mouthed the words.

"Nah, she was over here waiting for this other girl I know, Sheila. Sheila had a dentist or hair appointment or something else from the neck up. I don't know. I was just flirting with her, just messing around. You know me."

"Uh-huh."

"So she's not interested in me, which I know is weird, right? But she is diggin' you, my friend! Yeah, she would not stop asking about you after you left. Thank god her friend showed up to put an end to all that jabbering.

Tommy this, Tommy that. You know if it's not about me, I lose interest." Richie laughed alone at his little joke.

"Yeah, yeah, I know. She's very pretty and seemed nice. So she's older than me, am I right? What's her story?"

"I knew it! She caught your eye too! Pretty? Pretty? Man, the chick is gorgeous. She's *maybe* two years older than you, I suppose. That just can't be a problem!"

Tommy felt his face flush with warmth. Knowing that it sure sounded like she was, perhaps, as interested in him as he was in her started his stomach churning with butterflies. He replayed in his mind how she was so kind to him, the way she inched closer to him, how she touched him and looked at him.

Tommy leaned forward in his chair. "A problem? Not a problem. No! What should I do? Should I ask her out or what?"

"Oh my god, Tommy of course! No way she says no to you. Call her! Then you can ask her 'her story', 'how old are you?', 'where do you see yourself in five years?', and 'blah, blah, blah'. Can you ask her why she's not hitting on Richie?"

"Her number please."

"You're not going to ask her about me, are you?"

"Still waiting for her number."

Richie read off her number and Tommy nervously but excitedly copied it down on a scrap of paper.

After they hung up, Tommy began to pace and think. What should he say to her? What should they do? Where should they go? Tommy was known for being a planner. He could not ask her out without thinking about everything. His mom called it a blessing and a curse whenever she'd see him futzing about an upcoming event. He did not want to disappoint. He did not want to look foolish. He had to show people they could count on him. Falling short was not to be tolerated. His father certainly reinforced that.

He spent the rest of the evening thinking. Dating made him uneasy. Where should they go? A place to eat. Somewhere nice, but not so nice they would feel out of their element. Ann & Joe's fit the bill. He'd eaten there many times with his family. The restaurant's owners, Ann and Joe Townsend, were always kind to him when they frequented the nearby gas station. So it was decided he would stop there on his lunch break and make reservations. Now came the hard part. He needed to call her. He wondered if she would go out with him. Then the butterflies flooded his stomach again. He thought he should wait until the afternoon before calling, hoping nerves wouldn't get the best of him. Of course, they got to him and he avoided calling her all day.

The Girl - The Young Man

May 24, 1977, Tuesday morning, 10:34

SHE LOOKED IN THE rear-view mirror, smacking her lips to check her fresh lipstick, touched her hair gently with both hands, and gave herself a wink and a smile.

The mid-morning sun glinted off the hood of her car, windows down, filtering in fresh, warm air. She could feel a calm happiness surround her as she arrived at her destination.

Tommy was in the garage, changing the battery in a customer's car. It had been another busy day.

Ding-ding!

He had to deal with yet another customer. His dad had just taken off to make a bank run. "Dammit, what a day," he muttered as he casually walked out towards the gas pumps. A sharp-looking silver Datsun 240Z sat in the drive. Could be a new customer. Maybe a regular has a new car. He turned to grab a rag, wiping the spots of grime off his hands.

The driver of the Datsun pressed the horn, letting it honk for a solid five seconds. "All right, all right! I'm coming! Just hold your horses," yelled out Tommy as he ran around to the driver's side.

"May I help ... " and the rest of the words just stayed stuck in his throat as he stopped dead in his tracks. A smile crossed his now-red face.

"Hey stranger. I hope you can help me." The driver slyly looked up at Tommy and smiled that smile he'd thought so much about the previous night.

"Rita!" Tommy spun around and held his hands against the side of his head. "I was thinking about you this morning. And now ... ."

"And abracadabra! Here I am. I knew you were magical."

He could feel his face flush again. "What are doing, um, here? I mean, I'm glad you are here and ... geesh, am I glad to see you."

"Thought I'd take a chance you were here. So this is the family business," she said, looking past Tommy at first, but then her eyes fixed on his. "Very nice. I like what you've done with the place."

"Well, for a gas station, I suppose."

"I think it looks terrific. And so do you. I love that cute little uniform," she said, reaching out and tugging on his shirt. "I see you have your name stitched on your shirt, too. Is that so you don't forget your name? I know I don't need to be reminded!"

Tommy laughed a nervous laugh, gulped hard, and spoke rapidly. "So listen, Rita, um, I was just thinking that ... would you go out with me, Rita? Like to eat or something? Sometime? If not, OK, but I hope you will ... if you're not busy, I mean."

Rita laughed. "Oh sweetie, of course. There is one condition or else the deal's off." Tommy looked quizzically at her. "You don't need to be so nervous around me. I already like you, OK?"

"Sure, I'm sorry. It's just that I'm, I mean, you're so, well, I like you too. Ahh geez, I'm all tongue-tied, sorry."

"Is this you *not* being nervous? Care to try that again?"

"I sure do." Clearing his throat and standing tall, an emboldened Tommy responded, "Rita, it is such a pleasure to see you again. I simply must inquire, vis-à-vis, about your availability for dinner tomorrow. I know of an establishment of excellent repute. Ann & Joe's Ristorante. You know it's fine dining if it's a 'ristorante'."

"Why sir, it would be an honor," she said, holding her hand out. Tommy leaned down and softly kissed the top of her hand.

"Plus, we can wear jeans at this joint if we want," he whispered, still bowing.

"Did you just make a joke? Oh Tommy, I just love it!"

He leaned against the side of the car with newfound confidence and smiled at Rita. They gazed silently into each other's eyes.

Ding-ding! Tommy jumped, their moment interrupted.

"Call me and let me know when you're going to pick me up. Oh, and I'll be in jeans," she said, laughing as she put the car in gear. With a deep exhale, she drove away. She had been as nervous as Tommy.

Smiling, Tommy turned around, stunned to see this customer, on this day.

His smile disappeared.

The Daughter - Breaking The News

May 24, 1977, Tuesday morning, 10:41

"Morning, Tommy," she turned to face him, exposing puffy eyes and unkempt red hair. "I only need gas today. Just gas."

"Miss Werner, oh my god. I feel so bad for you and your family. Let me know if you need anything. Gosh, your dad was such a nice man. I was sorry to hear that he had passed away. I'm going to miss seeing him."

"Passed away, Tommy? Passed away? It's not like he sat down in his car, fell asleep, and didn't wake up! No, he didn't just pass away," her voice was rising now.

"Oh, I'm sorry. I didn't mean to upset you."

"It's OK," she said, looking up at Tommy. At that moment, she understood. "You don't know, do you? You don't know what happened, what they did to him. And you have no idea how he died, do you?"

"No, I don't know … ."

Speaking low, slow, and emphasizing every word, she said, "They threw him in his car, robbed him, took him to one of his construction sites, and killed him. They shot him, Tommy! They fucking shot him in the head!" She slumped in the driver's seat and sobbed. "Please, just get me some gas. I've spent the last two days either talking to the police or the coroner, calling family, and … sorry, I don't know why I'm laying this all on you. Just the gas and I'll leave. Thank you, Tommy. And thank you for being nice to my dad. He always liked you." The tears began again. "Whoever did this is going to pay. I'll make sure they do. No matter the cost. Believe me, Tommy."

He didn't know what to say. Mr. Werner, murdered? He had never known anyone who was a murder victim. The killer was going to pay? How? He didn't know what to say. His vision narrowed and darkened as tears welled up in his eyes.

Kaylie broke the silence. "Oh, one more thing. Tommy, my boyfriend Adam, may stop by in the next day or two. Can you take care of him please and put it on our bill? I guess it's my bill now," she said slowly, shaking her head.

"Of course, Miss Werner. Anything you need, I'm here for you. My family is here for you."

"Thank you, Tommy. You've always been so kind." She reached out and patted his hand.

After filling her car up with gas, he stood motionless and watched as she drove off, almost sideswiping a parked car as she left the station.

Tommy was now left on his own. His shoulders slumped as he hung his head, stunned and angry. Anger at whoever did this. Anger at the world. A world where this was almost normal; it happened too frequently. He took the piece of paper out of his pocket and looked at Rita's phone number. Should he call her? Maybe she could talk him through this. "No, too soon," he said out loud. Despite the strong connection, he couldn't burden her with this news. Should he call Richie? No, he'd doubtless make a joke about it. What about talking to his dad? No, he knew that would not help. It would make things worse; no telling where his dad would take that conversation. That left him lost and lonely. He sat down in the office chair. He needed to be alone for just a while to collect himself.

Ding-ding! Ding-ding! Tommy pushed himself up from the padded seat, exhaling as he did.

"I'm fucking Pavlov's dog here. I need a better purpose than this!" As he trudged out to the driveway muttering, "Please, please, please, just don't be that jackass, Harrison."

"Tommy, check that front right tire. She's pulling quite a bit. You checked the tire pressure the other day, didn't you?" And, of course, it was Mike Harrison and his precious car.

Tommy kneeled down next to the tire and pulled out his tire pressure gauge with his shaking hand.

"One more thing, Tommy. Can you scrub off that front windshield for me? The wife and I took a pleasant drive out to the country yesterday. We did a lot of night driving. Lot of bugs still stuck on it."

"Of course, Mr. Harrison," said Tommy. Then, out of earshot, "Sometimes you're the windshield, sometimes you're the bug. Why am I always the bug?"

The Young Man, The Girl - First Date

May 25, 1977, Wednesday afternoon, 5:15

Tommy tucked in his shirt and looked in the bathroom mirror, smoothed back his hair, and straightened his collar. "Forty-five minutes to go. Be cool Tom. No big deal. You've been on dates before." He took a long, deep breath. "Forty-four minutes to go. Tom, stop looking at your watch and relax. You've been out with girls before. At least four or five times. Is five dates a lot? Doesn't sound like too many. So what if she's the coolest chick you've met?"

She was always on his mind. The way she looked at him and how her smile surprised him at the gas station. She was not like any other.

"Reservations made at Ann & Joe's, got your car washed and gassed up. It's a very nice restaurant, she'll like it. Thirty-nine minutes to go ... and you just looked at your watch again."

"Tommy, phone call," his mom called out.

Trotting downstairs and passing her, he asked, "Who is it, Mom?"

"Some girl, Rita or Ruta, I think she said," she said jokingly.

He froze. "I knew it! She's going to back out. Damn!" He picked up the phone. "Um, hello?"

"Tommy, it's Rita! OK, don't freak out and I don't want to sound desperate, but, hey, I'm ready to go out and I know it's early. If you're ready, what do you say we go somewhere before dinner and talk? Maybe the park? It doesn't matter. I would just like to see you."

Tommy sat down at the kitchen table and smiled. "Um, well, I'm ready too and, so ... you want me to pick you up now?"

"If it's all the same to you, I'd love that," said Rita.

"Yeah, sure, me too."

"OK then, I'll see you soon!"

Tommy sat there, a bit dazed, listening to the dial tone. "Oh, shit!" He had forgotten to say goodbye.

"Is everything all right, Tommy? Tommy?"

"Oh, hey Mom. Yeah, I'm all right. Better than all right. So I'm going to go now." He kissed his mom on the cheek before bouncing out the door.

"Have fun," she said, waving to his back. "Young love. Please don't break his heart, Rita."

Tommy climbed into his car, a 1968 Chevelle that he kept immaculate, inside and out. With a little help, he kept it running like new. It was one of the few things he and his dad did together. He slowly backed out of his driveway. A sudden car horn blast shocked him to attention.

"Watch where the hell you're going," said the other driver.

"Sorry! Damn Tom, get it together, pay attention."

He began fiddling with the radio dial, trying for just the right music. "Who am I kidding? I don't know what kind of music she likes." A quick flick of his wrist and the radio went silent. "I guess I could ask her about music. What am I going to talk about? Think Tom. How do you know Richie? Sheila seems nice. What's your dad do for a living? I don't know."

An older lady was in a car next to him at the stoplight, watching him talk to himself. He caught her looking at him. "Hi there, ma'am," he said with a quick wave. "OK light, change. Jesus. I'm still talking to myself." The light changed and Tommy sped away and the older lady had a story for dinnertime.

The route to Rita's place took Tom past the gas station. Tommy looked over as he drove by and there was his dad, arms waving in the air as he was talking to one of his parts suppliers. It was obvious that his dad was upset. "Sorry buddy," he said towards the object of his dad's ire, "you aren't the only one he goes off on." He thought seeing someone else feel his dad's wrath would make him feel better. It didn't.

Driving through the neighborhood was just a tour of customer's houses. Tommy did a lot of pickups and deliveries for them. There was Mr. and Mrs. Benson's house, Mr. Williams' house next door — he could never remember if his first name was Marvin or Marlin, so he just called him Mr. Williams. There was Mrs. Reed's house, a widower, a nice lady. "Oh no, Mr. Harrison's house." He made a cross-shaped figure with his two index fingers as he drove past, picking up speed as he went.

A couple more blocks and a couple more turns and he knew he would be at Rita's apartment complex. At once he felt excited and energized, nervous and scared.

He sat for a moment at a stop sign across the street from her building. "She's in there and she's waiting for you, Tommy. Do you believe that? Where is this going to take me? Only one way to find … ."

The almost comical honk of a car horn stopped his pep talk cold.

Tommy looked in his rear-view mirror to see a beat-up, oil-burning Volkswagen behind him. It looked like a young boy driving. What startled him more was the passenger; he was obviously directing his anger at Tommy. "Get your ass moving, come on! Go!" screamed the man.

Tommy raised his chin up and, still looking in the rear-view mirror, said, "Hey, I'm sorry." He pulled away from the stop sign and into the parking lot of Rita's apartment complex.

"Idiot!" came one last shout as the Volkswagen sputtered away.

Rita's apartment faced the parking lot where Tommy pulled to a stop. She was looking out the window as he arrived. This gave her the chance to see how he acted when he thought he was alone. It was not a matter of trust; Rita was just a very curious person. As she would later tell a girlfriend, "It makes me feel closer to him. I don't know why, though. Plus, he's so damn cute!"

Tommy entered the building, disappearing from her view. He trotted up the two flights of stairs to get to her apartment, Number 307. He rang the doorbell and waited. And waited a bit more. Finally, the door opened.

"Oh, Tommy, you made it over here so fast. I had no idea you were here."

"Really? Because I saw you watching me from that window, right there," he said, pointing to a window just above her sofa.

"I didn't see you do anything to catch my attention. Did you wave at me or anything?"

"Oh, I waved. Furiously."

"You did not. Your head was down the entire time."

"But you just said you didn't see me," mused Tommy.

"Oh, OK then. Guess I'm busted. Come in if you'd like."

"That would be nice, yes."

With that, Rita grabbed his left arm and pulled him inside her apartment. He shut the door behind him. She wrapped both arms around his waist, pressed her body against his, and kissed him hard on the lips. "Oh,

I'm sorry. It's just that ever since meeting you at Richie's and then stopping by your work yesterday, you're all I can think about. I'm not a weirdo, honest. I felt a connection with you from the start."

"I don't think you're a weirdo, Rita. I've felt the same way. I can't think of anything else except you. I nearly got in an accident driving here, thinking about you, thinking about our date. Maybe I'm the weird one."

They both laughed, then kissed each other, a long, slow kiss.

"Oh my god, Tommy, I can feel the passion. Can you?"

"I do Rita. I've never felt this way before."

"Neither have I, not like this. I want to tell you something and also ask you something."

"Sure, what is it?"

"You need to realize I'm not the kind of woman who sleeps around. It's not my style, immediately hopping into bed with a man. You do understand that, right?"

"Of course I do, Rita. I would never expect that of you. Let's not pressure us like that."

She looked straight into his eyes. "When it feels right, there's no pressure."

"You know that song, 'Lovely Rita Meter Maid' that Richie brought up?" asked Tommy.

"You're going to bring Richie into this moment?"

"No, no. I had a different Beatles song pop into my head when I first saw you."

"And what song was that?"

"It's playing in my head right now. *'Got To Get You Into My Life'*. Those lyrics are perfect for us."

"Now you have me in your life," said Rita. With that, she grabbed his hand and led him into her bedroom.

The Victim - Requiem

May 26, 1977, Thursday morning, 9:30

THE SUNNY SKY AND warm air were a stark contrast to the pall that surrounded the church. Tommy could feel the mood, or maybe it was just him: dark, sad, angry, and seeking answers. He sat in his car, motionless; gazing at a lone cloud as it floated by, casting a cooling shadow across the parking lot. The air conditioning was blasting across him as he tried not to sweat through his suit.

His father pulled up next to him, mom in the passenger seat. He had the power window next to his wife rolled down before he stopped. "Tommy, let's go! It's back to work after this. I've got Conrad covering for us right now. Can't leave him alone for too long." Not waiting for a response from his son, he rolled up the window as he pulled the car away.

Tommy wasn't quite ready for this, but he also wasn't ready for another lecture from his dad, so he shut down the car and followed them to the church, up the marble stairs, to the main entrance. Though he had driven past it hundreds of times, he had never been inside the Basilica of St. John's and marveled at the artwork, statuary, and ornate woodwork of the sanctuary.

A gentle murmur was hovering throughout the already crowded nave. Tony had a lot of family, friends, and business associates, but Tommy could not believe how full the church was.

"Impressive crowd, Dad. He sure had a lot of friends," said Tommy.

"Two rows up. There's room for us. Hustle up there and claim it," was his dad's only response. Tommy did as he was told and waited for his parents.

"Such a beautiful church! The view from here is magnificent, don't you think, Tom?" asked his mom.

"It sure is. The artwork, the stonework. Such talent. I'll bet the stories behind them are fascinating," said Tommy.

"Don't you find it beautiful in here, Louis?"

"Can you imagine the money for this? A church ought to be spending money for its congregation instead of all this," said Louis.

"Well, I love it, and I think it is one way to honor God."

"I see at least a dozen customers down there. Tommy, you see any of them?" asked his dad.

"Yeah, I see several."

"How was your date last night, dear?" asked Tommy's mom.

"It was awesome, Mom. Rita is so kind, down to earth. We've really hit it off so far."

"How was you dinner? You mentioned you got reservations at Ann and Joe's. Did you two enjoy your meal?"

"Oh, Ann and Joe's, yes. The food was really good. Rita liked it too," lied Tommy. He then tried to change the subject. "I've heard that Catholic Funeral Masses can be long. I wonder if they'll speak in Latin?"

"I can't answer either of those questions, son. We'll just have to see how it goes."

"Yeah, and that's fine. I was just curious."

"Tommy, when you to go back to the station, show Conrad some pointers. I want to make sure we can rely him on when needed. Days like today, for example," said his dad.

"You want me to help Conrad out, dressed in this suit? Should I go home and change first?" replied Tommy.

"I hope that was supposed to be a joke. Of course, change into work clothes first."

"It was a joke, Dad." Tommy just looked up at the domed ceiling. He wished he were up there or anywhere else, come to think of it. He thought about Rita. He replayed last night with her in her bed. How perfect her body looked and felt.

"I don't understand you sometimes, Tommy. How are jokes about work funny? Joking in church at that!" asked his dad.

Tommy looked past his mom to answer his dad, but didn't say a word. His dad was already looking the other way, arms folded across his stomach.

It was then that the casket procession started. Tommy stood and watched the casket as it was pushed up the center aisle to the base of the sanctuary. The white funeral pall fluttered silently as the casket was centered.

The processional music ended, leaving a solemn silence throughout the sanctuary, punctuated by the occasional breathless sob. Tommy could see Kaylie in the front row. Dressed in black with Adam softly rubbing her back, her shoulders bobbed up and down, in sync with the sounds of the sobs.

"That poor woman. It's not fair," said Tommy in a hushed voice.

Tommy's dad glared at him; his way of telling the boy to be quiet. Today, Tommy didn't care what his dad thought.

After the service, the three of them joined the receiving line. Tommy's dad leaned over and spoke to him. "We need to get back to work. Conrad's been by himself enough for one day."

"Dad, I plan to go to the cemetery for the graveside service," said Tommy.

"That cemetery is out in the country. We've got work to do. We can't do that, sorry."

"I'm going Dad, it's the right thing to do. It's respectful."

"Where's the respect for the business, huh? Or for Conrad?"

"Conrad? Really?" asked Tommy, making his dad's face go red.

"Lou, not here. Let him go. Tommy's right. It is the respectful thing to do. He can represent us out there," said Tommy's mom.

"Do what you want. I guess it doesn't matter to anyone but me," said his dad.

They were silent the rest of their time in line.

"I'll see you when I get back," Tommy called out as they left the church.

Only his mom responded, "Drive careful."

The Daughter - Dad's Place

May 29, 1977, Sunday morning, 10:10

THREE DAYS AFTER THE service, Kaylie had built up enough emotional strength to make the drive over to her father's townhouse. She had the arduous task of going through his things. Deciding what to keep, give away, or throw away, all by herself. An only child, this was her responsibility.

Adam and Patti, as well as several other friends, had volunteered to help. Eventually, she would need the help. On this day, however, she needed to go alone, alone with her own thoughts. It would also give her time to reflect. She had rarely been by herself since his death and craved that solitude.

Adam grabbed her hand as she turned to leave.

"I'm afraid this is too difficult to do by yourself, even for you. Can't I come with you?" he asked.

"No, Adam. This is something I have to do. I have to. And I'll be fine, don't worry."

"OK, I'll be here, just a phone call away."

Kaylie turned back towards him and hugged him. The embrace reinforced the love and appreciation they had for each other. This tragedy made that feeling stronger. He had been her rock, and she knew that, with him, she would somehow get past this nightmare.

She stepped back from him, still holding his forearms, and looked into his eyes.

"I love you, Adam. I don't know what I'd do ... " her voice cracked, unable to say, "without you." But he knew. He knew what she meant. He knew how she felt about him.

"I love you too, Kaylie, and I'll always be here for you. Whatever you need, you can count on me. And that I promise."

She nodded her head as she turned away, wiping a tear from her face. The gentle sobbing continued as she walked to her car. After she started the car, she decided fresh air would do her good. So she unlocked the two clasps that held down the convertible top, pressed a button, and watched the roof's fabric fold into itself. She spotted Adam watching her, waved at him, then blew him a kiss. He waved back and yelled out, "I love you!"

With a deep breath, she put the car in gear and started the short, fifteen-minute drive. As she drove, she thought every place along the way held a memory. The ice cream store where they often met, especially after her mom passed away. A side street where her car broke down one night and he was heading home, saw her and took care of everything. "You always took care of me, daddy," she said, tears flowing down her face.

Kaylie found herself parked in front of her dad's garage. She did not recall the drive. Preoccupied with other thoughts will do that. She thought about putting the car's top up and looked toward the sky. Instead of noticing the weather, she talked to her dad.

"Why did this happen, daddy? Why? Please give me the strength to do this."

She sighed a deep sigh and dabbed her eyes with an ever-present tissue. Bracing herself for the moment, she swung open the car door.

The landscaping surrounding the townhouse was striking: a cobblestone sidewalk, flanked by a variety of plants, large rocks, and mulch. Mature trees lined the front of all the townhomes. The automatic sprinkler had finished moments before Kaylie arrived, settling the dust and leaving everything wet. As she walked up to the front door, her heart raced. A small sundial stood next to the path. The sun danced across the water on its bronze face. The antiquated timepiece was a present she had given her father when he first moved in three years earlier. Though Kaylie missed her childhood home, she understood and supported him, even doing most of the interior decorating.

Hesitating, she lingered at the front door, wanting to stave off the moment a few seconds longer. She unlocked the door and entered. Stopping in the foyer, she took in a deep breath. She headed for the sofa and collapsed on it with a thud, her purse bounding off the cushion and onto the floor. Half its contents tumbled across the carpet. She burst into tears. The smell of her dad's cologne still floated in the room and she cried even harder.

Finding herself in need of a pep talk, Kaylie said, "That's enough crying. Let's get it together. Daddy would not want you putting this on hold. He would insist you move on."

Hands on hips, she took another deep breath. "Where to start?" she said. "I'll do the tough stuff first: photographs, gifts I gave him, anything that has a powerful memory attached. Everything else should be easy. You can do this."

Kaylie peered into his office and it's dark brown leather, high-back chair. She knew it belonged in her home. Walking over to the chair, she sat down, spinning back and forth. His spirit filled the room. He spent most of his time here working. She smiled at the plaques that hung on the wall: Kiwanis, Za-Ga-Zig, Chamber of Commerce, 1975 Businessman of the Year, and many others. She picked a photo frame off the top of his desk. Four-year-old Kaylie smiled back at her as she sat on her mom's lap. They were in a park, a blanket spread on the ground, celebrating the Fourth of July. "You are coming home with me tonight," she said to the photo.

Next to that photo was another one she had never seen. It showed her dad, sitting in his new car, driver's side door open, his left leg on the ground. He's smiling that huge smile that people always mentioned. There, on his left pinky finger, was a diamond ring. On that same wrist was his large watch. The diamonds above every hour drew oohs and aahs from all who saw it. "Those bastards have both pieces. I will get those back, daddy. They will not get away with this. If it's the last thing I do."

She set the frame face down, grabbed the Fourth of July photo, and walked out of the townhouse.

The Prosecutor - Is There Enough?

July 27, 1977, Wednesday morning, 9:51

JONATHON MCMASTER HAD BEEN the county attorney for the past fifteen years and worked for the office ever since graduating from law school. He had committed his life to public service and played a role in locking up thousands of criminals. He was nearly sixty-five years old and had his retirement planned for several years. His wife had wanted to retire to Arizona, and he grudgingly agreed. But life interrupted that plan when his wife died of heart failure in the spring. The sadness consumed him, and he knew it affected his work. It was time to step down and enjoy retirement. He had begun the transition process with his successor, James Sartori, who would hold a new title, Interim County Attorney, until elections were held in November 1978.

In fact, Mr. Sartori was his next scheduled meeting at ten o'clock and was already waiting out in the lobby. McMaster, impeccably dressed, strode to the glass door.

"Jonathon, good morning, sir!"

"James, good to see you. How's Miriam?"

"She is well, doing very well, thank you. She has been busy working with the twins lately since they're off to college this fall."

"Those two girls still planning a pre-med track?"

"They still seem eager about it and they know how difficult it will be. Miriam and I are so proud of them."

"Yes, yes, as you should be. Listen, we have several cases for review this morning, but I'd like to focus on this murder case from last May. The victim's daughter calls my office almost daily and I seldom have anything to tell her. Are you familiar with the Werner case?"

"Yes, I was rereading the case file this past weekend — so much for my golf game!"

"Ah yes, golf. That will be me every day soon."

"You deserve it, sir. This Werner case has been a tough one. Not a lot of usable physical evidence. No eyewitnesses to the actual shooting have come forward. The gun found earlier this summer has a partial print. The forensics folks have a partial on a cigarette lighter found at the crime scene. They are somewhat certain it matches the print from the gun."

"That somewhat certain part concerns me about this case. It's full of speculation. What we have may fill the jurors with doubt. I don't see how this can progress without some more substantial proof unless someone comes forward."

"Agreed. This could go cold. The detectives working the case are certain they know one of the bad guys, maybe two. They don't have the solid evidence to pin this on them. Nobody is confessing yet."

"I feel for the victim's daughter, but these non-stop phone calls! Every other day, asking for updates. There are none. It's taking up staff time we could use in more efficient ways. Talk to her and see if you can explain the situation," said McMaster.

"I will do that. I I have her contact information in the case file and I'll review the case with the lead prosecutor, Jennifer Nichols," said Sartori..

"My recommendation, James, but do as you see fit, is to set up a meeting with her and the lead detective, too. Review the case top to bottom. Highlight the gaps we need to fill before this can move forward. Just as important, let her know her father has not been forgotten."

"Of course, all excellent ideas. I'm on it."

Sartori walked down the hall of the old courthouse to his small office, stopping at his secretary's desk. "Heidi, I need to have you schedule a meeting with myself, Detective Jacobson, and Kaylie Werner. Her number should be in the Anthony Werner case file. Let's update Ms. Werner and discuss how we will handle communications going forward. I'll talk to Jen about this myself. Check my schedule and get this set up ASAP, please."

"Oh course, Mr. Sartori, I'll do that now," she said as she reached for her files.

The Daughter - Discuss The Case

FOR A LATE JULY day, it was cold and rainy when Kaylie trotted up the courthouse steps for her meeting. She shook off her umbrella in the entryway, then walked over towards the elevator, heels echoing throughout the building. She entered the antiquated-looking elevator, took a deep breath, and pressed two. The light did not illuminate, so she pushed it again. And again. "Come on, come on, come on!" She sighed as the doors closed and the elevator lifted her to the second floor.

The beautiful architecture of the one hundred-year-old courthouse, with its ornate ceiling towering fifty feet above, did nothing for Kaylie's demeanor as she walked, determined and with purpose, to room 207. Just inside the door was a receptionist. "I have a meeting with Mr. Sartori. My name is Kaylie Wer —"

"Kaylie Werner, yes. Right this way." The receptionist led her to a small, windowless conference room. "Sit wherever you want." The receptionist turned on her heels and shut the door behind her.

"Nice attitude! Damn!" Kaylie took a seat along the far wall. She was the first to arrive, which gave her a chance to review the notes she had written.

The door opened and James Sartori walked in and Detective Jacobson followed. She rose from her chair. "Please don't get up, Ms. Werner. I'm Assistant District Attorney Sartori and you might remember Detective Jacobson, but it's now Senior Detective. Congratulations on your promotion, Charles."

"Good to meet you, Mr. Sartori. And I remember Detective Jacobson. Senior Detective now? Did you get that title for time served, or is it accomplishment-based?"

"Ms. Werner, I appreciate the frustration you must be feeling, but ... " began Jacobson.

"Unless your father had half his head blown off by some low-life, you have no idea, sir, none!"

"You are correct, ma'am, in that I have not had a loved one murdered. I have, however, worked on many of these cases. I've seen firsthand the pain and suffering these crimes cost. Because of that, I have dedicated my career to solving these crimes. Your father's case is at the top of the list, I promise you that."

"Ms. Werner, Charles, I'd like to go over what we have so far. We can discuss what we are missing, and what are our plans going forward. Of course, the goal is to bring to justice those who perpetrated the crime. I will also state, Ms. Werner, that this office shares the detective's goals in this case," said Sartori.

"I appreciate those words very much and I apologize for my short temper," said Kaylie.

"Ms. Werner, there is no need to apologize," said the district attorney. "Granted, we don't share in the intense loss you have — we couldn't possibly — but we do share in your desire to bring this to its rightful conclusion. I will turn this over to the detective. Charles."

"Thanks, James. Ms. Werner, we … ."

"Please, call me Kaylie."

"Thank you. Kaylie. We have been reviewing the crime scene photos and forensics gathered from the scene. We have some prints, smudges actually, inside the car and we found a lighter outside of the vehicle that has a partial print we are working on. Please, tell me a little about your father. Would he put up a fight? Or would he try to negotiate his way out of a problem? Would he be passive and follow orders?"

"Without a doubt, he'd negotiate at first. If that failed, he'd have no problem getting into a fight. He would usually win those battles, too."

"While we do not know if he tried to negotiate, we're certain he put up a fight."

"How do you know that, detective?"

"He had defensive wounds on his left hand. We believe he was struck with the butt of a gun, causing a wound. It is possible that he intended to jump out of the car before he was fatally shot."

"Charles," Sartori spoke up, "and don't we think this occurred on the freeway, given the exterior of the car?"

"Yes, the physical evidence does point to that conclusion," replied Jacobson.

"I don't understand. What kind of evidence?" asked Kaylie.

Sartori shot a glance across the table at Jacobson, who replied, "Ma'am, it's evidence that perhaps you won't be comfortable hearing."

"I'm not a child. There is a severe wound in my father's head, and I know what that means. Adam and I saw his body at the coroner's office, so don't hold back on me. If there are photographs in your folder that would help explain, I can handle it. Like I said, I'm not a child."

"Very well then, Kaylie," said Jacobson, "I'll show you *some* photographs of the crime scene, but I am not going to show graphic photos of your father. It will serve you no purpose, especially if you've already seen the wounds firsthand."

"I can accept that. What makes you think this happened on the freeway?"

"We're working on the theory that your father put up a struggle at some point. He may have tried to disrupt the driver somehow, though I don't have any direct evidence of that. Stronger evidence is the considerable amount of blood on the exterior passenger side."

"The *outside* of the car?" asked Kaylie. "How could that have happened?"

"Yes, the outside," continued Jacobson. "He may have tried to open the passenger door as a means of escaping. It's possible that he got it open, or partially open. During the struggle, he may have been shot twice in the shoulder. Those shots were fired from the backside of the front seat. They confirm the involvement of multiple subjects. The two shots would have made it more difficult for him to fight. It was at that point, and again, we are making assumptions, that he received the fatal wound to his temple." Kaylie's chin slumped to her chest. "I'm sorry, Kaylie. Do you want me to stop?"

"No, I can get through this. Go on please."

"By then, a considerable amount of blood was on the door's interior. It ran down the door and outside the vehicle. With the car moving at, say, sixty miles per hour along the freeway, it's obvious how there would be blood streaks extending to the rear wheel well. Exactly what we have here." He held up the photo, facing it away from Kaylie.

"Please, let me see it. It's OK."

Jacobson flipped it over on the table. A muted gasp came from Kaylie, and she turned her head away for a brief second. Gaining her composure, she looked towards the detective. "I don't understand how this is helpful."

"It's another piece of the puzzle. We are confident your father was abducted from outside his townhouse based on two facts. One, the garage door was wide open; which, according to you, he would never forget. Two, a witness observed a man sitting against a tree near the garage. We believe he is one man involved. Since the abduction occurred there and ended on Third and Seventh, it gives us the direction of travel. The amount of blood blown against the car implies freeway speeds. This assists us in determining the time of abduction. It also narrows down the time of death. These facts will only help us once we get to court."

"So, do you have any suspects yet? It is so difficult living with this. I go to the grocery store or the mall. I take a walk in my neighborhood. Everywhere I turn and see a stranger, my mind immediately asks, 'Is that him? Did you kill my dad?'. It's heartbreaking enough to not have him with us. The unknown just magnifies the suffering."

"Without getting into details — I can't give you names — we do have someone in mind. We're keeping an eye on this subject and tracking down leads that can, hopefully, provide us with solid evidence. We are always working with the watch commanders, making sure their officers are staying alert to cases like this. Many times we'll pick someone up on a minor charge and the next thing you know, they're ratting someone out."

"Like the movies?" said Kaylie.

"A little, just not as fast."

The district attorney straightened up in his chair and cleared his throat. "Let me summarize what we have at this point. We have some solid evidence that will be valuable in court. We have a person that we are keeping tabs on. If we can get more on this person, our hope is it will lead us to the second person involved. I'm confident we'll get anyone else connected to this crime. Detectives Jacobson and Winston are dedicating most of their time to getting justice for your dad. We are also having the police force reminded periodically of this case and to keep their eyes and ears open."

"This has been informative and very helpful. I had hoped for arrests by now. I'm beginning to see that I'm going to need more patience. Thank you, both of you."

"We only want justice. One last item I have, and please, detective, let me know what you think. How should we provide updates? How often should we contact you?"

"Well," Kaylie pursed her lips, "of course, any breakthrough I'd like to know right away. If it's three in the morning, call me. Otherwise, I'd appreciate a weekly call, even if there is no news. It doesn't have to be either one of you. Anyone on your staff can call me. I just don't want him forgotten because … ."

"We understand," the detective placed his hand on her shoulder. "This won't get swept under the rug. You and your dad will not be forgotten, and we will solve this."

District Attorney Sartori handed her his handkerchief. "Thank you, Mr. Sartori," she said as she wiped her eyes.

"I promise we will keep in touch."

"And I'll keep working this case to the end," said Jacobson.

Raising her head, Kaylie looked out the window. "Looks like the rain has stopped, and the sun is coming out. That's a positive sign, right?"

The district attorney smiled. "Let's hope so."

Detective Jacobson knew it would take more than better weather to break this case open.

No one present that day knew when justice would be served. It would be two years before the criminal justice system got their pound of flesh. Another five before many would feel that true justice was served.

The Rat - A Way Out

February 2, 1979, Friday morning, 3:12

JOHN BRODIGAN WAS DESPERATE. Desperate, and once again in prison. This time for a long stretch. He'd already done almost five years in prison before this, and he could not survive much longer. He needed a way out. A way out of the dingy, dull drudgery of penitentiary life.

"Why am I such a fuck-up?" He screamed into his thin, government-issue pillow. His cellmate, dozing in his bed, stirred and mumbled something, but John paid him no attention. All he could think about was getting out and trying, this time *really* trying to go legit, to stay out of prison, and to fix the broken relationships with his family. His dad had stopped coming for visits after the first year, and his mom six months later. It was just too hard to see the life that was now his and, with no light at the end of the tunnel, they simply gave up. His older sister could never bring herself to that dark and drab castle in the middle of nowhere. In fact, he knew she could not stand to be near him, not after what he had done.

And he certainly could not blame her. He could not come to forgive himself for how his life turned out; how it led him to this time and place. He was really looking for redemption, but was unsure if he would get that or if that was even something he truly deserved.

John closed his eyes, which only set his mind racing again, jumping rapidly from one thought to another, as it had every day for years.

In a flash, he saw himself robbing that hardware store, the gray-haired clerk and her terrified look as she opened the register ... mad dash to his car, cash in hand, a few bills escaping his grasp and fluttering across the parking lot ... tires screeching as he made his getaway.

The next second he's laughing, thinking about the drugs he will score with all that money.

The very next second came that loud thump. The sound that would haunt him for the rest of his days.

He just did not see that kid on his bike, but he knew something very bad had happened. He slammed on the brakes, jumped out of the car, and ran the half block back to that small lump in the street. The boy lay there, unconscious and bleeding. His orange bicycle with the white banana seat was mangled and flipped up on a bus stop bench.

John stood over the child, never saying a word. Not as he cocked his head from side to side, as if to decipher what he was seeing. Not as the crowd surrounded him. Not as the people's anger grew and a few of the younger men that gathered began to push and curse him. Not as the hardware store owner yelled at the crowd to stop him. Then they pummeled him, knocked him to his knees, and kicked him unconscious, just like the little boy. He didn't say a word when the police scraped him off the street and slapped handcuffs on him. He didn't answer them when the police asked about the handgun laying in the front seat of his car. When the emergency room nurses and doctors asked him what his name was, what allergies he had, and what surgeries. He remained silent. John became a mute for several days.

Right then and there, John gave up rather than sit through a trial. "Throw the key away. I don't care."

He got twenty-five years. Even he didn't think that was fair.

So there he sat again, another felony attached to his name. A funny thing happened to him over those first few months; he once again pictured himself as the victim. The Marines robbed him of a solid career, a life. Society wouldn't give him a decent job. That kid, that fucking little kid, should not have been riding his bike in the street. He just could not bear another ten, fifteen, twenty-five years. He knew his only shot was to make a deal. To tell someone the secret he had kept. Once he shared this, there would be no going back. It was bound to destroy lives. And to him, what made matters worse yet, he would become a rat.

"Better a rat on the run than a caged one." He had made up his mind.

He planned to use his phone privilege after breakfast to contact the attorney that defended him in his latest case, laying out what he knew and what he wanted in exchange — he wanted out as soon as possible, immunity in that old man's murder case, and maybe even the Witness Protection Program.

The Rat - We Need To Talk To The DA

February 2, 1979, Friday morning, 7:45

JOHN BARELY SLEPT THE rest of the night.

"I can't eat this shit, not today man," he said to the inmate next to him, who promptly ignored him.

He peered at the pale blue and gray walls in this combination lunchroom/gymnasium. He ached to make that deal. He'd been in prison long enough to know to keep quiet. When he was on the phone with his attorney, discretion was required. Snitches *would* get stitches in here. Sometimes even worse. He didn't want Dale or Big Man tipped off on his plan.

Silence was the order of the day.

The runny, pasty, and almost yellow eggs looked worse than usual today. Stirring them around on his plate only made them worse. He nibbled at the bacon. "Bacon's not bad," he thought to himself. "Watered down OJ, as usual." The permanent, musty smell of the prison and the occasional smell of passing prisoners put an end to eating. He walked slowly towards the trash, emptied his tray, and set it under the food-splattered sign that read *PLACE TRAYS HERE*.

His internal monologue turned to the matter at hand, his freedom. "Got the lawyer's number in my pocket, wait for the far-end phone booth to open up, and hope that public defender is in the office. Gotta stay cool, don't talk loud. They need to get me to that prosecutor soon!"

John made his way past the kitchen, peeling off to the left. Most of the prisoners were, despite the cold weather, headed right to the yard. He tried being casual. "No big deal, John, just going to use the phone."

He was relieved to find the far phone booth vacant. His pace quickened. He reached the end of the phone bank and sat down with his back to the wall; he wanted to see anyone coming.

After the public defender's office accepted the charges, he was connected to a receptionist. "County Public Defense Association, this is Samantha. How may I direct your call?"

Cupping his hands around the mouthpiece, he told her, "This is John Brodigan, and two years ago Mark Stedman defended me in a court case and I have to talk to him. I have a way of getting out of prison, but he's gotta help me."

"I'm sorry, John, but Mr. Stedman went into private practice last year. If you can hold, I will find out who has your case file."

"I got nothing else to do, sweetheart," he answered, but it was too late. He was already on hold. He began picking at the small stickers inmates would put on the walls; everything from Bible verses to stickers off of a banana bunch. It was something bored men did. And for no reason. "Is that Smokey the Bear?" he peered closer, admiring someone's handiwork, "Shit, that is funny!" Someone had marked up the famous '*Only You Can Prevent Forest Fires*' slogan by scratching out the letters r, v, n, and t in the word 'Prevent' and used a marker to insert 'ON' before 'Forest'. "Only You Can Pee ON Forest Fires! Ha, good one. That is fucking funny right there!"

"Mr. Brodigan?"

Still laughing, "Yes, I'm still here."

"Mr. Brodigan, your case has been assigned to Scott Lucas."

"Can you transfer me so I can talk to him?"

"I'm sorry. He's in court this morning."

"Fuck! Sorry, I didn't mean to say that. I need to talk to the man."

"Mr. Brodigan, I've worked at this desk for almost five years. That was pretty tame, OK? What I can do is leave him a note that you need to speak with him. He usually makes trips to your prison once a week, if not more often. I don't have his schedule in front of me, but once he is back from court, he can put you on his calendar. Then we can contact you through the prison's liaison office to let you know when to expect him. Will that work for you, sir?"

"Can he come up this week?"

"Mr. Brodigan, today is Friday. It will have to wait until at least next week. Again, we will be in touch. Is there anything else you'd like me to pass along to Mr. Lucas?"

"No. It would be great to talk sooner. But you're right, this is Friday. I just lose track of the days in here. Hey, you've been helpful, but that's all I need. Thanks for listening and I'll wait to hear from you."

Without saying goodbye, he hung up the phone and stared at the floor. "Another long wait. Seems like that's all I do here ... wait."

***

February 6, 1979, Tuesday afternoon, 1:24

"Inmate!"

John Brodigan flinched awake. "Wha ... what?"

It was a guard. "Inmate, you have a visitor. Let's go."

"A visitor, who?"

"Do I look like your personal valet?"

"Well, shit, the uniform alone, I'd ... ."

"Do you want to see this visitor? Yes or no?"

Brodigan leaped down from his bunk. "Of course, sorry for the ... ."

"Save it, let's go."

The men walked past empty cells, down an open set of stairs, and to the small meeting rooms set aside for legal conferences. These rooms were much nicer than the common visitor areas, with bright, fresh paint, and photographs of landscapes and cityscapes, plus it didn't smell like the rest of the prison.

The guard opened the door to the second room and motioned in Brodigan. Sitting at the table was a young, rotund man in an ill-fitting suit. The man stood up as Brodigan entered, extending his hand. "Mr. Brodigan, Scott Lucas from the public defender's office, good to meet you."

"Scott Lucas! Let me shake your hand. I'm so glad to see you today. Somebody at your office said they'd let me know you were coming, but I didn't know. That's OK, you're here and we need to talk. Damn, thank you for being here!"

"Of course, Mr. Brodigan. I believe Samantha let you know that your previous representation, Mr. Stedman, has moved on."

"Yeah, she said that, and that's OK."

"Sam also mentioned that you had a way of getting out of prison. What did you mean by that?"

"I'm stuck in here for years. I admit I did the crime. I admit that, and I feel like shit about the poor little kid. I have some information about another crime that happened a couple of years ago. And I know how it went down. I'm hoping that by telling the DA I can get free."

The attorney shifted in his chair. "I see. Two questions to start. What crime? And how do you know this?"

"It's a murder case. I saw it happen because I was right behind them when it happened."

"I don't understand. What do you mean you were 'right behind them'?"

"I was following them in my truck and I saw the flashes from the gun."

"And why were you following them?"

"Yeah, that's where it gets hairy. We were just going to rob the guy and steal some construction tools. But the supposed mastermind freaked out and blew the old man's brains out."

"You're telling me you participated in a murder and you want to confess? You also expect to get released for the current manslaughter charge? You also expect no charges for this other murder? Is that *all* you want? Because that will be a tough sell. They're going to want a pound of flesh."

"That murder case gets colder by the day and I can heat it up. Can you at least talk to them and see what they can offer? I just can't live like this much longer."

"OK, John, I will talk to them, but I don't want you getting your hopes up. I'm sure they will ask for some time. A little more time for manslaughter. Some for the murder. Who knows, maybe they'll feel generous when I see them.

"I'm just asking for a chance."

"What's the case? Tell me what you know."

"Do you know about the Werner murder? Found shot dead in his car next to a house he was working on?"

"Of course, I've heard of that. That was you?"

"That's what I'm saying. It wasn't me. At least, I didn't shoot the guy, but I know who did. I know the whole story."

"That was a high-profile case when it happened, and I know they're still working hard on that one. There might be hope, after all. It's a pretty big deal."

"Hell yeah, it's a big deal. Rich, white guy murdered. Matters a lot in that town."

"You know the prosecutor will need something he can sink his teeth into. Something specific, like a name."

This caught Brodigan off guard.

"John?"

After a few seconds, Brodigan replied, "That's a big piece of the puzzle. Without an offer, I don't want to tell them his name. I could get fucked on the deal."

"That's why I'm in your corner, John. You have to trust me."

Brodigan laughed softly, "Trust. OK, trust." After a few seconds of silence, he added, "Tell them it was Dale Bowers."

"Dale Bowers. Got it. How do you know this guy?

"We have the same friends. The two of us have worked together. Stupid stuff like mugging drunks outside of bars, breaking into houses, small-time shit like that."

"Anyone else involved in this murder?"

"I'm not saying anything more about the murder case until they give me what I want. I may need this to negotiate."

"Let me talk to them. If they push for a name, I'll tell them. To be clear, you will have to give them the names of all involved."

"I know, I know. Just get it done."

Scott Lucas walked past his client and tapped on the door. "Guard!"

The Public Defender - Let's Make A Deal

February 7, 1979, Wednesday morning, 9:14

"This is Jennifer Nichols, who's calling, please?"

"Ms. Nichols, this is Scott Lucas. I'm a public defender representing a client who may have some information on a murder case that your office is working."

"I see, Mr. Lucas, is it? What case are we talking about?"

"The Anthony Werner murder."

Her eyebrows raised as she sat up straight in her chair. "And what kind of info does your client have?"

"First things first. The guy's in prison on a manslaughter conviction and he wants a deal. He's asking for immunity in the Werner case and wants consideration for early parole."

"Jesus, it doesn't hurt to inquire, I guess, but that's a huge ask."

"Trust me, he's got firsthand knowledge of the murder. He's been doing a lot of soul-searching and wants to come clean."

"Soul-searching you say? I hear that happens a lot in prison. So far, I'm not impressed. Plus, I don't know you or your client, so I won't commit to anything just yet. Who is this guy?"

"James Brodigan. He's being housed at Brinkmeyer Penitentiary, doing twenty-five for robbery and manslaughter."

"Wait, wait, wait. The guy has already killed somebody. He's involved in this Werner killing, *and* he aspires to be paroled?"

"And immunity."

"No fucking way. Not only would my boss never go for it," she said as she tossed her pen on the desk, "but I hate the offer already."

"He'll name the shooter and will lay everything out. How it happened, who did what. Everything."

"That would provide solid intel, Mr. Lucas. But no way we do that deal. My office would look heartless. I just pulled that case file — our office tried that case also. Do you even know the details of his manslaughter case?"

"I'm not familiar with his case. Give me the highlights."

"He robbed a hardware store, tried to get away, and there was a little kid riding his bike. Your client ran over him. Christ, a little kid!"

"I did not know."

"Would you like to face that kid's parents and say 'Hey, we value this case over yours, you OK with that?' No one in my office is doing that."

"As counsel, I must present to you the offer my client has asked for. If there is a counter-offer, I will take it to my client."

"I understand the process, Mr. Lucas. As it stands, my offer sounds a lot like laughter. As a professional courtesy, I'll have staff review your client's current case and see if we can reach an agreement. I'll get back to you, perhaps with a counter. Expect a call from me soon. Expect very little out of my counter."

Jennifer slammed the receiver down, leaving the public defender with only a dial tone.

"Kerri," Jennifer called out to her receptionist, "where is Sarah?"

"Lunch, but she should be back soon. Can I help with anything?"

"No, I ... come to think of it, yes. Get everything we have on John Brodigan."

Holding a notepad, Kerri entered the room. "Brodigan. Got it. Should I let Sarah know?"

"Yes, do that. Both of you can work on that. I need the info today."

The Prosecutor - Now We're Talking!

February 7, 1979, Wednesday morning, 9:35

THE NEWLY APPOINTED COUNTY attorney, James Sartori sat in his comfortable, dark-paneled office reviewing a stack of notes he had jotted down the previous night. Unaware that she walked into the office, his Assistant District Attorney, Jennifer Nichols, dropped a sheaf of papers in front of him.

"What's this?" he asked.

"This is huge. Remember that murder we reviewed? Must have been your second day here? The construction owner from two years ago? Let's see," continued Jennifer as she leafed through the binder, "here it is, May twenty-first of 1977."

"Oh yes, Warner? No, no, Werner. Anthony Werner. We've always known the actors involved, but no witnesses. We didn't think the evidence was strong enough. What have we got here?"

"It looks like we have another jailhouse snitch *and*, thanks to technology, some solid forensic evidence."

Sartori sighed and looked up at Jennifer. He began leafing through the papers, holding up a document or a photograph for a closer look. "Hmmm, a career criminal who is now talking. Any idea of what his angle is?" asked the county prosecutor.

"According to the inmate's public defender, he'd like to have some consideration for some help to get him paroled. For all we know, he's figured out right from wrong."

"A prison revelation of some sort?" He laughed to himself. He admired the ADAs grasp of detail and at this moment felt she would help his office out immensely. She had tremendous potential in law and he hoped she would stay put and not defect into criminal defense. To do battle in court with her would be a challenge.

"Then there is the additional evidence. The lead detective wants to review some evidence. They re-analyzed some prints found on the gun, the victim's wallet, and a lighter found near the murder. Two years ago, they found a few partial prints, but they weren't complete enough to ID anyone. But, today they can take those partials and run them through the FBI's database, IAFIS. They got five hits from IAFIS and narrowed it down to one man, a Dale William Bowers, who lived here when the murder occurred. Not surprisingly, he is one man known to cavort with our convict."

"One of them?"

"Yes, he is indicating there were three men involved in the death of Mr. Werner, including our snitch. He's looking at some hard time for armed robbery and a manslaughter conviction while fleeing the robbery."

"And this is where we come in. If this guy is going to come clean, we could offer him something. What are you thinking?" asked Sartori, leaning back in his chair.

"Well, sir, I'm OK with immunity on the murder charge, but the manslaughter case, no. The guy killed a little kid. Two years is not long enough. I say we give him the immunity he wants and also relocate him. By relocation, I mean to another penitentiary where he does at least another nickel."

"I like it. Offer him that. If he balks, tell him he can enjoy his twenty-five years right where he is. We already know who we are after, this Bowers guy. We can leverage that, too."

"Agreed. Shall we meet with his attorney?"

"Not we, you. This is your case now; bring it home."

"Thank you, sir, I won't disappoint!" she quickly turned and left the office, shutting the door behind her.

Sartori smiled and got back to work.

Jennifer walked back to her office, which she shared with her paralegal, Sarah.

"Well, don't you look happy," exclaimed Sarah.

"And why shouldn't I? I officially have the lead on a murder case, a big one!"

"Congratulations Jen! How can I help?"

"By being the best paralegal I know. Pull the files on the Werner murder from 1977." Sarah was scribbling notes as fast as Jennifer was talking. "I also need you to review everything Kerri is pulling on a prisoner by the name of James Brodigan. I know he is doing twenty-five for manslaughter at Brinkmeyer, but I want his entire history. There should already be a file on Dale Bowers. I need to know his entire criminal record. If he's had a partner in crime before, I need a name. I'll need contact information on the detectives currently involved in these cases; hopefully Jake still has the murder case. Oh my god, this is exciting!"

"Isn't it though! I've got your back, Jen. You know I do."

"Of course I do. I hope you are ready for some long hours. I want to nail this case."

"Consider it done," said Sarah as she grabbed a file cart and headed off to the file room.

The Prosecutor - Counter Offer

February 7, 1979, Wednesday afternoon, 4:15

"OK Jen, you can do this. Just take some deep breaths. You've worked your entire life for this chance."

She paused, looked at the phone number, and made the call. Soon the uneasiness evaporated. She was in control and knew it.

"Scott, Jennifer Nichols with the DA's office."

"Good afternoon, very good to hear from you," came Scott's reply.

"Well, let's see how you feel in fifteen minutes."

"I'll be fine either way. I hope you will be good with it, too."

"Don't worry about me. I've read your clients' criminal history report. I've read the file on his manslaughter case. This guy is not a boy scout. But I'd bet you already knew that."

"Of course I do," said Scott

"Here's my only offer. I'll tell you why we will not negotiate on this."

"Now I'm intrigued. Go on."

"We know who pulled the trigger in the Werner murder and our investigators are working several solid leads and our evidence is lining up. Does the name Dale Bowers mean anything to your client?"

Jennifer heard the audible sigh from the other end of the phone. "So the name means something. You see why he may not be the hot commodity he thinks he is?"

"What are you offering?" The defense attorney felt defeated already.

"Your guy tells everything he knows, names everyone involved, and *confesses* to his part in the crime. In return, he gets immunity in the murder case, and he gets shit for the manslaughter case. He killed a kid, Mr. Lucas. At best, we'll try to get him housed out of state. It's a simple ask of the court. Perhaps as a protective measure."

"But he could spend another twenty years in prison. That's his entire motive for talking. We all know that."

"Let him spend the rest of his life there. I don't care. You're his lawyer. Appeal the fucking case if you can. Either way, that's my offer. I'll need an answer by the end of the day tomorrow. Anything else to cover regarding this offer, Scott?"

"No, nothing else. End of the day tomorrow and I'll have an answer."

Jennifer hung up the phone and smiled.

***

February 8, 1979, Thursday morning, 8:44

"Open gate seven," the guard spat into his radio. With a loud clank and high-pitched metal-on-metal screeching, the gate opened. "Right this way," said the guard as he pointed Scott Lucas down the hall. "Your guy is in room C-104, second on the right."

"Thank you, officer," replied the attorney.

Without saying another word, the officer took a seat at the end of the hallway and waited.

"Is my client already in there?"

The officer nodded yes; eyes cold and shark-like.

Lucas opened the door to room C-104, exhaling as he entered. "John, good morning. How are you?"

With a heavy thud, the door slammed behind him, causing him to flinch.

"It's just a door, Scott, take it easy!" Brodigan laughed a little.

"Caught me off guard is all," he said as he sat down across from his client.

"Tell me you got what we asked."

"Not everything. So you know, that seldom happens."

"Fuck! What did they offer, then?"

"You get full immunity on the murder if you testify and tell them everything you know, names, places, explain the crime from start to finish."

"So far, so good. What about my current charge?"

"That's the part that didn't fly. No relief in your sentence, but they will try to move you out of state."

"Nothing? I'm handing them convictions, man!"

"See, that's the thing; they're already on to Bowers and given enough time, they feel they will nail the guy. Your testimony could speed that up, but not enough to do you any big favor. A child is dead because of you. You're stuck with that."

"I can give them Thompson, too. Shit, he drove the damn car. There's this Steve guy, Steve Rudolph or Randolph, something like that. He led us to that dead guy. He's the reason we targeted the old man for robbery. Just robbery. I think Big Man knew Steve."

"Who is Big Man?"

"Thompson, we call him Big Man because he's a little shit."

"Let me give them those two names. It shows good faith. They mentioned neither man, so they may have nothing."

"I'll stay put then. I know how this place works. Who to hang with; who not to fuck with. Yeah, I'll stay here. Dammit!"

"Look, I'll have a colleague look at your case. We can see if we have a viable appeal option. I'll get that started and see where that takes us."

"Why don't you do my appeal too?"

"My colleague specializes in appeals, plus my time has got to be focused on your testimony and ironing out any deals."

"OK, I understand."

"I'll give the DA a call when I get back to the office and give them those two names. Guard!"

⸻ ⬦ ⸻

February 8, 1979, Thursday morning, 10:26

"ADA Nichols, this is Scott Lucas again."

"Thank you for calling Mr. Lucas. What has your client got for me?"

"He's ready to take your deal and, as a good faith gesture, has two names for you."

"Glad to hear that he came to his senses. What are the names?"

"Gordon Thompson, aka, 'Big Man'. He was in on the murder."

"We're familiar with him already, but it is additional corroboration. And the other name?"

"Steve Rudolph or Randolph, he wasn't sure of the last name."

"That is a new name, thanks. And how does he fit into this?"

"He gave them the victim's name, let them know he was a potential target to rob. The only other thing my client mentioned about him was that Thompson knew him."

"I'm comfortable with our deal now. Consider it done."

"I'll let him know, thanks!" said Scott, but the ADA had already hung up the phone.

February 8, 1979, Thursday morning, 10:45

"Jake, this is Jen. Please tell me you and your partner have some time today or tomorrow to pick somebody up for questioning."

"Hey Jen, today is not going to happen. We're both swamped. Tomorrow looks good. What have you got?"

"The Werner case. Brodigan finally broke. He gave us the names Gordon Thompson and another name. He wasn't clear on the last name, either Randolph or Rudolph, but the guy's first name is Steve."

"Let me look at the file." After a pause, "OK, now I remember. Thompson was probably the driver. Winnie," Jacobson yelled across desks to his partner, "your salmon guy got ratted out and we have another name. We're going to go get him tomorrow."

"I'll see if I can't figure out Steve's last name and get an address. I'll get a warrant and grab him tomorrow. You want to watch the interrogation?"

"Yes, it's a must. And please, someday explain to me 'salmon guy'."

"I'll call you after he's in lockup. And Jen, expect little out of the 'salmon guy' story."

The Police - An Accessory To Murder

February 9, 1979, Friday morning, 8:15

Due to wintry weather, Steve was laid off from work. He was more than happy having the house to himself.

"Yes, breakfast of champions!" said Steve as he poured milk over an enormous bowl of Froot Loops. He glanced up at the wall full of family pictures. Not his family, but his girlfriend's. It was, after all, her house where he lived now. "Cheers you little shit," as he locked eyes with a photograph of his girlfriend's son, outfitted in his baseball uniform. He buried himself in his recliner. "Crap, I hope I didn't miss the start of … ."

"Steve! Steve Randolph, this is the police." They were pounding on the front door. "Open up Steve, we need to talk."

"What the hell?" He looked out the side window and there, blocking his driveway, were four squad cars, with their red and blue lights flashing. He walked over and opened the door. "What is this all … ."

"Mr. Randolph?" Detective Winston said, "We need to talk."

"I don't have a reason to talk to you. Get the hell out of here!"

"Not going to happen, Steve. My friends and I are not going anywhere without you. I have an arrest warrant for you," said Winston as he waved the warrant in the air.

"Bullshit. I ain't done nothing wrong."

"No bullshit. I bet you've been a good little boy of late. You did something bad two years ago.

"I have no idea what the hell you're talking about, man."

"No? You any good at math, Steve?"

"What?"

"Math, you know, adding and subtracting, that sort of thing. Math."

Steve just stared at the detective, who continued, "Tell me, smart guy, what do you get when you add Steve Randolph and Dale Bowers … ."

"I don't know any Dale," interrupted Steve.

"You and I both know that's bullshit. Think back a couple of years. Now, back to your math problem. Steve, that's you, plus Dale Bowers, minus the life of Anthony Werner. What's that sum up to you, Steve?"

"Beat's me."

"Well, Steve, it equals you are fucked. Turn around. You're under arrest as an accessory to murder."

Steve placed his hands behind his back. "I want a lawyer."

"I bet you do, Steve. Let's go." Detective Winston escorted him to a waiting squad car, reading him his Miranda rights along the way.

⸺•◦•⸺

February 9, 1979, Friday afternoon, 12:42

Steve sat waiting in a dimly lit interrogation room. Cold and damp in the bowels of the police station, his hands sat in his lap, handcuffed. The door creaked open and in walked a young man in a gray suit, wearing an ill-fitting overcoat at least two sizes too large.

"Who the hell are you?", Steve asked as he sat back in his chair.

The man extended his hand. Steve raised his shackled hands and shrugged.

"Oh, I see, sorry. Um, I'm Underwood, William Underwood," the man said as he sat across the table. "The Public Defender's office has assigned your case to me."

"My lawyer, huh? Can you get me out of here?"

"I am not a miracle worker, Mr. Randolph, but why don't you tell me your side of the story?"

"That cop said I'm an accessory to murder. Well, buddy, I'm no Harvard-educated guy, so I don't even know what he's saying to me."

"They have accused you of being an accessory to murder, first-degree murder no less. What that means is they are accusing you of providing information to a certain person or persons. That person or persons used that information to assist them with a murder."

"But I ... ."

"Let me explain first. You did not go to Harvard, remember?"

"All right, sorry. Go ahead. Did you go to Harvard?"

"Where I received my law degree is not important, but the charges against you are. Let me explain the charges again. The police are accusing you of providing key information to one or more individuals that led to the murder of Mr. Anthony Werner. Do you understand that?"

"Yeah, I do."

"This means you are facing up to twenty-five years in prison if found guilty. Do you understand that, Mr. Randolph?"

"Twenty-five years? I just thought he was going to rob him, not kill him. Hell, I'm starting a family now with a fiancée. She has this great kid I get to play ball with. I can't have that taken from me," said Steve.

"So you are telling me you had some involvement?"

"I'm not saying that," his cheek trembled.

"Well, that wasn't a question. You just told me, your attorney, that you committed a crime. I can read you pretty well too, and I'm thinking right about now that you are getting scared. As well you should. You need to make a deal. You tell them your part and maybe we can keep you out of prison. They want those involved in the murder a lot more than you. So we may be able to negotiate with them. If we're lucky."

"You mean become a snitch? I can't do that!"

"Can you do twenty-five years in prison?"

Steve hung his head, banging it on the table.

"I didn't think so. I'll go talk to them. Guard!"

In a room down the hall waited the ADA, Jacobson, and Winston.

Underwood stepped into their room. "He's ready to talk." He turned and walked back to his client.

"Let's chat with him before he changes his mind," said ADA Nichols.

The trio stood up and hurried over to Interrogation Room Three.

"Mr. Randolph, I'm Assistant District Attorney Jennifer Nichols. I believe you've met these two detectives earlier today."

Steve nodded. "What do you want to know?"

The trio sat down across from Randolph and his attorney. For ten uncomfortable seconds, no words were spoken.

"OK, I'll go. How do you know Mr. Thompson?" asked Jacobson.

"Thompson? Who's Thompson?" replied Randolph.

"Counselor, is your client playing with us?" asked Nichols.

"No, he honestly doesn't know many last names," replied Underwood.

"Do you know someone who goes by the name Big Man?"

"Sure I know Big Man."

"Good, but someone else was involved, correct?"

"He told me about Dale and I ended up meeting that psycho," said Randolph.

"We've heard that about him," said Jacobson.

"Yep, that dude would explode. And for no reason. No one knew why. It was weird to see."

"Steve," said his lawyer, "I think it best to only answer their questions."

"OK. I ain't got anything to hide, but you're the lawyer."

The Prosecutor - Building The Case

February 9, 1979, Friday afternoon, 2:05

"SIT DOWN MR. BRODIGAN," said Assistant DA, Jennifer Nichols. "You suddenly don't like your deal? Think long and hard about this. We have enough on you to charge you along with the rest of your friends. We want a murder one conviction on Bowers and Thompson, which your testimony is going to give. Without it, we'll still put them away on murder two, at least. Oh, and if you back out now, you go along with them."

"Can I have a minute with my client?" asked Scott Lucas.

"Take your time. I'll step outside," said Jennifer.

"It would be advisable for you to keep their original offer. I agree with her. I think they would bury you if you don't."

"They know about Thompson, shit. That's out the window. You know what being a snitch in prison means?" asked Brodigan.

"I'll ask her to revise the offer and have those guys housed somewhere else. It's not foolproof, but it may be the best we can do."

"I don't like this at all. I knew I shouldn't have gone along with that fucker's idea. Bowers has always been trouble. Should have left them high and dry after I saw those gunshot flashes."

"I'm sure there's a lot you'd change in your life right about now. I'll have her come back in," said Scott. He opened the door and stepped into the hallway. She noticed him and held up one finger and nodded.

"She'll be right back."

When she returned, she asked, "I need your definitive answer. What are you going to do?"

"He's going to stick to the original deal, but ... ."

"There's always a but. But what?" asked Jennifer.

"It's a simple ask from us. No need to get upset," the attorney said, hands raised in the air. "He's going to be labeled a snitch. He might have a better chance if they housed Bowers and Thompson elsewhere. That's it. That's the only other ask."

"Couldn't be easier to do," said Jennifer. "As policy, we ask that co-defendants serve their time in separate facilities. We don't want them scheming together all day for years. They end up working on elaborate alibis or pointing the blame elsewhere. Always bullshit. They've done enough of that. So we're all set. Right Mr. Brodigan?"

"Yeah, about as good as it gets."

"OK, I think we're done here. Back to county jail for the next few days. We'll need a formal deposition. Mr. Lucas, my staff will be in touch soon. Gentleman, I wish you well. Guard, we're done with this prisoner."

"Why do I feel like I'm still fucked?" asked Brodigan.

"Because you are. It's the life you chose. Maybe you can work on turning it around while you're inside," said Lucas.

"Brodigan, stand up. We're going back to county lockup," said the guard.

"Home, sweet home," said Brodigan.

———◦◦◦———

February 10, 1979, Saturday morning, 10:15

"Detectives, you have your teams lined up?" asked Jennifer.

"We've got two tactical teams, four men each, and eight uniformed officers for each objective. I'll be with the team that grabs Bowers. Winston will lead the team for Thompson," said Jacobson.

"Good. Randolph will be tucked away in a neighboring county's jail for the night, and Brodigan is already in our county jail. He has a fake drunk and disorderly charge and private accommodations today and tomorrow," said Jennifer.

"We've got a man near the house where Bowers has been flopping the past two weeks, another one of his upstanding friends. Guy by the name of Daniel Green. His rap sheet is long and is known to be violent. The team is aware of that. There's a diversion planned," said Jacobson.

"When does the fun start?" asked Jennifer.

"The teams will meet at the station at four thirty tomorrow morning. We have simultaneous entries set for five fifteen. Surveillance has never seen either of them up and about before 10:00 am. Their dreams are going to get interrupted."

The Task Force - Go Time

February 11, 1979, Sunday morning, 4:30

"Ladies and gentlemen, may I have your attention, please? I am Detective Charles Jacobson. I will be directing this morning's operations. Some of you already know the details. At any rate, I will review them. I have assigned you to either the White Team or the Blue Team. There are two boards here in front. If you have not yet done so, familiarize yourselves with them. These detail our targets and have the rudimentary blueprints of their current location. These are both no-knock warrants. The element of surprise is crucial.

"I will be leading the White Team. Our target is one Dale William Bowers. I have a warrant for his arrest for the murder of Anthony Werner. This murder occurred in 1977. We believe this subject was the triggerman and should be considered armed and dangerous. An associate of his, Daniel Green, is providing room and board for our target. Mr. Green is not a subject of this murder investigation, but we will also bring him in as a material witness. I have that warrant as well. Mr. Green should also be considered armed and dangerous. The uniformed officers will set up a two-block perimeter. I also want three tactical team members here, at the southeast corner of the house. This is where Daniel Green's bedroom is located. Our go time is five fifteen. On my go, we will proceed with entry through the front door. Tactical, I want you to break these two windows to draw Green's attention away from the front. We believe Bowers sleeps on the couch directly inside the door. Let's make this quick; in and out in two minutes.

"My partner, Detective Jay Winston, will lead the Blue Team. He loves being called Winnie, so use that moniker at every opportunity. Winnie, the floor is yours."

"Well, fuck you very much, Jake. Gentlemen, our target will be one Gordon Thompson, aka, 'Big Man' but don't let that nickname fool you. Gordon here is a little guy, five-foot two-inches and about one hundred pounds soaking wet. He was the driver of our victim's car and will face the same murder charge as Mr. Bowers. While not known to be violent, we understand he's pretty timid, keep in mind he is facing life in prison, so be cautious.

"He has been living alone in the Longmore Apartments, unit 304. Our subject has lived in this complex for several years. He knows the apartment complex very well, so he could be slippery. Let's be sure our perimeter is tight. So we'll be humping up three floors. The tactical team will make entry also at five fifteen. Prior to that, uniformed officers will have set a perimeter around the apartment complex. I also want two tactical members stationed behind his apartment. His apartment has a balcony. Let's be prepared for an escape path there. Jake?"

"Thanks, uh, Detective Winston." This drew laughter from the team members. "We will take those arrested to the county jail. However, the White Team will unload any subjects in the front and the Blue Team will unload their subjects in the back. Wait for my all clear before doing so. The ADA, Jennifer Nichols, wants our subjects to believe the others involved in the murder are still on the loose. It should help her control the narrative for a while.

"Questions? Let's load up and go. Stay safe everyone, that's my priority for all of you."

The tactical teams loaded up in unmarked police vans that were led by one patrol car and followed by three. Two blocks from the station, the teams split and headed to their objectives.

The Killer - Busted

February 11, 1979, Sunday morning, 5:15

THE VAN'S SIDE WINDOWS were frosting over. The temperature had dipped to fifteen degrees overnight and remained there during the entire operation. Detective Jacobson sat in the van. With him sat the tactical unit members. He would follow them through the front door. The others had dispersed from separate vehicles moments earlier. A porch light lit up the target's house. The houses on either side were dark. He clicked on the mic. "This is White Team leader. Status check. Perimeter team?"

"Perimeter team in place."

"Tactical, secondary subject?"

"Secondary in place."

Off mic, Jacobson asked his team, "Everyone here ready to go?"

Heads nodded the affirmative.

"Door."

With that, the van door slid open and the team trotted towards the front door, forty feet away. At ten feet, Jacobson clicked on the mic again. "Go! Go! Go! Go!"

The two tactical members, one with a battering ram, the other with an M16 rifle, lead the charge. The ram crashed into the door, forcing the deadbolt lock through the doorjamb. The hinges were pulled from the frame. Men flooded into the living room. And there he was, confused. Dale Bowers was still in his dirty jeans and socks. In unison, the team trained their guns on him and yelled, "Freeze!" Windows were breaking on the back side of the house. Heavy footsteps were heading towards them, coming down the hall.

"Dale, we gotta go ... " said Green. He froze for a few seconds, taking in the roomful of heavily armed men. He held a pistol in his right hand.

"Gun! Gun! Gun!" said Jacobson as he trained his service weapon on Green. Simultaneously, a tactical officer trained his M16 on the subject, too.

"Drop that fucking gun, Daniel," said Jacobson. "Twelve officers are surrounding this place."

"Well shit, Dale. I guess it's over," said Daniel. He raised his gun towards Jacobson but was cut down by two short bursts from the M16. He never fired a shot.

Jacobson got back on the mic, "Shots fired! Shots fired! Subject down."

Daniel Green was dead. His body lay flat on its back, eyes half-closed. He was dressed only in a pair of boxers. The tactical team officer had fired two, three-round bursts. An officer checked Green's pulse and found none. All six 5.56mm rounds hit the homeowner in the chest. The dead man was handcuffed in front and his loose handgun secured.

Dale looked on in disbelief. "You killed him! Jesus! And then you hand-cuff him. Stupid assholes!" said Dale.

"Turn around Dale," said Jacobson. "Dale William Bowers, you are under arrest for the murder of Anthony Werner."

"I didn't kill nobody. You all did, though. I saw you shoot Dan down like a dog. Like a fucking dog, man!" he said as the handcuffs were tightened.

As he was led outside, Detective Jacobson read Bowers his rights. "You want to talk, Dale? I'd like to hear your side of the story," said Jacobson.

"Just take me to jail," said Dale.

Grasping the handcuffs by the chain, Jacobson led Dale over to a waiting squad car that would take him to the jail.

"You got nothing on me because I didn't do anything. But I saw you guys kill Green just now. Then you'll be the one in cuffs."

"Believe what you want to, Dale. I don't need to defend my men to the likes of you. But if I were you, I'd start thinking about how we knew you did this. How did we know where you were staying? Somebody is talking, Dale. Getting worried now?" Jacobson did not wait for a response. He slammed the door in Dale's face.

Even with the windows rolled up, Dale's voice was easily heard. "You know, detective, you're a coward hiding behind that badge. I see you out-side of here and I'm going to fucking kill you! You hear me? You're a dead man!"

Jacobson was on top of Bowers in an instant. "You think you are going to kill me? You're the coward, Dale. Shooting a defenseless man in the head! Everyone knows about your temper tantrums. Your buddies are laughing at you. Hell, I've laughed at you. You think I'm bullshitting?"

"I knew you were an asshole," replied Bowers.

"Yeah, you have a lot of buddies? Other than that psycho Green, who's now under a sheet? At this very minute, you have zero friends. You'll see what we have on you. Put two and two together. Your stupid ass will figure out that you are alone. Fucked and alone."

Jacobson slammed the door and walked away. He could hear Bowers screaming again, but kept walking. "Your day is coming, you prick!" he said as Jacobson walked back to the van.

The Accomplice - Busted

February 11, 1979, Sunday morning, 5:15

At the same time the White Team crashed through Daniel Green's front door, the Blue Team struck. Gordon Thompson's apartment door was no match for the battering ram. It easily tore through the deadbolt and door jamb. The force of the ram pulled the screws from the flimsy hinges, sending the entire door crashing to the floor.

Big Man was in deep REM sleep dreaming that he was driving a brand new car. The noise of the tactical team destroying his door woke him. Confused, he thought it was part of his dream. As he sat up in bed, voices screamed at him, "Freeze! Don't move Thompson!"

Unsurprised, he raised his hands above his head. Detective Winston slid between two tactical team members and stood next to the sleepy, surprised man. "Get up Big Man. You're done."

"Who are you?"

"Detective Jay Winston, Mr. Thompson. We're here to arrest you."

"No way. I've been straight for almost a year."

"The offense we're here for was committed almost two years ago, sir."

"I don't understand, honest."

"You helped Dale Bowers out by driving a car. How about now? Does that jog your memory?"

Thompson's shoulders slumped.

"Turn around Gordon," said Winston. "You're under arrest for the murder of Anthony Werner. I'm going to read you your rights now, so pay attention."

After Mr. Thompson was read his Miranda warning, Detective Winston asked, "Do you want to speak to me about this charge, Gordon? Before you answer that, you should know that some friends of yours are talking. I wonder who asks for a deal first? How about it Gordon?"

Thompson sighed a deep, long sigh. "No. I think I need my lawyer."

"OK, let's get you off to jail. Gentlemen, have someone stand watch and tape this apartment. Ident will process the scene within the hour. I'll come back after Gordo and I have a staring contest downtown. I think I'll win."

"Do you have a warrant? You gotta have a warrant." asked Thompson.

"Oh, found your voice, did you?" asked Winston, "Care to share anything?"

Thompson shook his head no.

"As you wish. Yeah, I've got a search warrant, right here," he said, tapping his breast pocket.

"Can I see it, please?" asked Thompson.

"Sure. It's a legal document full of legal mumbo-jumbo," said Winston as he showed the warrant to Thompson. "Hmm, you're handcuffed behind your back. You won't be able to read this right now."

"Tell me why this is happening."

"I told you why and you asked for your lawyer. At that point, we stopped asking questions about the case. If you want to talk, do it through your lawyer. I'm not even going to ask if you need to use the bathroom. Talk to your lawyer about the search warrant. It's going to happen no matter what you do."

"Geesh, now that you mention it, I do have to pee."

"And we need to get you downtown. Let's go." Jacobson looked past Thompson to an officer, "Officer Jensen, will you escort the prisoner to the transport wagon? Remind transport the drop off today is on the north side of the building. North."

"Yes sir, detective," said the officer. "Let's go Thompson. We're going to take the stairs. You've got the transport all to yourself. This way."

Thompson was marched down the stairs and out the main entrance of his building. By now, dozens of residents had gathered. Most recognized Thompson and called out to him. "Hang in there Gordon!" and "Innocent man, right there!" and, "We love you, be strong!"

The officer seated Thompson in the back of the van and secured his seat belt.

February 11, 1979, Sunday morning, 6:48

Detective Winston was waiting in front of the county jail when the prisoner transport pulled up next to the curb. Jail staff unlocked the rear door of the van, followed by the reinforced interior door.

"Let's go prisoner," yelled one of the jailers.

No response.

"Prisoner, stand up, let's go!"

Winston walked to the rear of the van, joining the jailer.

"Gordon, you OK?" asked the detective.

"Yes," came a weak response from inside the compartment.

"You going to come out? Or do you need some help? We will come in and get you."

"I'm coming, dammit!" said Thompson, who appeared at the exit and stepped down towards the waiting jailers. They took hold of his elbows, one jailer on each side, and led him indoors.

After they passed, one of the police officers came up to Winston. "You see all those tears? What a pussy," said the officer.

"That's a good sign to me. I think he's broken. He knows he's whipped. Once these guys know that, they'd sell their own mother to get six months knocked off a sentence. Maybe he starts talking soon."

Winston stepped into the building and headed down to the interrogation room where he sat and made notes on today's arrest, and prepared himself for the next day's interview. If it happened at all.

ADA Nichols stepped in and sat down across from detective Winston.

"Everything go OK with Thompson?" she asked.

"It went smooth. He seemed confident when we started talking to him. Then I read him his rights and he asked for a lawyer."

"You know we're not talking to them until tomorrow, right?"

"Oh, I know. It's a quiet place to prepare, make notes, and reflect on the day," replied Winston.

"You don't seem like the reflective type."

"What type of person am I?"

"Frat boy type. Don't get me wrong, I liked frat boys. In college."

"Frat boy? I'll take that. What's tomorrow going to look like? Does Thompson have representation yet?"

"He's been assigned a public defender, Leslie Garmen. I've been up against her before. She's good and she's fair. Dale Bowers drew Stephanie Langley to represent him. She's new and I don't know a thing about her. We've got Bowers tomorrow morning at nine thirty and Thompson at three thirty. So be ready. I've already let Jake know the schedule."

"Jake, you call him Jake now?"

"Sure do. Is that a problem?"

"Nope, not at all. I'll see you in the morning. I'll bring Jake with me," said Winston, chuckling to himself.

"Get some rest, Jay," said Nichols. She smiled at him as she shut the door.

"Jake? I thought I was the only one who could call him Jake. What a day!"

The Killer - Interrogation

February 12, 1979, Monday morning, 9:25

THE PROSECUTION TEAM OF ADA Jennifer Nichols and her paralegal Sarah Chapman were already seated in the interrogation room's mirrored viewing area when Detectives Jacobson and Winston entered the main room.

"Good morning Ms. Nichols, Ms. Chapman. I hope we're all ready for this guy. He's quite the sociopath with a short fuse," said Jacobson, waving at the mirror.

Footsteps interlaced with the jangle of chains grew louder. As did the voices, unintelligible at first, but then, "I'm telling you, he attacked me while I was handcuffed!"

"Mr. Bowers, that is not the most serious issue to be dealt with today. Is this the room, officer?" asked Stephanie Langley.

"Yes, it is, ma'am," replied the jailer. He directed them in with a wave of his hand.

The new arrivals sat across from Jacobson and Winston.

"Good morning, I am Stephanie Langley. I am with the Public Defender's office and I am representing Mr. Bowers today."

After introductions went around the table, Jacobson spoke up, "Your client has been charged with murder one, kidnapping, and armed robbery. These charges, as I'm sure you are aware, could lead to life imprisonment without parole."

"Yes, I've informed my client of those details and we intend to challenge them all in court," said Langley.

"Well, good for you, Ms. Langley. Is that your idea or his? Because the evidence is mounting every day," said Jacobson as he turned his attention to Bowers. "It's looking pretty bleak for you, sir."

"Bullshit. Bleak? All you have are words coming out of the mouths of career criminals. Every one of them is a fucking liar and you know it."

Jacobson half-smiled and shook his head and looked directly at Bowers.

"Don't you smirk at me, you little bitch, because … ."

Jacobson sprang up from his chair, sending it into the wall and teetering over on its side. "Because what, Dale? What are you going to do? We're going to have a problem if you keep talking like that. A big problem!"

"Jake, take it easy," said Winston as he tugged on his arm.

Winston retrieved the chair. "Here boss, have a seat." Jacobson sat down.

"That's the temper I told you about, Stephanie," said Bowers. "I feared for my life."

"Yes, I can see that. Care to explain yourself, detective?" asked Langley.

"This interview is about the murder of Anthony Werner. I suggest we focus on that. I'm not on trial here," said Jacobson.

"You expect my client to discuss these very serious allegations while under the threat of physical harm by you?"

"I will not litigate that issue here. That's not my job. Bring that up with a judge. Good luck. I have a spotless record, and there were several witnesses there yesterday. They will all testify that it was your client, and your client alone, making threats. And you sir," Jacobson said to Bowers, "pull that shit again and I'll add a threat on a peace officer charge to the list. Back to the reason we're here, please. Ms. Langley, thoughts?"

"Yes, let's continue and we'll discuss the charges at hand. Dale, it is in your best interest to remain calm. Detectives, ask away."

"Dale, I'll just get right to it. Did you kill Anthony Werner?"

"No."

"What if we had a witness who claimed he helped set up this score?"

"That would be a lie."

"Excuse me, detective. Do you have this witness you mention? You know I have to have access to any witness you have," said the attorney.

"Uh-huh. We have someone who admits to assisting in these crimes. I'm sure the DAs office will provide you with all that information. That's not my job. Anway, Dale, our witness labeled you the ringleader of the scheme. What would you say to that?" asked Jacobson.

"I'd say you know a lot of liars. Maybe this person is your killer. Ever think of that?" shot back Bowers.

"We did think of that. To that point, we have someone else involved in the crime. He's in our custody right now. In fact, he's in this very building and we'll be talking to him this afternoon. What do you suppose he will say?"

"I don't know, since I'm not involved in any killing. I suppose, to answer your question, you'd have another liar on your hands."

"So everyone but you is lying? Is that what you're saying?"

"It is. They're all liars."

"Sounds like you associate with a lot of liars, Dale."

"Detective Jacobson, I know you are doing your job. I also know you are trying to get him agitated. Before we came in here, I advised him to take the fifth. He said no. He wants to tell you what he knows about this case. Which is nothing. He is not involved. Beyond that, do you have any real questions for my client?" asked Langley.

"Just trying to get my bearings with your guy is all. I've been involved in a lot of murder cases. I am aware of the process we have in front of us. I don't need a public defender on her fifth case, telling me how to conduct myself."

"Fifth case? What the fuck?" said Bowers.

"I may be new, but I also know you have a serious evidence problem. As you said moments ago, let's get back to the reason for our get together, shall we?"

"Fair enough. I'm just trying to point out to your client what he's up against before he enters a plea. We have three accomplices who are going to talk to save their own skin. We have the murder weapon with a partial print, probably yours, Mr. Bowers. We have three partial prints inside the vehicle where the murder occurred, one of them in blood. All three are probably yours. We have someone directly involved who is definitely going to turn on you, another involved who might turn on you. Plus, we have a guy who gave you the details surrounding Mr. Werner. There are many other witnesses. One witness heard arguing that night. They also saw a light-colored Dodge pickup haul ass out of the neighborhood. Dale, who owns a light-colored Dodge?"

"I don't know anybody who'd even own a Dodge."

"Do you know where you were May 19, 1977?"

"No, do you?"

"I believe I do, Mr. Bowers. Do you know a Mr. Gordon Thompson?"

"Does not sound familiar."

"He's also known as Big Man?"

"Oh sure, we did some time together. His name's Gordon?"

"What about John Brodigan?"

"I think Big Man introduced us once. Big Man knows him way better than I do."

"One more person. Steve Randolph. Do you know him?"

"Can't say as I do, sorry."

"Ever fire a handgun?"

"Nope. They're too dangerous."

"I get it. Keep your side of the story a secret. Maybe during discovery things will go better. Ms. Langley, do you have any questions for us?"

"No, we'll probably get the charges dropped shortly after the arraignment. You really don't have much to hang your hat on." She looked at the one-way mirror. "The ADA must realize it is time to drop the case."

"Confidence. I admire that when it's well placed."

"We're done talking. My client and I will need to meet in case there is an arraignment."

"Sure, we appreciate your time. Oh, one thing I almost forgot to ask. Dale, are you a smoker? I mean, I know the answer because I can smell it on you, but I'd like to hear it from you."

"Yeah, I smoke, so what?"

"Your mom and dad. Where do they live, here in town?"

"No. They live out of state."

"You mean New Mexico, right?"

"Yeah, so? Keep them out of this."

"Did you ever find your Zippo lighter?"

The color washed out of Dale's face.

"We found one. Found it under a Cadillac. You don't look so good. No comment, Dale?"

"We're done here. Jailer!" said Langley.

The jailer stepped into the room. Langley asked him, "My client and I need to confer. Is there a room we can use?"

"Yes, ma'am. Follow me."

The three walked down the hallway, Dale's chain rattle grew fainter and then silent.

February 12, 1979, Monday morning, 9:45

Nichols and Chapman left the screening room and joined the detectives.

"That went quick and did not go well," said Jacobson.

"Oh, to the contrary, Jake. I think all of our goals were accomplished," said Nichols.

"What do you mean?"

"I wanted this guy to start feeling cornered, despite all of his denials. He knows all those three men you mentioned. He'll figure out that one of them is going to turn on him. Maybe more than one."

"Did you see his face when you said the word, Zippo? Classic look of a guy knowing he's screwed. Good job!" said Nichols.

"Sorry I lost my shit," said Jacobson.

"Hey, I don't care. He should have had someone like you when he was growing up. Maybe we wouldn't be here and Mr. Werner would be alive," said Nichols.

"I'm just not able to keep quiet when someone, especially a low-life such as Bowers, shows disrespect like that," said Jacobson.

"I heard there was a bit of a kerfuffle involving you and Bowers, Jake. Should we talk about that?" asked Nichols.

"You were party to a kerfuffle, Jake?" asked Winston with false incredulity. "I don't know if that's happened to you before, Jake. Jake, is it true? Jake, say it ain't so."

"What is wrong with you, Winnie?" asked Jacobson.

"It seems Bowers wasn't the only psychopath in this room today," said Nichols.

"To answer your question, Jen, yes, Bowers pushed my buttons yesterday and I overreacted. That's not going to happen again. Lord knows he'll probably try. Remind me of that, Winnie."

"Sure, I'll do that ... Jake. Sorry, Charles," said Winston.

"I'm going to recommend we add threats on a peace officer charges for that incident in the squad car," said Nichols.

"Well, I lost my shit as much as he did. Let's see this guy's demeanor after today. We may not need to pile on the charges. Then again, he is a hot head. He may threaten everyone in here before this case is over."

"Don't lose any sleep over it. Now, I'm sure we all have work to do before our next meeting. Sarah, what time is that second meeting?"

"Three thirty, this very room," replied Chapman.

"Very well. See you all then."

The two detectives grabbed an elevator to the first floor exit and walked across the street toward their office building.

"You want to explain that 'Jake, Jake, Jake' bullshit back there?" asked Jacobson as the two stood next to each other.

"You're going to find this funny as hell, promise!" replied Winston.

"I'm listening."

The Accomplice - Interrogation

February 12, 1979, Monday afternoon, 3:45

THE SAME FOURSOME OF Jacobson, Winston, Nichols, and Chapman stood outside the interrogation room, waiting. And waiting.

"You two going to play good detective, bad detective?" Nichols asked Jacobson.

"I am ready. Might be more like 'unpleasant detective'. I don't want to get him so upset that we lose him."

"Good idea. He'll probably invoke the fifth, anyway."

"Three forty-five and they're not here. What gives?" asked Winston.

"I'll find a jailer. Let's figure out the delay," said Chapman as she scurried out the door.

"Have a good lunch, Jen?" asked Jacobson.

"No, I had a bag of vending machine chips. You?"

"I talked this guy," he said, rocking his thumb at Winston, "into grabbing some tacos from Kate and Ken's Taco Shack."

"Oh, I love that old place. My stomach is jealous!"

"We were going to eat there before heading over to watch Thompson at his apartment. Before we placed our order, who drives by? None other than Big Man!"

"No, that did not happen! Really?"

"It's true. I was getting ready to grab a taco and a burrito. Thompson stopped that," said Winston.

"They'll be here soon," said Chapman as she hurried to her seat. "The accused was having a moment."

"A moment?" asked Nichols.

"He was crying. A lot. I asked his attorney, Ms. Garmen, if she wanted to delay our meeting. He'll be OK in a few minutes."

Five minutes passed when the familiar sound of jangling chains came echoing down the hall. In walked the diminutive Gordon Thompson. His lawyer, Leslie Garmen, towered over him, her four-inch heels adding to her five foot seven-inch frame. She was dressed in a sharp blue suit, jacket buttoned in the middle, covering a thin white blouse. An attractive woman, she caught the eye of Detective Winston, who subconsciously sat upright. She set her briefcase on the metal table with a thud and took her seat.

From the safety of the screening room, Sarah nudged Jen. "She's pretty. I hope she doesn't steal your man."

"You think my man is in there? Who?" asked Nichols.

"Who? Who are you trying to bluff? Jacobson, of course."

"I think she caught Winston's eye, the way he snapped to attention. Look, he's still eyeballing her. We should be quiet now, especially you, Sarah."

"Good afternoon everyone, we apologize for the delay. I know your time is valuable, but it could not be avoided. I appreciate your patience. I am Leslie Garmen with the Public Defender's office and I am here representing Gordon Thompson."

"Good afternoon, Ms. Garmen. I'm Detective Charles Jacobson and this is my partner, Detective Jay Winston. We have been working this case since day one."

"Very well, gentleman," said Garmen. "Shall we proceed?"

"Good afternoon Gordon. Are you feeling well enough to talk with us today?" asked Jacobson.

"Yes sir, I'm OK now. It's just been a tough run the past two days. I have a record, but I also want to turn my life around. I've kept my nose clean for over a year now. Stayed employed."

"And where do you work?" asked Jacobson.

"I work the meat counter at Brambilla's Grocery."

"Can you spell that for me, please?"

"B-R-A-M-B-I-L-L-A, Brambilla."

"Got it. You like working there?"

"I do. It's just a little grocery store, owned by an older Italian couple who gave me a second chance."

"Thank you Gordon. Do you know a Dale Bowers?"

"Yes."

"How do you know Mr. Bowers?"

"We did some time in jail together."

"And when was this?"

"I guess it was about three years ago. It was when I was serving time for burglary. I'm sure you could look it up if you needed exact dates."

"That's very thoughtful of you, Gordon, but that won't be necessary," said Jacobson.

"Hi, Gordon, I'm Detective Winston. Tell me something. Think about the past two years. Have you had any contact with Mr. Bowers? Do you think you've run into him, talked with him, anything like that?"

Gordon looked at his attorney, who shook her head no and slid a sheet of paper in front of him.

Reading slowly from the paper, Gordon said, "On the advice of counsel, I invoke my fifth amendment privilege against self-incrimination and respectfully decline to answer your question."

"OK, Mr. Thompson, you're going to do that. Tell me this. Have you been party to any activity, legal or not, with Mr. John Brodigan?"

The attorney tapped her finger on the paper.

"On the advice of counsel, I invoke my fifth amendment privilege against self-incrimination and respectfully decline to answer your question."

"Do you know a Steve Randolph?"

"We've met before, yes," replied Thompson.

"Ever been engaged in any illegal activity with Mr. Randolph?"

Finger tap.

"On the advice of counsel, I invoke my fifth amendment privilege against self-incrimination and 'spectully, sorry, respectfully decline to answer your question."

"Do you know, Big Man, that is your street name, correct?" asked Winston, "Did you know that murder one and kidnapping carry mandatory life prison terms each? There is no parole. You know that, right?"

"That's wha —" Thompson started to say but was interrupted by his attorney.

"Detective, I've advised my client of the charges against him, so quit trying to bully him or we walk out of here."

"Ms. Garmen, I'm just making sure he is aware of the gravity of the charges," said Winston.

"He is, and you are insulting him and me. Do you have any other questions?"

"Is he going to be able to answer any of my questions? Maybe we are wasting our time here. I want you to know, Gordon, that we have in custody, Dale Bowers." A stunned expression crossed Thompson's face, and the detectives saw it. "Oh, you didn't know that, did you? We also have your other friends, John Brodigan and Steve Randolph. Yeah, all three of your buddies. I'm sure one of them is going to make a deal with us. Someone always does."

"Can I make a deal?" asked Thompson.

"Gordon, please be quiet," insisted his attorney.

"You have exercised your fifth amendment privilege multiple times," said Jacobson. "I believe you don't want to talk about what you really know. That is how deals are made. Go back to your cell. On the way, discuss your options with your counsel. Jailer!"

Gordon looked over at his attorney again, confused. "Not a word Gordon, not here."

"Just so you know, Gordon, the first to talk usually gets the best deal. You don't want to talk, so just go," said Winston, waving them away.

The jailer stood in the doorway, then escorted them back down the hall.

Nichols and Chapman walked into the interrogation room. Both were laughing.

"That was just amazing!" cried Chapman.

"Fucking amazing! You two gave him, and his pretty lawyer, a lot to think about," said Chapman.

"You thought she was pretty?" asked Winston.

The Prosecutor - The Talking Accessory

February 14, 1979, Wednesday morning, 10:05

"Ms. Nichols, William Underwood, nice to meet you."

"Mr. Underwood, a pleasure. I understand you represent Mr. Randolph, our accessory to murder."

"Alleged accessory."

"Save it for court, Bill, because according to Detective Winston, we've got him dead to rights."

"My client would like to testify in the Werner murder case. He's not asking for a lot, probation, no jail time. He's got a fiancée. A soon-to-be stepson that he just adores. He doesn't want his mistake to detract from family time."

"And Mr. Werner's family? How do you think they're doing? I think they'd be doing a lot better had your client kept his mouth shut, don't you?"

"He's sorry the man was killed. That was never part of the plan. What do you want?"

"If your client testifies about everything he knows, he gets a year in county jail and five years probation. It's a good offer. In fact, it's the only offer I'm going to give. Otherwise, there's a good chance he'll have plenty of time to be better friends with his co-conspirators in prison."

"My colleague, Mr. Lucas, said you're quite the ball-buster and he nailed that."

"You bet I am, Underwood. You have two seconds to get the fuck out of my office! Never talk to me like that. Present the offer to your client, or I will see you in court, and I will break your balls. In half. Goodbye."

"Look, I only … ."

"The door is that way."

Sarah, Ms. Nichols paralegal, rushed into the room. "It pays to listen in on conversations sometimes! Holy shit, I almost felt sorry for the guy."

"He was getting me angry, the arrogant prick."

"Here is my impersonation of his new counter-offer; 'Uh, Ms. Nichols, we're fine if you'd like to crush my client's balls. Uh, I brought a hammer.'"

"Love it, Sarah! Plus, I'd take that offer," said Jen.

------◆------

February 15, 1979, Thursday morning, 8:19

Sarah poked her head inside of Jen Nichols' office and upon seeing her behind her desk said, "Well, you are in the office today."

"Of course. Mr. Sartori caught me on the way in. What's up?" asked Jen.

"Randolph's attorney called thirty minutes ago and agreed to the terms you proposed yesterday. A year in the clink, five years probation, and he sings like a canary, ma."

"You watch too many Cagney movies. But thank you Sarah. Can you update the files for me, reflecting that offer and get the paperwork sent to Underwood?"

"Already done, and a courier is on his way."

"You're the best! Watch all the Cagney movies your little heart desires!"

As soon as Sarah left her office, Jen called Detective Jacobson. "Jake, Jennifer Nichols. How are you today, sir?"

"I'm well, thanks Jen. I certainly hope I'm glad to hear from you."

"Yes, we've got another piece of the puzzle nailed down. Steve Randolph will testify for us."

"That is good news! Did you get a good deal?"

"I think we did well. A year in county jail as an accessory, then five years of probation."

"Well done. That should help tighten up a conviction."

"While I have you on the phone, I was wondering something. Would you care to have a drink with me tonight, my dollar? We can talk about the case. And get to know each other better?"

"Uh, Jen, that is tempting, and I think that's a great idea. Problem is, people can't stop killing people in this town. I'm headed off to the east side of the city."

"Oh, I see. I feel a little silly now, sorry."

"Don't feel silly. I've been wanting the same thing. It's just that tonight I've got a date with a dead guy."

"That was bad. You need to work on your lines," laughed Jennifer.

"Now I'm the sorry one. I need to stop talking. For my own good. Can I call you in a few days and we make that happen?"

"I look forward to your call, Jake."

Detective Jacobson hung up the phone and looked across his desk. His partner, Jay, sat there slack-jawed, looking straight into his eyes.

"What now, Winnie?"

"Did the ADA just ask you out on a date-date?" he asked.

"We plan on talking about work-related things, too. I have three points to discuss," said Jacobson. "One. Yes, she asked me out on a date. Two. Why would you act so surprised? And three. Stop listening in on my phone calls. How many times has this been discussed?"

"Let me address these concerns in order," Winston said, as he cracked his knuckles.

"And that right there, knuckle cracking. You sir are a knuckle-cracker and you know it sends me up a wall!"

"But it brings me so much joy, just knowing that. Frankly, I don't even need to crack them. When I'm around you, I *want* to crack them. But I digest, er, digress, sorry. One," he started, all the while mocking Jacobson's points, "I was under the impression that dating an ADA was some kind of policy violation. It does not sound right. Two. Have you looked in the mirror? OK, that was hurtful and just plain mean. Let me erase that." He took his right hand and fluttered it back and forth in the air. "There. It never even happened! Two. When did you last have a date? Three. Impossible. I'm a trained detective. Remember that."

Jacobson put his suit jacket on and headed out the door.

"More dead people?" asked Winston as he followed him out the door.

"I'm afraid so."

"What are you two going to name your kids?"

The Daughter - They Finally Got Them!

February 14, 1979, Wednesday afternoon, 12:45

"Hey honey, those detectives just pulled into the driveway. Adam!" said Kaylie.

Adam came bounding up the basement stairs. "Who's in the driveway?"

"The two detectives from Daddy's case. Oh my god, you don't suppose ... ?"

They hurried to the front door, arriving just as Detective Jacobson rang the doorbell.

"Well, that was quick," laughed Jacobson.

"Afternoon and Happy Valentine's Day. Can we come in? We are about to make your day happier," asked Detective Winston.

"Of course, yes!" said Kaylie.

"Please, please, get out of the cold," added Adam as he led the two inside the warm house.

"Can we sit down somewhere, perhaps at your dining room table? He has some documents to show you," said Jacobson.

"We can do that. Let me clear our lunch plates," said Kaylie. "Please, sit."

Kaylie asked from the kitchen. "What can I get you to drink, gentlemen? I just made a pot of coffee."

"Sure, much appreciated," said Winston.

The other two men nodded in agreement.

"Make it coffee for four, honey," said Adam.

Kaylie returned with matching coffee cups in one hand, the full coffee pot, and trivet in another. She set down the cups, followed by the trivet.

"Any cream or sugar, gentleman?" she asked. All three shook their heads no.

Kaylie poured the coffee, sat next to Adam, and looked across the table at the detectives.

"That coffee smells terrific, thanks! You're probably wondering why we are here, correct?" asked Jacobson.

"We do, since our weekly update was just two days ago. Does this mean you bring promising news?" asked Kaylie. She looked at Adam, eager, worried, and confused.

"We're proud to say that it is more than promising. The last few days have been frantic and we've finally made some arrests!"

Kaylie's hands cupped her mouth and nose, muffling her words when she said, "Oh my god, yes. Thank you! Thank you! Thank you! Adam, do you believe this?"

"What wonderful news!. What can you tell us about them?" asked Adam as he handed Kaylie a tissue.

"I'll let Detective Winston walk you through that. Detective."

"Thanks Jake. So, we have made, technically, four arrests."

Kaylie interrupted, "Did you say four arrests?"

"Yes ma'am. Four men," said Winston. "Three of them were directly connected to your father's murder. The fourth led those three to your dad. These photographs may show up in the newspaper, but we wanted to present our information before tomorrow morning."

He began ticking off the information with each photo.

"Dale Bowers. This is who we believe pulled the trigger. Like the others in this folder, he has an extensive rap sheet. Burglary, drunk driving, assault, and battery, among other crimes. Mostly misdemeanors, just a lot of them. Bowers has a forceful personality. He's definitely the leader of this gang.

"Gordon Thompson. We believe he drove your father's car from the townhouse to where we found it at Third and Seventh. He's a long-time associate of Mr. Bowers. They've even spent time in jail together. He's a follower and, from what we've heard, Bowers dictates this guy's every move.

"And here is John Brodigan. Former Marine. Lots of arrests, including a recent one that jumpstarted this process. We believe he drove a pickup truck, following your dad's car. The truck was going to be used to carry off construction tools. Those tools would have been pawned for cash. We have an eyewitness that saw a truck fitting the description, leaving the scene that night."

"They stole equipment too? Killing daddy was not enough?" cried Kaylie.

"No, they did not get that far. They got spooked and had to run," said Jacobson.

"My partner's correct. Our witness heard some yelling, likely from these subjects," said Winston.

"Our last arrest is a Steve Randolph. He knows Gordon Thompson." Winston tapped on Thompson's photo. "Mr. Thompson contacted Randolph on Bowers' behalf. Are you following me on that? It can get tricky."

"Yes, I think we understand," said Adam.

"Good. Randolph had done odd jobs for your dad in the past. We checked with Patti for any payroll records on him. There were none, as your dad would sometimes pay day laborers cash. It was through Randolph that Bowers learned of the cash your dad carried and he knew of the diamond rings your dad loved."

"Oh, daddy! I knew he shouldn't have done business that way," said Kaylie.

"How do you know this?" asked Adam.

"Good question," said Jacobson. "We had to make some minor deals with Brodigan and Randolph to strengthen our case against Bowers. He's the primary target for us."

"They are minor concessions," added Winston. "For their testimony, one might get a little time taken off his current felony sentence. That is for a crime unrelated to your father's case. It's still possible that he'll be moved to a prison out of state. Snitches in prison rarely last long. That's Brodigan we're talking about, by the way. The other concession is for Randolph. The DA will ask for one year in jail and—"

"A year? Oh hell no!" said Kaylie.

"Please, let me explain," said Winston. "He ties a lot of loose ends together and the DA is willing to trade that off to get the men directly involved. I'm not defending him at all. He thought they only meant to rob your father. He's also getting five years probation, so if he violates that, he'll join his friends in prison."

"So it sounds as if it's true. This should have just been a robbery. What happened to make him kill daddy?"

"Kaylie," said Jacobson, "while questioning the guy who drove your dad's car, before he lawyered up, he hinted that there may have been a struggle while they were driving down the freeway. That's when the shots were fired. Our jailhouse snitch, Brodigan, confirmed seeing three flashes in the car as he followed them."

"When does this go to court?" asked Kaylie.

"That's difficult to say," said Winston, "but it could be a couple of months unless their lawyers try to pull some delays. The DA's office can answer that better than I can. I believe that Assistant DA Jennifer Nichols plans to contact you soon to explain her team's process. I'd look for a call from her today or tomorrow."

"She is going to be very busy for several weeks," added Jacobson. "They will be meeting with us and the coroner. She'll also have a lot of depositions to take. I would expect she'll want to depose you, Kaylie, and perhaps Adam. That doesn't mean you will be called as a witness. She likes to cover her bases."

"Another possibility to prepare yourself for," said Winston, "is there may be multiple trials. The DA's office has not said if they'd ask to have them tried together, or separately. That's not solely their decision to make. The court and the defense lawyers may work that out. I'd also advise that you be aware they could make plea deals and a trial never happens. Jennifer will talk to you before anything is finalized. You will have input on that decision. Ultimately, it's the DA's call. She can better explain the process."

The Justice System - Killer Depositions

March 2, 1979, Friday morning, 10:05

THE COUNTY'S OFFICES HAD several rooms on the second floor of their six story building. The rear of the building had the primary entrance used for depositions and the lawyers accompanying them. Purposely placed away from street view. The designers believed this would give those being deposed a sense of privacy. This, it was hoped, would lead to more honest and complete answers to questions.

Each room was painted in muted colors. Some in soft blue or light green, others in eggshell white, the rest in pale gray. These colors were selected for the same reason, to produce informative answers.

After being chosen District Attorney, James Sartori instituted that change. These were the most visibly noticeable changes made, but he also embarked on changes that affected his employees. The staff's office space was upgraded at the same time. New desks and chairs, office furniture, and break rooms were modernized. Employees were encouraged to decorate their desks or offices as they saw fit. The first week of Sartori's new appointment, he crafted a letter to all employees to open the line of communication between employees and management. He reminded them that, as a team, they were here to serve justice. He stressed that to him, serving justice meant finding the true perpetrator guilty, not finding any criminal guilty just to pad the staff's win-loss record. On the wall, high above the team's small sea of desks and offices, were two simple words, spread out in an arc pattern that read, *Truth, Always.*

Steve Randolph and his attorney, William Underwood, checked in at the security desk in the back of the building. A sheriff's guard led them up one flight of stairs, down a narrow, well-lit hallway. The guard stopped the group in front of room 212. "Gentlemen, someone from the DA's office will be with you soon. Make yourself at home." He opened the door for them. Once they were settled, he walked back to his post on the first floor.

"Nice looking rooms they have here," said the attorney.

Randolph crossed his large, hairy arms, leaned back in his chair, and stared at Underwood.

"I know. Who gives a shit, right?" asked Underwood.

Before he could answer, the door opened. Jennifer Nichols entered, followed by a court reporter.

"Gentlemen, I thank you for your time.

"This questioning is recorded by an electronic device and by an appointed court reporter," she said, pointing at the court reporter.

"Ms. Nichols, before we begin, has there been any reconsideration of your offer for my client?" asked Underwood.

"If I reconsidered at all, your client would not like it. I'm not reducing the terms. Period."

"Had to ask. Proceed."

"Let the record show that today is March the second, 1979. It is 10:10 a. m. This is a formal deposition related to the Anthony Werner murder case. Case file number is 77-42FE107. I am Assistant District Attorney Jennifer Nichols. Before me is Steven Jacob Randolph and his legal representative, William Underwood.

"Mr. Randolph, you are aware of the charges you are facing and come here of your own volition to discuss your involvement. Is that correct?"

Randolph looked at his attorney, who nodded at him. "Yes, that is correct," he replied.

For the next two hours, she grilled him on every aspect of his involvement. What conversations, and with whom, did he have concerning the victim? When did he sense the victim would be an easy target? Did he feel any remorse? She asked about his family life and his work record. She confirmed his criminal arrest record. Dozens and dozens of questions that she asked to help form a picture in her mind and, ultimately, in the minds of the jurors.

Her staff would spend the rest of the week taking depositions for all the witnesses she intended to call to testify. They included all the big players, Dale Bowers, Gordon Thompson, John Brodigan, the detectives, and the coroner and his staff. Also included were those who had one small but important piece of information, the older couple, Henry and Doris Mitchell and the dog walker, Vern Danielson.

At the end of the week, James Sartori stopped in Jen's office. "How did your depositions go this week?" he asked.

"In a word, fantastic. In three words, they're all screwed!"

"Got to love your confidence, Jen. I hope you can bring this home."

"I have no doubts they're going away. Murder one is iffy, but murder two shouldn't be a problem."

"Very well. If you need more resources, give my secretary a call."

"Will do. Have a great weekend, Jim."

The Justice System - And Justice For All?

June 1, 1979, Friday morning, 10:30

THE VINTAGE GOVERNMENT OFFICE space was dingy and tired looking. In contrast, the upbeat and jubilant people crowded into the conference room.

"We won!" cried out Sarah Chapman to her boss, ADA Jennifer Nichols.

The ADA walked over and gave Sarah a hug. "Thank you for the arduous tasks performed and the success we attained," said Nichols.

Stepping up to the center of the room, District Attorney Sartori called for attention. "Please everyone, if I may." The room got quiet. "Thank you. It's good to see all these smiling faces here today. It's encouraging after everything this office has endured the past two and a half years.

"I'd ask we remember why we are here. Why all that hard work? Justice for Anthony Werner. May he rest in peace. I had Jen invite Anthony's daughter Kaylie Carlson and her husband, Adam, and I'm glad to see them," he pointed to the couple standing in the back, near the door.

"This was a rather unique case. Fitting all the bits and pieces together was quite a task. All of you played a vital part in this. And we can't forget the team leaders in this case. ADA, and if I don't watch my back, she'll have my job someday, Jennifer Nichols! And the person I consider the top crime solver this community has, Senior Detective Charles Jacobson. Not only did they show skilled leadership, but showed everyone that the District Attorney's office and the police department can not only work together, but thrive. It hasn't always been that way and I thank you two! Jen, come up here and give us a few words, please."

"Sure thing, Jim. We had four trials that came out of one case. Even though we compromised when needed, I'm pleased with the results. We sent a co-conspirator to jail for a year, followed by probation. John Brodigan turned state's witness. He was one of the three involved in the case. To be clear, he did not receive the get out of jail card that he originally requested. He'll spend years where he belongs. We were also able to have a career criminal, Gordon Thompson, sent away for a long time."

"See ya, Big Man," yelled someone in the middle of the crowd, causing a great deal of laughter.

"Yes," continued Nichols, "that is his nickname. The main character, Dale Bowers, had to be taken off the streets. Career criminals are common in our line of work, without a doubt. They don't get worse than this guy. The life term evaded us — a disappointment indeed — but he won't be walking free for a long, long time."

"Thank you, Jen. Take time to celebrate this huge win. Just don't go overboard! We've still got other bad guys to take down," said Sartori. The DA quietly left the gathering.

"Jen, I want to thank you so much. It's been quite a ride," said Kaylie, as she grasped the ADA's elbow.

"Kaylie! So good to see you today. Glad you and Adam could make it. My only genuine regret was we couldn't make first degree murder stick, especially for that animal, Bowers."

"They're off the streets. That's all that matters right now. I'm not happy with the verdict; a life sentence only seems fair."

"That reminds me. There was a couple in the gallery that sat behind you. They seemed very upset at the verdict, too. Do you know them?"

"I think you mean Tommy and his girlfriend Rita. Tommy worked at his family's gas station until he went to college. Dad was a customer there. My father thought the world of him. This hit him as hard as it did us, it seems. Rita has become of friend of mine. She calls me often and brightens my day each time. We've done lunch a couple times too. Rita and Tommy make a terrific couple. She was planning on being a lawyer but ended being a school teacher. He's doing some freelance engineering work. I heard he graduated near the top of his class at Stanford."

"Stanford? Impressive. No, I just remembered seeing them a lot. We could have asked them here today."

"I'll let them know you mentioned them. They'll appreciate that. Now we're going to talk about you, Jen! Have you ever gone out with that detective? Detective Jacobson? He's a cute one and he has an engaging personality."

"Well, if the DA were standing here, I'd feign confusion. I'd have to add that I never thought about it. That would be unprofessional!"

"But he's not here," said a smiling Kaylie.

"Oh, in that case, yes, we're dating. It's difficult though, with our jobs, you know. We both work seventy or more hours a week. That makes it difficult to even grab a burger some days."

"Well, I thought I could sense some sparks. You two look good together!"

"That's very kind of you. He's a good man," said Jen. She smiled at the detective.

June 3, 1979, Sunday afternoon, 1:15

Kaylie finished drying the stone off and stood back to examine her handiwork.

"Good job, Kaylie. It looks great," said Adam.

"Thanks. Dad used to do this for mom. I'd like to continue that tradition, if you don't mind."

"Mind? Sweetheart, this will be a wonderful tradition. I loved and respected your dad. I'm just a little sad that I never knew your mom."

"She would have adored you!"

"What's not to be adored?"

Laughing, Kaylie gently pushed him away. "OK, Mr. Adorable, can you put these cleaning supplies in the trunk? I'd like to have some time alone. You understand, don't you?"

"Of course I do. I'll start the car up and get the air conditioner going. It's really starting to get hot out here."

"Thanks, Adam."

After Adam stepped away, Kaylie bowed her head, as if in prayer.

"Mom and dad, those trials are over. I won't have to listen to the details about what happened. And hearing all those lies! I'm just glad the jury could see through them. Maybe my nightmares will subside now that they are in prison. I'll be a grandmother before they get out. Just saying that makes me sad and mad at the same time. Neither of you will see any kids Adam and I will have. Mom, cancer took you from us. I will fight that disease any way I can. I won't give up. Dad, those degenerates took you from us. I will make it my mission that their sentences are served. Cancer and those murderers picked the wrong person to mess with!"

Kaylie unbowed her head, tears in her eyes. She briefly touched the top of the headstone and got back into the car.

"You OK, Kaylie?" asked Adam.

"Yes, that felt good to do. Thanks."

"Are you ready to go home?"

"Yes. Home please, kind sir," she said as she looked in the vanity mirror. "Dang wind blew my hair all around."

"Your hair is starting to get longer, isn't it?"

"Mom wore it just on her shoulders. I'd like to do that to remember her."

"That's a beautiful thing to do. It looks very nice too."

The Killer - Prison

May 3, 1979, Thursday morning, 9:35

THE LONG, GRAY BUS, with a faded light blue *Department of Corrections* logo stenciled on the side, came to a dusty stop just outside the main gate of the prison. Most of the prisoners had experienced the trip before and appeared bored. Four of the sixteen men were first-timers and obviously afraid; wide-eyed and wary. A large, serious-looking corrections officer stepped aboard the bus and whispered something to the driver. They looked at the prisoners and laughed.

"Inmates!" the serious one screamed. "I am Corrections Officer Lewis, but you will address me *and every other* corrections officer at this facility as only *Corrections Officer*. Example. When you receive an order, the only response is *yes, Corrections Officer*. I don't want to hear anything else. Not, *yes sir, Corrections Officer, sir* because this is not the fucking military. It's a fucking prison, understand?"

The prisoners were silent. The driver looked up at C.O. Lewis and just shook his head.

"Ladies, a response is required!"

Dale was staring out the bus window, taking in his new home's massive stone walls that were lined with razor wire. From his vantage point, he could see two guard towers looming, their cold, window-eyes glaring down on the prison yard. There was movement in a window. A man wearing a blue shirt, crisp and starched, long gun in his hands, paced. The tower guard slowly bent down, placing an elbow on the windowsill. He took aim. Dale thought he might be a target. He couldn't be sure and either didn't care if he pulled the trigger or hoped he would. He just didn't know. Plus, he hadn't listened to a word Corrections Officer Lewis had said.

"You, what's your name, boy?" Lewis kicked Dale's shoe, startling him out of his daydream.

"Dale, it's Dale, man."

Smiling down at him, Corrections Officer Lewis asked quietly, "Is Dale your last name cuz it sure is pretty and it sure as shit is not on my list here?"

"It's Bowers. Dale Bowers."

"No, your name is," he glanced back at his clipboard, "Inmate 11-2359604. You see gentlemen, you all have the same first name, and it … is … inmate! Wasn't that nice of the state?" He slowly made a half-circle with his upturned arm. "And did you, Inmate 11-2359604, not just hear me say how to address every corrections officer you interact with?"

"Nope," Dale replied with a full grin.

Lewis smiled back as he leaned into Dale's face, their noses almost touching. "Once more, you will address us as *Corrections Officer*. Do you understand that? Do you have any problem with that?"

"Nope." Lewis glared at Dale with this response. "Sorry man, what I meant to say was 'Nope, *Corrections Officer*.'"

"You see, you can do it. Not so hard, was it? Anyone else need a little one-on-one time to review this simple directive?" Silence. "Good! Any questions?" Lewis scanned the bus from front to back, but no one moved. No one, that is, until Dale raised his hand.

"For the love of god! Inmate *whatever-the-hell-your-number-is* what do you want?"

Batting his eyes, Dale replied, "Corrections Officer, I was wondering, do all the guards have the first name of Corrections? Wouldn't that be a coincidence?"

The two men locked eyes. "Get the fuck off of my bus! All of you. Now! Jesus H. Christ you all stink!"

Dale smirked at the officer as he started to pass by him, but Lewis stopped him with a firm hand to the chest. "That was a mistake, son. A *big* one."

"Good to know, dad."

"Oh, you're going to fall hard, boy. Get the fuck out of my face."

Dale laughed under his breath as he jaunted down the bus steps and into the sunlight. The red-faced corrections officer pulled out a pen and paper from his pocket and angrily made a note about this new inmate. It read in part, "Needs to be broken."

The other fifteen inmates on the bus followed Dale through the layers of security gates; each one impressed with his guts in the face of authority.

Of course, this was Dale's plan from the beginning. His years of county jail time had taught him well — taught him how to survive in this dangerous environment.

May 3, 1979, Thursday afternoon, 1:20

"Open A-24," the corrections officer spoke into his shoulder mounted microphone. Seconds later, an electric motor kicked into action. A hard click of metal signaled the release of the door lock. The barred doors opened slowly. "Home sweet home inmate."

"Wow, this is roomier that I ever thought possible. Corrections Officer, does that window open?" asked Bowers.

"All the way in, genius. Your roommate is still in the hole. Don't get lonely on us."

"I should be fine, Corrections Officer," said Bowers as he smartly saluted the guard.

"Pal, I served in the military and I'm not going to let some chicken-shit pussy like you disrespect those who served."

"I'm no chicken-shit pussy and you don't scare me at all. Look at you bragging about it like you're Audie Murphy or something. I'll bet you were more like what's his face, uh, Andy Griffith guy in *No Time For Sergeants* when he was in charge of the shitters. You remember that movie?" asked Bowers.

"Problem is, you should be scared of me. I hold all the cards. You've got shit. Hell, you are shit, inmate. I've seen that movie about five times. Funny, funny movie."

"It was OK," said Bowers.

"Shut up inmate! The funniest part was when Andy's character got himself a title, PLO. Remember that?"

Bowers just crossed his arms and looked away.

"You just got your first assignment. Starting tomorrow, *you* will be my PLO — Permanent Latrine Orderly, until I say you're not."

"You can't do that to me."

"I just did. Close A-24!" the iron door slid back in its tracks, locking the door with a solid clank of metal. "Let that sink in, Inmate 11-2359604. Yeah, you could say I've got your number!"

The System - Budget Cuts

January 3, 1984, Tuesday morning, 8:00

"Governor Prescott, we just don't have the money to maintain the prison population that we are experiencing today," said Ronald Collins.

"Director Collins, what will it take to maintain the status quo?" asked the governor.

"Sir, our accounting staff, working with your accounting office, has determined that we would need more than $150 million this year alone. And that's just to tread water. We need to build two facilities for men and one for women. Only then will the situation improve."

"How soon does that need to happen?"

"I'm not being crass, but this should have happened five years ago."

"My staff," the governor nodded to his Chief of Staff Hal Taylor, seated in the back of the office, "has advised me that the $150 million won't be available, this year or next. Options?"

"If the legislature won't act … ."

"They won't believe me. Those liberals think we toss too many citizens into the system as it is. Their leadership is pushing for even less money for your department."

"Because of the overcrowding, we're fighting off ACLU lawsuits left and right. Our legal expenses associated with those court actions were over $2 million last year and believe me, will be double that this year. That's money we don't have, sir. The only way we can keep operating within budget is to lighten the load."

"You're talking about letting inmates out early?

"Yes, I am," said Director Collins.

The governor tapped his pen on the desk. "How many releases are we talking about?"

"We have to let forty percent out, at least."

"Jesus Christ, Ron. Can we stagger those releases over several years?"

"The numbers won't work without releasing them during the first quarter of this year."

"Interesting. I'm going to confer with my staff later today, but I think we can work this to our advantage."

"Sir?"

"We let everyone know it's because of our liberal legislative friends. They can't find it in their kind hearts to punish people. They are responsible for this mess. We can let them know that this mass release will happen unless they push their representatives to pay for it. If that doesn't work, hey, it's an election year and this administration will look like we're tough on crime, they aren't. They get the blame, I get the votes."

"Who decides what prisoners get released?" asked Director Collins.

"I appointed you to this position was because I believed in your judgment and expertise, Ron. Backroom talk indicates a review of department finances is headed your way. Make sure all is in order. I want an announcement to the press. Make it in two days. I'll leave the all the details up to you. Just keep my staff in the loop," replied the governor.

"Very well, I'll handle this. Thank you, sir."

The director turned and left the office. The governor looked at Chief of Staff Hal Taylor and said, "Problem solved. You know what's beautiful about this? It will not be popular, but I won't get any of the blame."

"That's why you are the governor, sir! Did you want me to set up a staff meeting?"

"No. That was just for Director Collins' benefit. Besides, we just talked to your staff, right?"

"Very true. Will that be all, sir?"

"No, my plane leaves in four hours for the Keys and that beautiful lady is waiting for me there. Plus, I get out of this cold weather. If any emergencies crop up over the next three days, my secretary has the hotel information."

"I hope you and your wife enjoy your time away. You deserve it."

"My wife? She's not going. She hates these political conferences."

"As I said, enjoy your time away."

"Something tells me I will. Take care, Mr. Taylor."

The System - Press Release

January 5, 1984, Thursday afternoon, 4:00

"Did you see this?" asked Kaylie. "I just don't believe it! No! This cannot affect those, those … ."

"What's going on?" asked Adam.

"This newspaper article. It's bullshit," she said, tossing the paper across the kitchen table.

PRISON SHORTFALL ANNOUNCED
WILL RESULT IN THE RELEASE OF THOUSANDS OF FELONS
CURRENTLY HOUSED IN STATE PRISONS

By Brenda McLemore, Staff Political Correspondent

Director of Corrections, Ronald Collins, announced at a press conference today a shortfall of $150 million for each fiscal year, 1984-86, exists. This deficit will lead to the release of thirty percent of all prisoners being housed across the five state penitentiaries. At the end of 1982, the latest statistics available, listed 7,211 prisoners incarcerated. This could mean that nearly 2,200 inmates will gain their freedom early.

When pressed about the reasons for the shortfall, the director cited inadequate funding from the legislature.

"For too long, we have asked this legislature for funds to build additional facilities. Each time we have pleaded with them, we were refused."

When asked if any stop-gap funding has been requested, Director Collins has pointed to the governor's annual budget requests and State of the State speeches. The director also stated that he has met with several members of the legislature to iron out any differences. He added that those members, "never came back with a feasible solution."

Speaker of the House Michelle Stenson acknowledged several meetings have been held with the governor's team and Director Collins. She also indicated that without budget cuts elsewhere, "no funds are left to address this problem." Adding, "I lay this at the feet of our governor, whose policies have dictated incarceration for far too many non-violent crimes. I fear if the releases planned occur, this will lead to a flood of violent offenders pushed, unprepared, back into our communities. I will also call for a financial review of the Department of Corrections. This is needed to ensure that taxpayer dollars are spent wisely and for their intended purposes."

Governor Prescott was attending a conference this week and was unavailable for comment. His chief of staff, Hal Taylor, stated the "legislature has turned a blind eye on this issue," and added that the liberal leaning House of Representatives is "more concerned with pampering offenders than punishing them."

Director Collins stated that, for this plan to be effective, the prisoner releases will occur "in waves, not dribbles." All releases must be done before March 31, 1984. He also indicated that, should the release be required, victim services will attempt to contact anyone affected by the early discharge of offenders.

"That is so wrong. You don't think they'd let your dad's killers out, do you?"

"Adam, I just don't know. 2,200 releases? I will call the prosecutor's office and find out for sure. They can't get away with that! Daddy had a lot of connections with politicians. Maybe I can do some asking around. Those killers have to be punished. You can't imagine how I'd feel if those guys don't stay put!"

"No, I've got an idea. I could let them know they'd be safer staying locked up than having to face you."

"That's not funny, Adam. I can't believe you said that!"

"I'm sorry, but I wasn't kidding."

———◆———

January 6, 1984, Friday morning, 8:00

"This is the office of Assistant District Attorney Jennifer Nichols. My name is Kerri. How may I be of assistance?"

"Kerri, this is Kaylie Carlson, and I must speak with Ms. Nichols as soon as possible."

"Certainly, Ms. Carlson. May I tell her the reason for your call, please?"

"She'll know but, OK. This concerns the article in the paper yesterday about the early release of a huge number of prisoners."

"We've been getting a lot of calls about that today. At present, we have nothing to add because we just don't … ."

"Kerri, I'm going to stop you right there. My dear, I'm sure you are doing what has been asked of you. I'm not, I will not, take a canned answer for this. We're talking about the people who murdered my father."

"Ms. Carlson … ."

"Please, call me Kaylie," she interrupted.

"Thank you. Kaylie, I can assure you this office does not know any details. Who will be released? No one knows yet. The Department of Corrections has not provided that information. What I will do, Kaylie, is have the ADA call you personally when she is free."

"Perfect! That's all I'm asking for right now. Let her know she can call me anytime, even late at night. I'll give you my number." Kaylie gave her the number, hung up the phone, and waited.

The Young Couple - The Daughter

March 27, 1984, Tuesday morning, 9:10

THE LATE MARCH MORNING started warm and the sweet perfume of fresh cut grass filled Rita's bedroom. Tommy was lying on his side, half-awake, a filtered sunrise silhouetting his close-cropped brown hair. Rita ran her fingers through it. "Such a beautiful boy," she said.

"I'm twenty-four years old, you know?" One eyelid opened, then the other. "My god you are beautiful. The sunlight makes you even more gorgeous. Such a perfect face framed by your golden hair. Angelic!"

"There's that creative writing class in action! Go Cardinal!"

"Hey! Don't make fun of my school. It's Stanford University for god's sake! It's true though. You look fantastic. Hey, what time is it?"

"Just after 9:00. Why?"

"Damn, I told dad I'd pick up some auto supplies for the station and drop them off. Care to join me?"

"Car parts and a gas station, both in one day? I am such a lucky woman."

"Yes, you are! Now go, get dressed, lucky woman!"

"Going to be a bossy boy today, are we? I like that!" she wiggled his nose between her thumb and index finger and bounded out of bed. "Jeans OK?"

"Sure. Want to grab breakfast somewhere after we drop that stuff off?"

"Yes, I'm famished. You name the place. You pay for it."

"Maybe I'll get dad to pay, since we're providing a delivery service for him today."

"Even better."

———◆———

March 27, 1984, Tuesday morning, 10:17
Ding-ding! That familiar ring brought back mixed emotions for Tommy. He had many positive interactions with customers, some not so wonderful. Those experiences were OK with him. They helped shape him. Then there was his dad.

"How's your father been to you lately?" asked Rita.

"It's been better than before. He still tries to run my life even though I don't live under his roof. Guess that will never go away."

"Hey, I need those supplies back in the storage room," yelled his dad from behind a customer's car.

"See what I mean," said Tom. And then, "Consider it done, dad."

"Want some help?" asked Rita.

"I'll take care of it. You just sit there and look pretty!"

"Oh, go on!"

"But you are gorgeous!"

"I meant, put that shit away so we can go eat! Let's go!" said Rita.

"Now who's the bossy one?" said Tommy. He turned to look at Rita; they were both laughing as he walked away.

"Hello, Mr. Newton!" yelled Rita with an exaggerated wave.

From underneath the hood, Lou nodded.

"With that personality, how is Tommy possibly your son?"

Tommy stepped back outside, but stopped to think. He saw his dad working on a customer's car. Exhaling, he strolled over to the car. He recognized the customer sitting in her car. "Mrs. Prentiss, so nice to see you again," Tommy said.

"Oh, Tommy! I heard you were back in town. It's good to see you again. Your father told me you did very well at that college of yours."

"Thanks, I hope you and Mr. Prentiss are well. Hey dad, those supplies and parts are put away. We're heading out for breakfast."

"Breakfast? It's after 10:00 a.m."

Tommy walked back to his car in silence rather than make a scene in front of a customer.

"Thanks," called out his dad.

Tommy waved and drove away.

"So you say your dad's not so bad, huh? Seems like the Lou Newton I've always known."

"At this point, I'm just happy I don't live and work with him anymore. It limits my exposure to shit like that."

"I'm sorry that you've had to deal with this," said Rita, resting her hand on the back of his neck.

"I'm hungry. Does Nick's Place sound good?"

"It does. But it doesn't matter where we go or what we do. As long as you are there, I'm happy, Tommy."

"I just love you, Rita! Nick's it is!"

"To Nick's Place!"

Tommy and Rita pulled into Nick's parking lot. The cafe stood there many years, but Nick, and later his daughter, had taken care of it inside and out. The exterior had a fresh coat of white paint and powder blue trim. Even the parking had a fairly new layer of asphalt put down along with bright yellow parking space lines.

"Not too many cars today. Probably a good table for us," said Rita.

"I'm starving. A three-egg omelet with hash browns and bacon is in my future!"

"Sounds good, if you're eating for five!" joked Rita. "Is your dad treating us today?"

"You know, I didn't even ask him. He was already full of attitude today, so I wasn't going to bother to ask him."

"Yeah, I noticed his body language. Anything going on with him?" asked Rita.

"I haven't heard anything. After you, my dear," said Tommy as he opened the door to the cafe.

"Why thank you, kind sir!"

"Sit anywhere you want Tommy, Rita. We're not too busy today," said Rose, who ran the place ever since her father, Nick, passed away several years ago.

"Rosie! Thanks," said Tommy.

"Tommy Newton? Oh my god, it is!" It was Kaylie, sitting in the corner.

"Kaylie. I didn't know that I'd ever see you again. How are you?" asked Tommy.

"We were doing good until earlier today. And sweet little Rita! I've missed you!"

"Hi Kaylie, I have missed you as well. I cherished our little get-togethers. My gosh, I love your hair. Such a beautiful auburn color. I'm so jealous!"

"Why thank you Rita. I get this color from my mother. She grew hers much longer, down past her shoulders. I like it a bit shorter, not as daringly short as yours, which looks terrific! I also keep hearing good things about you."

"You're too kind, Kaylie! But tell me, who's been singing my praises now?" joked Rita.

"None other than one, Mr. Lou Newton."

"That didn't happen," said Rita. She shot Tommy a bewildered look.

"Yeah, no way," chimed in Tommy.

"He certainly did. He thinks you are good for Tommy. I understand you're a teacher in town."

"I am teaching over at Coolidge Junior High. My second full year and I love it. I was considering a law degree and still thought about it until I took my LSAT. That made me change gears, but it turned out for the best."

"Plus, she's the girl's basketball coach," said Tommy.

"Very nice. I went to Coolidge, forever ago! Plus, I've forgotten my manners. You both remember Adam."

Rita extended her hand. "Very nice to see you again, Adam."

"You too, Rita," said Adam.

"Good to see you, Adam," said Tommy. "How is your investment firm doing?"

"Things are really taking off. I may have to take on another financial planner. If you know of any good candidates, send them my way."

"I'll keep an eye out for you. Kaylie, you said things were going good. But not now?" asked Tommy. "I'm not trying to pry, just concerned."

"No, you're fine. You knew my father quite well. You should know this, too. It's been on my mind since January when the news broke. Maybe it's nothing. Maybe it's a big thing. The prison system is planning on releasing almost one-third of the prisoners due to budget problems. I'm just sick about it. What if they let my dad's killers go early? It's only been five years, you know. Justice? That would not be justice!"

"They can't do that," said Tommy. "Not for murder, can they?"

"That's just wrong," said Rita. "What can be done about it?"

"I don't know. But I'm considering my options."

"I'm telling her we should sit tight and see where this goes before we do anything," said Adam.

"Would the classic cliche, 'Write your congressman' help?" asked Tommy.

"Some clients have mentioned that this is happening outside of the legislature. I mean, the governor has a big hand in this, as does prison management."

"I will wait, we just have to be prepared," said Kaylie, "and consider our options. But I'll say it here and now — they will rightfully pay for what they did, even if they get out of prison early."

"We're on your side. If we can help, reach out. I hope it doesn't come to that," said Tommy.

"Thanks, Tommy. He's one of the good guys, Rita. Make sure you hold on to him," said Kaylie.

"He's not going anywhere, not if I can help it!"

"We'll let you finish your meal. It was great to see you again," said Tommy.

"Same here, take care," said Kaylie.

The two grabbed a table next to the window.

"I just don't believe that is still planned!" said Tommy. "I was hoping she hadn't seen that article. That was back in January, right?"

"Right around the first of the year. That will be rough for them. It's just not fair and, frankly, it pisses me off they could let them free."

"How can we stop it?"

"If only your 'write your congressman' idea really worked. Politicians at that level do as they please. To hell with everyone else. I think we should stay in touch with Kaylie. Make sure she is OK. She seems very nice but has had some terrible things happen. I'll keep in touch with her," said Rita.

"You're right. Let's keep an eye on her. Maybe some moral support. So, what looks good?" asked Tommy.

"Coffee. I need coffee!"

"Me too. Rose? When you have a minute, we'd like some coffee."

"Tommy, you're like family here and you know what I'd tell the family?" asked Rose.

"Get it your own damn self? Something like that?"

"Oh, exactly like that, sweetie!"

"See what I put up with?" Tommy walked over to the coffee maker.

The Killer - Early Release

April 5, 1984, Thursday afternoon, 4:00

The phone rang as Kaylie walked in the door, groceries in hand. "Miss Werner?" asked the unfamiliar voice.

"Yes, this is Kaylie Carlson. Werner was my maiden name."

"Mrs. Carlson, this is Rachel Bruner with Victim Services. Was your father Anthony Werner?"

Kaylie's knees weakened. "Yes," she replied.

"Ma'am, I'm calling to notify you that Dale Bowers is to be released within the next six weeks."

"No. There has to be a mistake. This man killed my father. He shot him and he's only been imprisoned for five years!"

"Mrs. Carlson, I am sorry, but there has not been a mistake. This is all a part of the budget shortfall with our prison system."

"I knew about the shortfall. Such a pathetic failure for the government. But how can this man be freed?"

"According to the memo we received from Corrections, they devised a formula to determine those eligible for early release. Each inmate was interviewed on a wide range of subjects. Remorse for the crime committed. Plans for the outside world. Did the inmate attend courses that would help him face the outside world? Those kinds of things. A prisoner's record while he was being housed by the state is a big factor. Mr. Bowers kept his nose clean for five years. Perhaps a lawyer can offer you better advice than I can. I'm sorry Mrs. Carlson."

"But the man has to be punished!"

"I understand your concern, Mrs. Carlson. I must discuss the other two men."

"No. Don't you dare tell me!"

"I'm sorry, but they are also scheduled to be released this year."

"You have got to be kidding me! Lady, this is one mean fucking joke."

"Ma'am, I'm sorry, but I am not joking. The records I have in front of me indicate that Gordon Thompson has a tentative release date of May 7 of this year. John Brodigan is scheduled for release the second week of May, this year."

Kaylie's phone fell to the floor. Andy looked up from his newspaper.

"What's going on?" asked Adam. "Is this about your father's killers?"

"Bowers is getting out. The person who actually ended daddy's life will walk around us. The others are getting out next month. All three are going to be free. Adam, we have to do something."

"We'll make this right. We have to!"

April 11, 1984, Wednesday afternoon, 1:35

Tommy stopped at the gas station to see his dad before his long weekend with Rita. He sat on the counter, watching his dad help a customer read a map. Tommy smiled. He enjoyed helping people out. Even little things like giving directions. He was happy to be on his own, more accurately, away from his father. Looking around the office, he saw the daily newspaper. Front page, below the fold, was a headline that caught his eye.

THE EARLY RELEASE OF CONVICTED FELONS HOUSED IN STATE PRISONS TO BEGIN NEXT WEEK.

By Brenda McLemore, Staff Political Correspondent

Director of Corrections, Ronald Collins, announced at a press conference yesterday that a shortfall of $150 million will indeed result in the release of up to one-third of the current prison population. When pressed for a list of offenders and their expected release date, Director Collins responded, "We cannot provide the public with a list such as that. What we are doing is advising those impacted by the offender. They will be told of the expected release date ... ."

——◦——

April 27, 1984, Friday morning, 8:45

He didn't think he could be so lucky. Part of him felt he deserved his freedom. The prison system was overcrowded, that much was obvious. The governor ordered a review of all inmates eligible for release. He was headed back into society. Ready or not.

He didn't flinch when the gate slammed shut behind him. He didn't care he would be on probation virtually the rest of his life. He was no longer Inmate 11-2359604. He was once again Dale William Bowers. Dartmoor Maximum Security Penitentiary was no longer home. He just smiled and walked to the waiting car, an old white Chevy chugging out clouds of pale blue exhaust as it idled awkwardly.

He opened the passenger door, tossed his duffel bag in the backseat, and slammed the door. "Hey sis," he said as he sat down in the front passenger seat, not looking at the driver, Brenda.

"Dale," was all she said. Silently, she put the car in gear and it lurched down the road. Dale watched the high walls and guard towers fade from view, vowing never to go back.

An hour passed in silence before anyone spoke. And it was his sister. "One month, Dale, and that's it, and you gotta be out. Stay the fuck away from my two boys. Don't bring anyone around. And be gone. In one month. I'm being way too generous. I didn't even want to pick you up. I hate you have to stay with us for even a minute. I'm only doing this because our father called me, begging. Giving me the same old song and dance. Family always being first, no matter what. Sometimes I think that rule isn't always right. Like when an unforgivable mistake is made. Guess what I think is an unforgivable mistake, Dale?"

"Oh, gee I don't know Brenda, killing some fucking old man. If I asked for your forgiveness, would that set us straight?"

"Too late for that."

"Look, all I want … ."

"All I want is for you to be gone in one month."

"I want to be on my own, believe it. I hope it doesn't take more than a month."

"I guess you don't understand. Midnight, May thirtieth and you are gone. You never come back. We need an understanding, Dale. Otherwise, you're getting out here and now." Her jaw was set firmly.

"All right. Fine. A month" He rested his chin in his hand and watched the world fly by. Despite being free, he felt trapped again.

Another hour of silence passed before they pulled up in front of an old, weary house. It sat in the middle of a neighborhood of other old and weary houses. Yards littered with old cars, tires, and bags of garbage. No one seemed to notice or care. They did not appear to pay attention to the new visitor, either. If they did, they probably didn't much care. Everyone there had their own problems.

"Listen, Brenda," Dale asked his sister before they got out of the car, "do you suppose mom and dad would take me in? My P.O. would have to clear it first. Obviously, I need out of here."

"You know they'd take you. They got that old trailer behind their house. Ask them about that. You're right — you need to leave all this trouble. Could be how you get your shit straight."

"Plus, it'd get me out of your hair."

"You got that right. You should call them now. The phone's right over there, my dime!"

The Accomplice - Early Release Too

May 7, 1984, Monday morning, 10:05

HE DIDN'T WANT TO leave, but also knew the remaining inmates would despise him. Gordon Thompson had spent the last five years trying to improve himself. Gordon started to make positive changes in his life. His thirty-five-year sentence was his wake up call.

Within ten months, he earned his GED. He knew convicted felons would have a difficult time getting a job. A felon without a GED may as well stay in prison. That was enough motivation for him. With a few college credits under his belt, he developed a dream of being the first in his family to graduate from college.

"This release will delay my goals, sir," said Thompson to the prison's career counselor, LeRoy Wilson.

"I understand your situation, Gordon. You're one of the few inmates to devise an actual plan to better yourself. I'm going to reach out to some schools on the outside. Maybe I can place you somewhere that will allow you to grow," said Wilson.

"I appreciate you trying to help me out, Mr. Wilson. Wish I'd had someone on my side earlier on in life."

"Gordon, I have to ask you this. This morning I read your updated file, and it says you are going back to where you lived at the time of your arrest."

"That's correct, sir," replied Thompson.

"Why are you putting yourself in the same environment that helped imprison you?" asked Wilson, holding his arms open.

"I feel I took something from that community. I got this second chance. Maybe I can benefit the city in some way. I'm wanting to pay them back."

"You also took a lot from that man's family. Have you thought about them?"

"That's all I do some days. I've written that man's only kid, but she has not written back, not tried to call. I can understand why, so I will not push that."

"That brings us to where you are today. Please, make the most of this chance. You'll never get one like it again. Here's a packet of information for you. Job possibilities, adult education classes, housing, financial aid. My card is also there if you need to talk. Take care of yourself, Gordon. Do right by yourself and others," said Wilson as he shook Thompson's hand.

"I will, sir. Thanks for all this information. I'll dive right into it. My release processing starts in ten minutes, so this has to be goodbye, Mr. Wilson."

"From here on out, call me LeRoy. Goodbye Gordon."

Gordon picked up his duffel bag and the binder that Mr. Wilson created and headed towards the prisoner's Release Processing Center and his new life.

May 7, 1984, Monday evening, 9:42

The rain had started just after the prison transport van, with a cargo of twelves riders, dropped Gordon and the others off at the bus station. Every passenger released gained his freedom because of the budget issue. A group of taxi drivers, known as the *Convict Conveyor Corp* by the locals because of its primary business, stood by, waiting. The cab drivers almost only ferried freed convicts home or relatives journeying out to visit incarcerated loved ones. The local taxi drivers made the ten mile round trip to and from the prison with the enthusiasm of a carnival pony giving a kid a ride, walking in circles. While never the friendliest drivers, they were less so now that at least one-third of their business would soon disappear. Their disappointment came early as they observed that the twelve ex-cons would be taking one of the next three busses that left between now and 6:20 the next morning.

Gordon's bus was scheduled to depart at 6:20 the next morning, taking him back home. Home, where he partnered with Dale Bowers and John Brodigan in the infamous Anthony Werner murder. He sat alone in the bus depot, away from the other ex-cons. For once, he was serious about changing his life. The conversations he had with his counselor in prison kept replaying in his mind. In one, Mr. Wilson advised him to "always walk away from known ex-cons, even if you owed them or they owed you. Whatever was owed would pale in the price you would end up paying. It will be your money, your freedom, or your life. Don't give that power to anyone. It's your power, Gordon."

Gordon watched the other released prisoners as they laughed, smoked, and cursed at each other. "I'm going to follow your words, Mr. Wilson. I have to do that. My life is not over yet."

"Hey Big Man. Hey!"

Startled, Gordon looked up to the sight of ex-con, Will Dunlap, looming over him. Dunlap was the closest thing to a friend he had in prison.

"Greenie? Crap, what time is it?" asked Thompson.

Greenie, short for Greenthumbs, got his nickname by growing acres of marijuana in his family's farm fields over several years. When finally arrested, authorities estimated he had grown five tons of marijuana in his gardening career.

"I don't know. About two in the morning. Want a hit?" he asked, holding out a joint.

"Man, you know I can't. I've talked to you about this. I have to stay clean, shit. I mean, I got caught up in this murder and it about ended my life. But God gave me another chance. I know He did and I'm not fucking it up this time."

"It's just a way to celebrate. No cops are around, one pull, man."

"Not going to. I appreciate that, but with respect, no thank you."

"You talked to that Mr. Wilson guy at the prison way too much."

"He's a pretty smart man," said Thompson, "and I'm going to stick to his advice."

"Smart? If he's so damn smart, explain how a dude goes to college and he spends all that time and money. For what? Working sixty hours a week in an old building that smells like rotting vegetables and dealing with people the likes of us?" asked Dunlap. "Sounds like a first-class idiot to me, but if you want to follow his advice ... ."

"I'm disappointed in you, Will. You've known for months that I'm trying to turn it around and here you are, tempting me like this."

"Tempting you? Man, do your thing, dude. Going to turn your life around? Who will want a convicted felon like you, someone who helped kill a man? What would they want you for? Tiny little bitch like you might find circus work, but you ain't never going to amount to shit, Big Man. None of us will. You don't get it!" With that, Dunlap turned and walked away.

Still sitting down, back against the bus station's wall, Gordon watched as Dunlap walked towards the other end of the station. He felt numb and betrayed. As his former friend's footsteps grew quieter, he whispered, "I will amount to something. My life has a purpose. It has to amount to something. If it doesn't, why be here?"

The Accomplice - Paroled

May 11, 1984, Friday morning, 6:05

John Brodigan was already awake and had been since three. The anticipation was too great. This time tomorrow he'd be waking up in his own bed. His brother Jimmy came through by finding a place for John to live. Having peace and quiet when he wanted and partying when the mood would strike was something he missed. He wouldn't miss the noises of prison. The screaming and fighting. Doors slamming shut. Echoing footsteps of a corrections officer walking the floor at two in the morning. Checking each cell with a flashlight, sadistically banging it on the inmate's bars while they slept. The ever-present threat of violence followed him around wherever he went. While in prison, he never sought it out, but it would find him. He was not one who normally backed down from a fight. He promised himself he would stay out of trouble when he was freed. Even he didn't believe that.

He was thinking about the last meeting he had with the prison counselor. He promised him when he said, "I'm going to do my best to stay out of trouble."

"How will you accomplish that, John?" asked the counselor.

"I really don't know. Trouble will follow me around and if they're not already inside, hell, I open the damn door and let them right in. Like when I let those guys right in and believed their shit."

"This is where you can be strong. Lead your own life and don't let them direct your life."

"They probably won't be coming around anymore."

"But others might. Some people out there may ask you to break the law again. Fight that urge to follow them."

"I'm going to try. I've got to get a job. You have to have money to live. I just hope someone takes one chance on me."

"Me too John, me too. What else is on your mind before you leave?" asked the counselor.

"Well, it's just — no, forget it."

"What is it John?"

"I've been having nightmares lately."

"Given your situation, that sounds rather normal. What are they about?"

"It's really just one that repeats itself every few nights. The old man that got murdered. I still don't feel like I played a part in his dying, like the courts do. But that guy keeps showing up next to my bed while I'm sleeping. The only reason he wakes me up is his blood drips on my face, hits me like rain. I look at him and he answers my question, knowing it without me saying it. He says, *I will be avenged. When you least expect it, John. You won't be able to avoid it.* And then I wake up, shaking."

"It tells me on some level the remorse you have is real. Do you have the information about the psychologist I mentioned?"

"Yes, it's in my bag."

"Call him. Tomorrow. Get that therapy going. It will do you good."

He promised he would.

He rolled on his side, facing the middle of his room. He could see that his hygiene kit was gone, photographs off the wall, everything on his side of the cell was bare. A medium-sized, prison issued duffel bag sat on the floor at the end of his bed. It contained nearly every earthly possession he would take out of prison life into the next. It was now 7:00 a.m. and checkout was at 8:00 a.m.

"Checkout. That's what that guard called it. Like this is some fancy hotel. Asshole."

"Who you calling asshole?" yelled the prison guard. Not the checkout guard, which made John feel relieved.

"Me sir, I'm the asshole," said Brodigan.

"Says on my clipboard that you are the lucky asshole today, Brodigan. You ready to go?"

"Yes, I guess so."

"Well shit, man, I'm not taking you to the gas chamber. Let's go," barked the guard. And then, "Open 71A."

The locked door creaked open. Brodigan grabbed his duffel bag and walked out of his cell for the last time. The guard tapped him on the back. "That way. Go," he told Brodigan who walked slowly, guard in tow.

The two men worked their way through a maze of locked doors and checkpoints until they reached the intake/outtake window.

"Name?" asked the guard behind bullet-proof glass.

"Brodigan, John Brodigan."

"Been expecting you, Brodigan," he said. "This envelope contains your release papers, identifications, government food vouchers, and $150 cash. Sign here," he said, swapping the envelope for the legal paper. Brodigan signed the document and slid it back inside the cage.

"You need anything else from him?" asked the first guard.

"No, he's good to go. Good luck, sir."

"Thank you," said Brodigan.

"This way to freedom, John." The guard held one last door open.

"You called me John! Thank you."

"You're not an inmate anymore. You're a regular citizen now. Don't disappoint."

"Thank you again, um. I don't know your name."

"Reggie, I'm Reggie."

"Thank you Reggie."

"Goodbye John. Exit clear for opening," yelled Reggie.

John walked out the gate and waited for his brother, who was late.

The Accomplice - One Meets A Fury

August 4, 1984, Saturday morning, 12:19

THE BAR DOOR SWUNG open, banging against the wall. John Brodigan stumbled out and made his way to his pickup. He always left it unlocked; nothing to steal there after all. The night was cold and he was drunk. He sat and waited for the engine to warm, nearly falling asleep.

He didn't know that he was being watched. He had no reason to think so. Parked on the street and set back several feet from the bar's parking lot entrance, they sat in their warm car. A man and a woman. Watched. Waited.

"That's him, it's Brodigan," she said.

"Uh-huh, I'd recognize that piece of shit anywhere," said her partner. "You ready to do this?"

"I am. I'm ready to get a taste of justice."

"Me too. Long time coming."

They had already spent many days and nights surveilling this target and knew where he lived. He was followed for hours. His habits were noted, looking for weaknesses. They were certain he would go straight home. They headed that way to wait for him. Over coffee that morning, they both agreed they had enough intel on him. They had been planning this most of the summer. They were confident their plan would work and they would slip away unnoticed. They parked one street over, as they had done many nights, under a large maple tree that shaded the car from most of the streetlight. He carried a paper grocery bag under one arm, his other arm around her shoulders, under her long red hair. A narrow alley provided a path from the street to the target's backyard. They stepped over a half-trampled chain-link fence and walked to the back door. Unlocked, as usual, they slipped quietly into the kitchen. He placed the bag on the counter. Dirty dishes were piled in the sink. A leaky faucet became a metronome, counting off time as the water plunk-plinked into an old mug. They executed this like a military operation. He took his place beside the front door, pressing his back against the wall. She stayed in the kitchen, crouched low, guarding the back door. They both had handguns and, once in position, they drew them from the small of their backs, hidden between a shirt and jeans.

John Brodigan lived alone in a small, sad house. His brother, Jimmy, found the house for John. Jimmy plunked down the deposit and two months' rent in his own name. It was doubtful the landlord would allow an unemployed convict to rent the house. Old sheets of various colors hung in the windows for privacy, tacked down with roofing nails at the top of the window casings. The city had issued several warnings about the unkempt yard. John recently mowed it, though it looked like a hayfield. The trash that was normally scattered throughout the yard, old car parts, paint cans, beer bottles, and the like were now tossed together up against the front of the house. That was as organized as he got. The interior of his house matched the exterior. The empty walls spoke to the lonely, sad existence that was his life. To him, all this went unnoticed. To him, at least it wasn't prison where he was forced to endure the sights, sounds, and smells of cellmates. At least here, the stench was his and his alone.

Despite his intoxication, Brodigan was able to make his way home and pulled slowly into his driveway. It was 12:45 a.m. He sat there for a few minutes, the truck still running. He waited for the song on the radio to finish. He could feel himself almost drift off to sleep, but managed to shut off the engine and open his door. The now cool night air felt good. He lingered in the cab for a moment, leg dangling towards the ground.

The lights of his truck had illuminated the back wall of the kitchen; both intruders saw this and tensed up, getting ready. After five minutes, she slowly poked her head into the living room. "Where the hell is he?" she asked. Her partner shrugged his shoulders. They heard the truck door slam shut, its driver drunkenly, as well as loudly, singing a song that had played back at the bar.

She cast her eyes to the ceiling and whispered to herself, "Be quiet! God, even his singing voice is repulsive."

The rusty hinges on the metal screen door squawked as Brodigan opened the door. The front door was also left unlocked. Upon entering, he noticed the figure of a man now facing him. "Who the fu —." Before he finished, a pistol butt across his jaw knocked him out. As he fell to the floor, his arm crashed down on a small table, flipping it and its contents on the floor. The two intruders hastily drug the unconscious man over to the couch, set him down, and tied his hands and feet with a few lengths of thin rope pulled from their bag.

When he regained his senses, duct tape was across his mouth, muffling his yelling. His eyes flared with confusion and rage at the two unwelcome guests.

"Hello John," said the redhead, "we're going to have a little talk."

The taped mouth garbled John's speech.

"Now, you are going to be quiet. We will talk to you, and you will listen. Otherwise, the tape goes back on. You understand?"

He nodded his agreement. With the gun in her hand, she motioned to her partner to remove the tape. He grabbed a loose edge and quickly pulled the tape off, causing the new prisoner to yelp in pain.

"Some tough guy, eh, hon?"

"No kidding. Not much of a badass." she said.

"What the hell do you want? I ain't got no money. I mean, shit, look around."

"As I said, we're going to talk now."

"Hey, I know you! I remember you two from court. Yeah, that's right. Is this what this is all about? That old man getting killed?"

"That *old man* meant a lot. To lots of people. And that *old man* had a name. Anthony Werner. You got that?" he said to him, "Show some respect. Or are you even capable of that?"

John didn't say anything, he just hung his head.

She grabbed his chin with her index finger and thumb and forcefully jerked his face towards hers. "We need some information, John."

"Yeah, sure. Like what? I'll tell you anything. I just want to be left alone."

"We all know that you don't have a problem turning on your so-called friends. Snitching got you out of this mess until now, didn't it, John? We're going to need you to turn on them again."

"They aren't friends of mine, not by a long shot, honey."

This was met with a sharp back-handed slap across his cheek. "What did I just tell you? Respect. Show some respect and some dignity. Don't you fucking call her honey again!"

"Yeah, yeah, all right buddy. Just fucking relax, man,"

"No, you fucking relax, man, or I'll just shoot you right now! We can get that information elsewhere. And I'm not your buddy."

She continued, "Your cohorts, where are they?"

"What the hell is a cohort?"

She shook her head. "Oh my god, read a book once in a while. Lots of little kids read and they probably know more than you. Cohorts are your partners in crime, and we have to know where they are."

"It's not like I hang out with them anymore. In fact, I plan on avoiding them since I kind of fucked them over, ya know?"

"Sure, but you hear things. I know you do. In fact, I'll bet you snoop around because your life depends on it."

He looked at the ceiling and exhaled. "Yep, I hear things alright."

"Such as?"

"Well, Big Man is out of prison."

"We know they are both out. Are they back in town?"

"I heard Big Man, that's Gordon, Gordon Thompson, found a room at one of them crappy old downtown hotels, but I don't know which one, I swear. Plus, he's waiting for some government assistance for an apartment on the east side. Maybe he's in an apartment now."

"And Bowers?"

"Oh, little lady, you'll want to stay away from him. He'll eat up a pretty little thing like you."

Instantly, the barrel of the gun was jammed hard into the bridge of his nose by the male intruder. "What did I just say about respect? If I tell you again, it's going to get ugly."

"Babe, it's OK. Let's just get the information we need and move on," she said.

"Sorry man," said Brodigan.

"Apologize to her, not me."

"Sorry, sorry ma'am."

"Dale Bowers, what do you know about him these days?" she asked.

"He moved into a trailer after prison. Somewhere in New Mexico, but I ain't never heard exactly where. His dad owns the place. I swear I'm being honest. Fuck, I need a drink!"

"We know you've had enough to drink tonight," said the man. "Yeah, you've been followed."

"Shit, you people are cra ..." he saw the gun raise up and caught himself, "No, no, no. I'm sorry I just about said that. You've been following me and I had no idea. You guys are good."

"We'd also like to know the real reason for the murder."

"Besides Dale being batshit crazy? It happened like they said at the trial. Now, I wasn't there, but Big Man told me all about it. The old, I mean, Mr. Werner, grabbed the steering wheel and Dale just reacted, *pow-pow*, and shot the guy. Didn't kill him right away, though. He should have stopped there. Dale didn't want no witnesses, so he shot him in the head. They were still going down the freeway. I saw the flashes because I was following them. I couldn't believe it. That was not the plan, I swear. It was supposed to be a robbery, nothing more."

"So let me get this straight," she said, taping his mouth back up, "he got shot twice in the shoulder?"

Brodigan nodded yes. The man flipped on the stereo. Brodigan's eyes widened. The man turned up the volume.

She spoke loudly in his ear, "Like this?" and she pressed her gun against his left shoulder blade and pulled the trigger twice in rapid succession. Brodigan screamed loudly at first, then, with eyes bulging, his breathing got very heavy. With each rapid breath, the duct tape pulsed in and out. "Put another strip of tape across there," she told her partner.

The victim faded and started to lose consciousness. "John," she said, "John, you need to stay with us OK? It's very important that you know what's going on and why. You need to feel the same pain your cohort handed out. See how I used the word cohort in a sentence?" He could hear her speak, but was getting confused as the pain overwhelmed him.

She continued, "John, we are only here for justice. You did so little time in prison. We have to even the score. You're a man of the streets, so I think you understand. What's about to happen to you will happen to the others. Do you understand me, John?"

He began to sob.

"Why are you crying, John? Because of what you did? Because you know what's next? I hope you feel sorry for the death and misery you caused John. Do you feel sorry, John?"

Through the tape came a muffled yes.

"Thank you, John." She gently put her left hand on his knee, looked into his eyes, and smiled as she lifted the gun to his temple and pulled the trigger.

"Leave the stereo playing like that. I want someone to complain," she said, "and we should probably leave now."

The vigilantes slipped away into the night. They would now be the hunted, too. But they knew that already.

The Police - This Guy?

August 4, 1984, Saturday morning, 2:30

"Yes ma'am, we'll send a car out," said the police dispatcher.

The noise had been too much for Brodigan's neighbor, Nancy Seymour. She was aware of her neighbor's violent past, so she kept quiet and steered clear of him. He normally would be kind enough to shut off his music before he passed out. But not on this night. The music had been blaring for nearly two hours. Enough was enough.

She sat by her front window, barefoot, bathrobe opened in front, a long Oakland Raiders jersey hung to her knees. Her lips held a cigarette; the rising smoke causing her to squint.

"About damn time," she said as she saw the squad car pull into the driveway, behind Brodigan's truck.

After a couple of minutes, two officers hopped out and walked towards his house, flashlights scanning the front of the house.

"That is pretty loud," said Kent Bancroft, the first patrolman.

"It'd piss me off too. I'll knock. Just keep your eyes open. We're rarely welcome around here," said the second patrolman, Norman Skinner.

"You got it Norm."

"Police department, open up!" He paused for a few seconds. "Let's go, open up. You gotta turn that music down. Open up, police!" He waited a few seconds. Still no response. "Well, dammit, let's look around Kent."

Officer Bancroft went to one side of the house, down a narrow alley. There were no windows on that side. He was looking up at the second story when he heard his partner yell, "Kent, front of the house, now!"

Bancroft came running and stood next to Skinner.

"Look in this window. We've got a body."

"No shit," he said as he pointed his flashlight in the window. "Yep, that is one dead guy."

"Grab the tape," sighed Skinner. "I'll call it in."

Bancroft trotted out to the police cruiser, opened the trunk, and pulled out two spools of yellow tape.

"Dispatch, this is Unit 712, responding to the loud music at 1443 Stimson. We've got bigger fish than the music. I'm going to need to have my sergeant respond to this address. We've got a 10-79, at least one male victim. Advise the coroner's office and the detectives on call."

"Copy that 712. We'll send uniforms over to assist. Time out 2:41."

The two patrolmen ran crime scene tape from the street, enclosing the front of the house when extra units started arriving. Five in total would report to the crime scene. Skinner spotted a rookie and tossed the tape to him. "Run across the backyard." Without a word, the new officer complied.

An unmarked car pulled up in front of the house. The two detectives climbed out.

"Oh, great."

"What's up?" asked Bancroft.

"The detective there on the left. Jay Winston. We got into it a couple months back. He didn't like how I handled a piece of evidence. I didn't like his shitty sense of humor."

"Well, this could be fun," said Bancroft.

"Detective Winston, how are you?" asked Skinner, walking up to meet him.

"Good. You remember my partner, Detective Jacobson?"

"Yes sir."

"It's sir now? That's different from the last time we met," said Winston.

"Enough Winnie. Let's go to work," said Jacobson.

"Fine. What do you have here, Skinner? And what have you touched so far?"

"Funny. See Kent, I told you he's a hoot."

Jacobson calmly stepped between the two men. "Gentlemen, let's be professionals here or you both can leave. Copy?"

Both men nodded in agreement.

"We got a loud music call, as you can still hear. No one answered our knocks. I peered inside a window, the one on the left. I could see a male. It was obvious he was deceased. Laying on his side. Lots of blood."

The detectives walked over to the window. Jacobson lit up the room with his flashlight.

"OK, I see you have got the placed taped off and uniforms here, good. Coroner's office?" asked Jacobson.

"They have been notified," said Skinner.

"Any idea if there is anyone else inside?" asked Winston.

"We've not seen or heard anything else."

"Let's get inside and shut that music down. Then we'll clear the house. Skinner, get me four uniforms, one on each side of the house. You and your partner will come in with us and clear the rooms. Be mindful of any potential evidence."

"Copy that. Hey, Bancroft, over here," said Skinner.

"Winnie, do your magic and unlock the door for us," said Jacobson.

Winston walked up to the door. With gloves on, he tested the door knob. It turned, allowing him entry. Winston looked at Bancroft and Skinner. "Neither one of you checked to see if it was unlocked? See what I mean Jake?"

"Drop it partner. Let's do our jobs. Officers, let's do this by the book. No mistakes," ordered Jacobson.

"Police department," shouted Winston, "police department. The house is surrounded. Make yourself known."

The uniformed officers cleared the house. First, to the kitchen. "Clear!" one of them called out. Then down a hallway illuminated only by their flashlights. They checked out the bathroom, a bedroom, and another room used for storage. "Clear!" "Clear!" "Clear!"

With a gloved hand, detective Jacobson powered off the stereo. He also found a light switch that turned on an overhead light, revealing the ugliness of up-close handgun violence.

Jacobson walked over to the body, careful not to step in any blood. No doubt the man was dead. "OK team, we have a white male, deceased. At least one to the head. It caused a mess so steer clear of the blood. Has the coroner arrived yet?"

Winston stuck his head out the front door. "Hey! Is the coroner here yet?"

"Not yet," called out an officer.

"Sorry Jake, not yet."

"Hey Skinner, we all clear?" asked Jacobson.

"Yep, there's nobody else here."

"Thank you, officers. Let's clear out of here until the coroner arrives on scene."

The four men left the house. Bancroft stayed next to the door. Skinner walked out to the yard.

Jacobson pulled his partner aside. "Winnie, I think we know that dead guy."

"Oh yeah, how so?" asked Winston.

"He was involved in that construction owner's murder and ratted his partners out."

"No shit? The Werner case, right?"

"One and the same. And I'm not sure, but it looks like he has two shoulder wounds and the head injury he received. I'll ask Walters what he thinks once he gets here. Dammit, where is he?"

"So, are you thinking he just now paid the price for snitching?"

"Maybe. Two shoulder shots and the head shot? It's just how Werner's case went down. I'm not positive what it is, except I'm positive that it is not a coincidence."

The Police - Where Were You?

KAYLIE HEARD TWO CAR doors slam. Peering through the peephole, she spotted the detectives.

"Oh shit, what do they want now? Can't they just leave me alone?"

One of the detectives reached over to ring the doorbell, but before he could, Kaylie quickly swung open the front door, startling both men.

"Mrs. Carlson. I'm Detective Jacobson and this is my partner, Detective Winston. Perhaps you remember us. We investigated your father's death."

"Yes, of course I remember you. We met numerous times," she said, eyes darting from one man to the other. "Again, what do you want?"

"Either late last night or early in the morning today, one of the men involved in your father's homicide was shot to death."

"I don't understand. I mean, I appreciate you telling me, but I suppose a phone call to let me know would suffice."

"There's more to it than that, ma'am," piped in Detective Winston. "We'd like to discuss this in private if we could please."

"I'd rather have this behind me, but sure, come in," she said, shaking her head and motioning them towards the living room.

"Ma'am, your husband is Adam Carlson? Is he home? We want to talk to him, too."

"No, he's not. He's teaching night class right now. You need to speak to him, too? What's going on here?"

"We may need to catch up with him later. I'll leave my card so that he can contact me," said Detective Jacobson, handing her his card. She casually flipped it on the coffee table. She waited for the two men to talk, her hands on her hips.

The two detectives gave each other a sideways glance. "Ok, Mrs. Carlson," began Jacobson, "as we said, there was a murder last night involving one of the men convicted in your father's case. It was John Brodigan, the man who drove the pickup truck. Has he ever been in contact with you since he was released? It could be to apologize or explain or intimidate. Anything like that?"

"Of course I remember Brodigan. I remember them all, every single day of my life. To answer your question, no, I wouldn't even care to speak with him after what he did. In fact, I'm glad that low-life is dead. I hope the others get theirs too. Pardon my French, but fuck them!"

"No need to apologize. We completely understand. Naturally, you never initiated contact with him or the other two men, correct?"

"Absolutely not! Victim Services contacted us when each of them was released, far too early if you ask me, and we just had hoped they would leave the area."

"So you were aware of the fact that Brodigan was living in town?"

"Well, no, I'm not saying that. I assumed that because you are in my home, the crime must have happened in town." She paused, then with a raised voice continued, "Hold on here! Are you implying this involves me? Do I need to call my lawyer?"

"No, we … ."

"If that's what you are saying, get out of my house. Unbelievable! Now you are saying … ."

"We're not implying anything, ma'am. These are questions we just need to ask as part of our investigation," interrupted Winston. "We'll be on our way if you'd like."

"Oh, I'd like that very much," said a defiant Kaylie.

"Just one thing I ask of you, ma'am," said Jacobson, "if anyone contacts you about this murder or if the other two involved in your father's death contact you, call us right away. Please, it's for your own safety."

Kaylie was already headed for the front door. Without a word, she swung the door open. She looked down as the detectives left.

"Thank you again," said Jacobson.

"Detectives, are the other two in town also?" she quietly asked.

"They might be, but I don't know their whereabouts right now. Stay safe and let us know if you see or hear of anything suspicious."

Kaylie slammed the door, nearly clipping the shoes of one of the detectives. She sat on the sofa, letting out a long, slow sigh. She needed to process this information. Were they suspecting her? She thought of her dad and what they did to him. What should she do next? Standing up again, fidgeting with her hair, she pulled back the drapes and watched the detectives leave. "Adam, hurry home. We need to talk. We really need to talk!" She snapped the drapes closed, briskly headed to the liquor cart, and poured herself a strong drink.

She sat down on the thickly padded sofa, drink in hand. Picking up the detective's card off of the table, she felt the raised lettering of the police department's logo and laughed. "Sure, I'll call you. Like you gave my father justice! You guys can't possibly give me the satisfaction my family needs." She tore the card in half, then half again, and tossed the shredded pieces back on the table.

Sadness and anger welled up inside of her as she sighed and slumped down on the sofa. Looking at her watch, she cursed again, as it would be at least two hours before Adam returned home.

The Accessory - Remember This

August 8,1984, Wednesday afternoon, 12:15

THE RAIN HAD BEEN unrelenting for the past five days, washing out construction work for Steve. He was fixing lunch for himself. His new wife worked full time and, with his stepson visiting his grandparents, he had the entire house to himself.

The doorbell rang.

"What now?" he asked, setting aside his half-prepared PBJ sandwich, chips on the side. He went to the front door and swung it open.

"Well, hello there, pretty lady," he said.

An attractive woman was in the doorway, standing in the pouring rain. To Steve, she looked to be in her late twenties. She also seemed distressed.

"Oh, thank goodness you answered the door. Yours is about the fifth house I stopped at. My car broke down a few houses up and I need to call someone to tow it. May I come in, please?"

"That's too bad about your car. Sure, please come in," he said.

The woman stepped inside, shivering. Her red hair dripping wet. "I'm sorry for getting everything all wet in your house, but I am soaked to the skin. I forgot my raincoat at home and then this. What a day! I must be a mess! Can you show me to your phone?"

"It's just water. Don't worry about it. Plus, you look terrific to me. The phone's in the kitchen, that way," he said as he pointed towards the kitchen.

"Oh, thank you! I won't forget this." The woman slowly walked towards the kitchen, her clothing sticking tightly to the curves of her body.

Steve took a long look, making a very audible, "Mmmm-mmmm. Me either baby."

She turned, smiled directly at him, and said, "Before I forget, I want to tell you good night, big boy."

He smiled, but then cocked his head. "Good night? What do … ."

The redhead's partner slipped inside the door, a short, heavy wooden baton in hand. One strong blow to the head later, the real *Big Man* was face down, out cold.

His assailant shut and locked the front door, closing out the sound of the rainstorm. He rolled Steve on his back and pounced on top of him. He then placed handcuffs on Steve's wrists and two pieces of old cloth around his head. One covered his eyes, the other was jammed hard across his mouth and between his teeth. It was a very effective gag.

In silence, the man and woman drug Steve to a nearby rocking chair. The male assailant pulled four short pieces of rope from his pants pockets and tied Steve's legs to the rocker. Once that was secure, he unlocked the handcuffs and tied their prisoner's arms to the armrests of the chair.

Simultaneously, the woman pulled the curtains, darkening the room. She turned on a floor lamp next to the rocking chair. The two sat on the sofa, waiting for Steve to awaken.

Five minutes passed before he started to regain consciousness. Moving slowly at first but, once he realized his predicament, he began thrashing around, trying to loosen up the ropes.

"Knock it off," said the man. "We're just going to talk. Then we'll be on our way."

Steve mumbled something, but it was inaudible.

"Sweetie, I think we can take the gag out. Steve, if my partner takes that gag out of your mouth, I don't want any yelling from you, OK? Otherwise, it goes back on."

Steve shook his head yes, and the gag was removed.

"What the fuck do you want? I hope it's not money because you're shit out of luck if you do."

She said, "No, Mr. Randolph, we don't need your money. Like he said, we'll chat for a bit and be on our way."

"About what? Do I even know you?"

"You may not know us, but you certainly knew Anthony Werner, right?" she asked.

"Oh fuck. Is that what this is about? I remember you now," he said, nodding at the redhead. "You were at the trials. Yeah, that red hair. You were there and your boyfriend or husband, too. Well, I didn't kill him, if that's what you're asking."

"We know you didn't pull the trigger. We saw you at the trial, explaining your part in this whole mess. The murder would not have happened without you and your big mouth. No destruction of lives. No need for us to do what we've done," she said.

"I did my time for that. I didn't just walk away from that bullshit. I'm with you. He should not have lost his life."

The male intruder picked the gag up off the floor and said, "All right, I'm sick of hearing your excuses." He once again shut Steve up by securing it across his mouth. "And you think a year is fair? A year!" Steve flinched.

"Honey, calm down, OK? Damn Steve, you pissed him off. That does not happen very often. And it's a bad sign for you," said the woman.

"You will not walk away from this. I guarantee that. You'll be reminded of your wrongdoing with every step you take. Every single step the rest of your days," said the man.

Steve began thrashing about again.

"Get it all out," said the woman. "There you go," she said as Steve relaxed. She nodded at her partner.

"Just remember today," said the man. He pulled a handgun out of his waistband. He placed the muzzle on top of Steve's left knee. Steve flinched. His eyes bulged as he shrieked. "Consider yourself lucky. This is a little .22 and you're not getting your brains blown out." Seconds later, one shot went off, boring through Steve's kneecap, shattering it into a half dozen pieces. The small caliber bullet bounced around the inside of his knee without passing through his body. He let loose with a primal, gut-wrenching scream. It was answered with a baton across Steve's forehead. The impact knocked him out and sent him crashing to the floor, rocker and all.

"I'm just about done," he said. He flattened Steve's left hand against the carpeted floor, centered his pistol on the unconscious man's hand, and fired. He repeated that to the right hand. "Now I'm done with this guy."

"One more man. Bowers. Then it's over," she said.

They left Steve on the floor, tied up and bleeding.

That was how Steve's wife found him two hours later. Very much alive, but a changed man.

The Police- We've Got A Live One?

August 8,1984, Wednesday afternoon, 2:13

"Somebody help him, please!"

"Ma'am, you need to give us room so we can help," said the paramedic. He removed the gag from Steve Randolph's mouth, exposing a deep red and purple bruising across his cheek and length-wise across his left ear.

"They shot me," said Steve. "I am so tired."

"Stay with us buddy," said the other paramedic on scene. "Let's get a tourniquet above that left knee. It looks like the bleeding has slowed, but I want that tourniquet in place."

The other medic grabbed his kit and kneeled down next to Steve's leg.

Standing in the doorway, raincoat dripping wet, was a uniformed officer dispatched along with the medic team. "Dispatch, this is 412 responding to the medical at 1711 East McManus. Can you send a sergeant and a couple of other units my way? I have an individual with a single gunshot wound to the leg, unknown origin and unknown severity at this time. Subject also has a single gunshot wound to each hand. These are through and through wounds. There are corresponding holes in the carpet."

"Copy 412, will advise."

"It looks like he is stable enough to transport. Are you his wife?" asked the medic.

"Yes, I'm his wife, Staci. Is he going to be OK?"

"He should be fine. We just need to get him to Franklin Regional. Will you be able to follow us there?"

"Yes, of course." She ran over to Steve's side as the gurney was raised. "Steve, what happened? Who did this to you?"

"Red, it was a red ... hit me ... that dead guy ... hit me ... red ... ."

"He's fading in and out. We gotta go. Coming through."

The police officer stepped out into the rain following the victim to the ambulance.

The wail of the emergency siren filled the neighborhood, then drifted away.

The officer stepped inside the house and could hear the woman's half of the phone conversation. "I don't care, mom, you have to keep him overnight. No, he can't come back here. The house is trashed, and there's blood on the living room floor. Of course it's Steve's. They fucking shot him mom. I'll call you from the hospital."

She hung up the phone and walked into the living room. "What a mess! Am I supposed to clean this up? I have to get to the hospital."

"Ma'am, Mrs. Randolph, is it? Be with your husband. I'm going to get the house taped off and secured. My sergeant is on his way here. Someone will stop down at Franklin and talk with you and your husband. Probably one of our detectives."

"OK, thank you, officer. He'll be the death of me," said Staci. With that, she left for the hospital.

"Dispatch, 412."

"Go ahead 412."

"Advise the detective that victim and victim's wife will be at Franklin Regional and not at my location."

"Copy that 412, will advise."

The officer pulled the yellow tape out of his raincoat and taped off the front yard.

—•◦•—

August 8,1984, Wednesday evening, 9:27

"The surgery went well mom. No, he's awake now and the police are ... of course mom, and ... because he was shot and ... . mom, I have to go," said Staci as she slammed down the phone.

Steve stirred a little in his hospital bed.

"Hey, honey, I'm right here. It's Staci," she said.

"Am I in a hospital? What the hell happened?"

"They think maybe somebody broke into the house and shot you, Steve. Do you remember anything?"

"Um, there were two of them. They didn't break in … ."

Detective Jacobson tapped on the door as he entered the room.

"Who the hell are you?" asked Staci.

"Good evening ma'am. I'm Detective Jacobson. I'm here to ask Steve some questions. And you are?"

"Staci Randolph, his wife. And you're not asking him anything without a lawyer present. I know my rights."

"Mrs. Randolph, I'm not here to arrest Steve. I'm interested in who did this to him. I'm on your side."

"OK. You can talk to him. He had surgery earlier and has only been in his room a couple hours. He's pretty tired."

"This shouldn't take long. Can I ask you a few questions too?"

"Sure. Go ahead, I ain't got nothing to hide," said Staci.

"Mrs. Randolph, were you at home when this happened?"

"No, I was working the assembly line at Toolz. I help make the sliding drawers for toolboxes."

"I have one of those at home. Very good quality. Why would someone have done this? Any enemies?"

"Steve was worried about those three guys getting out of prison. He kind of testified in court about them killing that guy. Maybe it was one of them?"

"It wasn't one of them!" said Steve, who tried to sit up in bed, but failed.

Jacobson turned to Steve. "No? Do you know who it was?"

"I don't know their names, but they said it was payback," said Steve.

"Payback? For what?" asked Jacobson.

"Like what Staci just said. For helping those guys out. Damn, I should not have done that."

"How many were there?"

"Just the two."

"Two of the men you testified against?"

"No, but they were both in court."

"I'm afraid I don't understand. They were in court? Doing what?"

"Yeah, court. They were just watching, you know, sitting in the crowd."

"What did these guys look like?

"It was a guy and a girl. She was real pretty," Steve turned to Staci. "Sorry honey, she's pretty. What can I say?"

"I'm glad you found her attractive, Steve. Probably why you let her in," said Staci.

"Mrs. Randolph, please let your husband talk. OK, Steve. The female. What did she look like? Black, white, Asian? Was she very tall? Heavy-set, skinny? That kind of thing."

"No, she's white, probably about Staci's height. What, five foot four? Skinny girl. Oh, red hair down to her shoulders. Except it was wet. Said her car broke down and needed to call someone. Then I got whacked in the head."

Jacobson underlined _RED HAIR_ on his notepad.

"You were struck in the head. Where did you wake up? At home or here in the hospital?"

"I woke up at home and I was tied up, gagged, and blindfolded."

"Did they say what they wanted?"

"Basically, they were there to get even. Because I set up that old man. That's what they told me."

"What did the male look like?"

"Just some white dude I don't know. But that fucker shot me, man!"

"Did they say anything else? Overhear them talking?"

"They said I was lucky to not get my brains blown out. They mentioned that I only did a year. Seemed pissed about that. Then he shot me in the knee. I think one of them must have hit me upside the head because I don't remember anything else until I woke up here."

"OK, Mr. Randolph, that's about all I have for now. I'll be in touch if I need more. Get some rest and heal those wounds. Mrs. Randolph, good evening."

As the detective walked out of the room, he could hear Steve ask his wife, "What's wrong with my hands?"

"They shot you there too, Steve. How do you not know that?"

As the detective reached the elevator, he clearly heard Steve yell, "In the hands? Who shoots people in the fucking hands?"

The Accomplice - Two Down

August 11,1984, Saturday afternoon, 5:10

"Gordon, I'm going to head home now. The front door is locked. If you could sweep up the floor before you leave, we'll be good until Monday morning. I got the shelves stocked," said the store owner, Vincent Brambilla.

"Sure thing Vincent, see you Monday, bright and early," said Gordon Thompson.

"Bright and early! Oh, and Gordon, there's a couple of bags of garbage next to the butcher's table. Toss them in the garbage too, please."

"Will do."

With that, Mr. Brambilla left the store. Gordon was alone.

"There he is. There's the owner. Leaving for the day," she said.

"OK, I'll go hide out behind the dumpster. When he drops off the garbage, I'll follow behind him and block the door for you," he said.

"This one I kind of feel bad about because he's trying to turn his life around."

"You want to back off and leave him alone?"

"No, he needs to die for what he did. He should have changed sooner."

"OK, good. Here we go." The man scampered over to the dumpster, hiding between it and the store wall.

The wait only lasted about ten minutes. The man heard the back door open. There he was; today's target. Thompson set the bags of garbage on the pavement. He kept the door open by sliding an old brick in the doorway. After tossing the garbage in the dumpster, he slammed the lid with a crash that echoed down the alleyway. Thompson casually pushed the brick aside and walked back inside the store. The man leaped from his hiding spot, catching the door with his gloved hand. After counting to five, he slowly opened the door and slid the brick over to keep it open.

His partner slowly walked across the street to the alley while he entered the grocery store.

The back door opened to a small, poorly lit storage area. A shelf stood against the wall. It leaned inward from the weight of the bottles of glass cleaner, bleach, and Pine-Sol. A stack of rags hung precariously on the middle shelf. The man drew his gun and walked towards some plastic insulating strips hanging down in the doorway. These strips provided a barrier between the two rooms. It was there he waited for his partner.

And there she was, touching his arm gently. He turned and looked at her eyes, touched her red hair. "You ready?" he asked.

"I am. Let's do this," she replied.

They both put their guns away. His in a concealed holster behind his back, hers in her large brown purse.

"Act like you didn't know they were closed. Get him to the meat counter," he said.

She nodded and headed towards the sound of Gordon Thompson whistling while he worked.

Her partner slipped inside the butcher's work area. He crouched behind the counter, bumping into ruthless looking butcher knives and band saw blades. He didn't notice, he just listened.

"Excuse me sir, I can't seem to find a butcher to help me," she said.

Thompson jumped and yelped, "Oh crap, you scared me, lady. The butcher? Well, we're closed, sorry. How'd you even get in here?"

"Well, through the front door! You silly man!"

"Did Mr. Brambilla let you in?"

"Who is that, sugar? So about that butcher. Friends are coming over and I need some meat. Can you help?"

"Uh, yeah, I think I can help with that," gulped Thompson.

"Lead the way, sugar."

"It's funny. We've been closed for at least fifteen minutes. Where have you been hiding?" asked Thompson with a laugh.

"Oh, you never know where I'll pop up. I like to surprise people. Do you like surprises, Gordon?"

"Sometimes, I do. You called me Gordon?"

"Isn't that your name? Sure don't hear that every day."

"No, I mean, how do you know my name?"

She tapped his chest and smiled. "Says on this badge, Gordon."

"Oh geez, of course," he slapped his forehead, "the name tag!"

"So Gordon, about that meat."

"Well, let's look and see. We have hamburger, steak. I mean, there's a lot to choose from."

"How long has this been sitting out? I want to impress my friends with some fresh cut steaks. Can you do that for me, please?"

"Well, I'm not supposed to, but heck, you seem nice. OK, let's go look and see."

Gordon walked past the meat case and opened the door leading into the workroom. The woman followed closely, one hand in her purse.

"Now, the latest delivery is in storage over … " Gordon's words caught in his throat as the man stood up in front of him, pointing a gun at Gordon's face.

"Surprise, Big Man!" said the woman.

"Oh fuck! You! I've seen you before. Oh no, I've seen both of you. My trial, right?"

"You catch on quick, my friend. Maybe not quick enough," said the man.

"I don't, I don't understand. What do you want with me?"

"Information, to start," said the woman.

"What kind of information, lady?"

"We really need to find Dale. We have something to pass along to him. Where's he at these days?"

"He's still in prison, isn't he?"

"You know he's not, so don't bullshit us," said the man.

"You're right, I lied. Sorry. So if I tell you, will you leave?"

"Sugar, I promise you we will leave. Just tell us," said the woman.

"I heard he went to live with his parents. They live in New Mexico."

"Ahh, the lighter!" said the man.

"You know about the lighter? Who *are* you?" asked Thompson.

"We're busy people, Gordo. Where at in New Mexico?" asked the man.

"Living in a trailer on their acreage. Outside of a little town, Edge-some-thing. Edgewater? Shit. You're making me nervous."

"Relax, we're almost done here. Edge-something?"

"Edgestone! That's it! Edgestone!" said Thompson.

"Good job! Thanks Gordon," said the woman.

She then fired two rounds, point blank, into Gordon's shoulder. He crumpled to the ground, moaning in agony. The man used his foot to push Gordon on his back.

"This is also the reason we're here, Big Man. None of you three pieces of shit got what you deserved from the justice system. Brodigan has been taken care of. Bowers will, too, thanks to you. I'm not going to lie to you. You'll be dead soon."

"Oh god no. I know what I did was wrong and I'm trying to turn my life around. Shit, I'm bleeding a lot. Please help me, man. How about you lady? Can you help me?"

"There's only one way I can help you now. Roll on your stomach."

Gordon sobbed but complied. He squeezed his eyes tight when he felt the gun against his temple.

The bullet ripped into Gordon's face. Exiting, it dug into the tile floor. The cracks made by the impact quickly filled up with his blood.

The Police - It Happened Again

"W E   H A V E   T O   F I G U R E this out. I'm telling you, these two are at the center of it and I think they're much smarter than the typical criminals we've dealt with," said Jacobson.

"They've got the motive, means and opportunity. Motive; revenge, pretty obvious. Means; they could easily get a gun in this town, they have financial resources too. Opportunity; hell, Victim Services called her and told her about their release. They had plenty of time to plan these crimes," said Winston.

"The way they were shot shows a solid knowledge of the case."

"Yeah, what do you make of that? Shot the same way her dad was. It's understandable but twisted too, right?"

"It's fucked up in my book."

"Why shoot up Randolph like they did? Kneecap the poor bastard and shoot his hands? His hands?"

"Two things come to mind. Even though he wasn't involved in the murder, he played a part and they had to send a message to him; the guy makes his living in construction, using his hands. Those three wounds will alter his career path, so he pays for it every day of his life."

"They've got some explaining to do."

They were back. This time with more purpose. Jacobson rang the doorbell to the Carlson's home but only waited five seconds before banging on the front door. "Mr. and Mrs. Carlson, this is Detective Jacobson again. Open up!"

Detective Winston stood back on the sidewalk, scanning the house for anyone peeking out a window.

"They're not home," said the Carlson's neighbor, Mr. Tucker.

"What?" was Jacobson's response.

"I said they're not home. Went out of town last night."

"Do you know where they went?"

"Depends on who wants to know."

The detectives walked across the yard, pulling out their badges on the way.

"Police," said Winston. "So where'd they go?"

"Oh, sorry. I didn't know who you were. You can't be too careful these days. I can answer your question; they said they were headed south for a few days. See where the road took them. They're a couple of hard workers, so I imagine they needed a break."

"Do you know what time they left?" asked Jacobson.

"Well, let me think. It wasn't quite dark yet. I'd guess around 8:00 p.m."

"You seem like the kind of guy who watches over his neighbors," said Winston.

"What do you mean by that? You saying I'm a snoop?"

"No, not at all. You spotted us. Have you noticed anything different about them the past few days, the way they act, the hours they keep?"

"Well, they come and go a lot. Guess that's not new. Seems like she's been kind of nervous the past few weeks."

"Nervous? Nervous how, sir?" asked Jacobson.

"Whenever she's coming or going, I see her looking all around. If a car goes by, she's taking a good, hard look at who's driving. It's like she doesn't want to get surprised or something. I don't know, just seems out of sorts for her."

"Fascinating Mister ... ."

"Tucker, Norvin Tucker."

"Mr. Tucker, have you noticed any strangers coming over or anything else out of the ordinary?

"I know her husband has been coming and going a lot in the evenings. Not sure why. Sometimes she's with him, but usually not. Aside from that, no sir, I haven't."

"We thank you for your time. Here's my card. When they come back home or if you see or remember anything unusual, I'd appreciate a phone call."

"Certainly. Glad to help. You fellas have a good day."

As the detectives walked away, Winston said to his partner, "Heading south, huh? South as in south to New Mexico and Dale Bowers?"

"God, I hope not, but the court granted him permission to live there with his parents."

"We've got to let the guy know he may have a visitor."

"Yeah, we do. I'll give the Edgestone, New Mexico police a call and have them visit Mr. Bowers. We have to give him a warning, the scum. I just hope we're wrong about this."

"The husband being out in the evenings? The night classes? That would be my guess, since she's not always with him. I'll make a note to follow up with them. Just how much is he teaching?"

Jacobson looked around the well-kept neighborhood; trash cans lining the street for the next day's pickup. "I don't know what's going on."

<hr>

August 12, 1984, Sunday afternoon, 2:21

Jacobson hung up the phone and looked at his partner.

"I take it Edgestone PD knows about the Bowers family?" asked Winston.

"Seems like they get called out there quite a bit. Alcohol induced domestic stuff. Usually mom versus dad, but sometimes the neighbors get involved. They have not seen Dale yet. However, the Edgestone Police Department consists of the guy I just talked to and three other officers. Granted, the town only has about 1,200 people, but that stretches them pretty thin. Bottom line, they'll notify Dale when they can and keep an eye out for the Carlsons."

"That's about all we can do. I'll give the Carlsons a call later this evening, just to see if they're home. Looking at the map, it's a bit of a drive to Edgestone."

"How far?"

"Best guess, it's a twelve hour drive so you don't just hop over there and back."

The Killer - Pure Revenge

August 18,1984, Saturday afternoon, 11:45

SUNLIGHT PEEKED THROUGH A gap in the heavy brown drapes, standard issue for roadside motels.

The TV provided background noise; *Gosh, ninety-eight degrees today. Not going to be fun for the New Mexico State football squad. They're still doing two-a-days. Expectations are high under second-year coach Fred Zechman, who last year ...*

The woman snapped off the TV. "You getting hungry?" she asked.

"I'm starving," replied the man as he buttoned up his shirt.

"Let's find a burger somewhere close. I looked at a city map they had posted in the office. Looks like his place is northwest of town. Not too far from here."

"Good, I'm hoping we can find the guy soon. I just want this done," he said.

"I know, me too."

"I'll load the car up."

They found a tiny cafe just two blocks from the motel.

"You know what's best about small towns? Corporate America hasn't sunk its talons in yet. McDonald's hasn't found Edgestone, New Mexico and we get the benefits," she said, waving her hand as if to present the cafe to him.

"True, this is a damn good burger."

"It's not just the food. It's the people. They're memorable to me. Like our waitress, snapping her gum the entire time she's taking our order, calling us sugar, and honey, and cutie. I think they care more about people than those shiny corporate places."

"That is a double-edged sword."

"How so?"

"This is memorable to you, right?"

"Sure is, I love it!"

"Who's saying we're not memorable to them?"

"Are you worried about any questions after we're done here? You barely look like yourself right now. You never wear a trucker hat and you've got that scraggly beard that can be shaved off. This isn't how my hair normally looks. I think we've got that covered. Oh, we should do the fake name game with the waitress!"

"Same names as always?"

"No, no. Surprise me."

"Can I take your plate, honey?" asked the waitress. The man avoided eye contact with his partner.

"Yes, please and thank you," he said with a laugh.

"Now what's so funny, sugar?"

"Oh, my wife and I were just talking about how friendly everyone is here. Like how you call me honey or sugar, instead of my name."

"Well, that's because I don't know your name, darling," said the waitress.

"My name is Nathaniel. This is my wife, Sophia."

"I love that name, Sophia. It's so pretty. I've got an uncle we call Nate. He might be a Nathanial. You ever go by Nate?"

"My brothers call me Nate, sure."

The shopkeeper bell above the door rang out. The women looked towards the door and saw the police officer enter.

"Hey, Harry, sit anywhere," she turned and looked at the couple and finished her sentence, "honey."

They laughed as the waitress turned to tend to the new guest.

"Coffee, Harry?" she asked.

"You know it Carol."

"We need to be cool. Don't look. But a cop just walked in, Nathaniel. Where'd that name come from? And Sophia?" she asked.

"Nathaniel Hawthorne and his wife Sophia," he said.

"Very nice, Nate."

"Sophia was a painter. Have you ever painted?"

"My bedroom. Once. I'm not allowed to paint again!"

"Good to know. You ready to move on?"

"I am."

"Carol, check please," he called out.

"Be right there, Nate."

"Nate!" she said, giggling.

------◇------

August 18,1984, Saturday afternoon, 1:09

The couple took off down the road. The sun, looming high in the cloudless sky, was baking the scrub land on either side of the highway.

Three miles from the cafe, she saw the turnoff they needed. "There, turn right on that gravel road." She studied the map. "It should veer to the right and then turn straight north." They slowly rumbled along the washboard road for a few minutes in silence.

"Look for a house with a mobile home set back a few hundred feet. He's supposed to live in that mobile home," she said.

"I'm not seeing a thing, are you?" he asked.

"Not a damn thing."

The car bounced its way across the rough road, up and over a rise. And there it was. They saw it at the same time. They looked at each other and smiled.

"I'll make a pass, drive a couple miles down the road, and turn around. Should give us a feel for the land," he said.

"Good idea. We've got to find out if anyone else is home. I hope not. We won't involve anybody else."

"A pity we have a job here. I wouldn't mind being a tourist. Beautiful country out here, don't you think?" he asked.

"I love it. You see all of this brown, sun-baked dirt. It seems lifeless, and then, boom! There's a wonderful rock formation that shoots up a hundred feet in the air. Right in front of you! Those rocks make the brown tolerable."

"I'd say the brown make the rocks even more wonderful."

"You're right. They do. Only a Nathaniel would see through that."

"Only a Sophia would appreciate that."

He slammed on the brakes, forcing the car to fishtail on the rough road. The car came to a stop. The dust swirled past them before drifting away.

"Look!" he said. "There's a guy walking along the road and it sure looks like ... ."

"Dale Fucking Bowers! He's going to walk right to us!"

The man took his foot off the brake and crept along the road, towards their target.

Dale saw the car. Instinctively, he knew why they were here. The Edgestone police had paid him a visit earlier in the week and warned him. He looked back down the road. Nothing. The other way, nothing. Except the car he saw skid to a stop.

"He knows it's us. See him looking around?" he asked.

"Here I am, all alone out in the wild. And now they're moving this way. Shit!" said Dale.

He looked around again. He stood next to an eight-foot wall of rock carved out of the terrain to form the gravel road. To his left was a hundred yards of scrub land, sandy and rocky with cane cholla dotting the landscape. He knew there was an ancient gorge nearby. It dropped down more than one hundred feet. None of his options gave him confidence, but he decided to use the gorge to get away from them.

"Dammit, he's going to walk across that open space. Go after him!" yelled the woman.

The car sped forward, kicking up dust and dirt as it accelerated down the road. Bowers was halfway to the gorge before they were parallel to him and pulled the car off the road.

The man cupped his hands to form a megaphone. "Dale, stop right there. We only want to talk!"

"Talk my ass! Get away from me!"

The pair took off running, guns drawn. Dale saw this and turned to run. He didn't see the cane cholla cactus in time and brushed the front of his left shoulder against it. Several barbs from the plant embedded deep in his skin. He instinctively grabbed at the injury with his right hand but lost his balance, falling against the rocky and sandy ground. He looked toward his pursuers, who were now bearing down on him.

He screamed once again as he forced himself to his feet and staggered next to the gorge's edge. He peered over the precipice.

"Stop right there, Dale!" yelled the man.

Without saying a word, Dale hopped over the edge, falling five feet before planting his boots firmly on the dusty edge. A natural path lay at his feet. He hoped he would not run out of room. Keeping his back to the wall would provide him with cover from gunfire. He could hear them calling out his name, but he kept quiet as he crept along the wall.

Dale slowly scooted another twenty feet. As he went around a small bend, the trail abruptly ended. The wall loomed twenty feet above him, nearly vertical. The tip of his boots hung over the lip of the path, knocking gravel off the side, falling fifty feet into a group of jagged, rocky outcrops.

"Dale, we see you, man. It's over. Why don't you climb up here so we can talk?" said the man.

"You want more than talk. The fucking cops told me what you did to JB and Big Man."

"Then you know we are serious. You also know we aren't going any-where."

Dale looked up the steep wall. He could see the couple peering down at him, each still holding a gun. He knew he was trapped. He turned and looked at the jagged rocks looming far beneath his feet. The cactus spines stuck in his shoulder were like razors anytime he moved.

"Dale, I just want to hear you say you're sorry," she said.

"I'm not sorry for shit, lady. This is my life. But you snotty little rich kids don't get it. You have no idea what it's like to be me."

"We're not those rich kids you think we are. Let's talk about that, Dale," she said.

"I'm done talking. Hell, you just want to shoot me down. I'm not a damn dog and I'm not an idiot. I've got one more thing to steal from you. My life! See you in hell."

With that, Dale used all his remaining energy to push himself off the edge. He fell without making a noise. He could see the couple reach out towards him, but did not hear their voices before he slammed into the rocks. His left shoulder blade squarely hit a small rock formation, causing numerous fractures. The impact twirled him sideways, spinning around twice before the side of his head crashed into a jagged boulder, splitting his skull open. The impact killed him instantly. His lifeless body dropped a few feet to another small ledge, his legs dangling and swaying over the edge. His upper body was lying along the rock's edge. Gravity took over and his body slid slowly off the ledge and dropped the final ten feet, crumpled in a lifeless heap.

"Oh my god!" said the man.

"He's dead, right?" she asked.

"There's no way he survived that."

"What do we do now? Should we leave him here?

"Damn right we're going to leave him. Let him rot. We need to leave. Now."

They ran up the slight grade and hopped in the car.

"I can't believe he did that! Why did he do that?" she asked.

"He saved us three bullets," he said as the car bounced along the road, headed towards home.

They drove on until dusk started to settle across the landscape. Exhausted, they pulled into a motel in another small town. They were halfway home.

In The End There Is A Beginning

August 19, 1984, Sunday morning, 8:27

SHE ROLLED OVER IN bed, facing him while he slept. He was in a deep sleep. Peaceful for the first time in months. She reached out her soft hand and brushed his clean-shaven chin. "I love you so much."

He stretched out his legs and smacked his lips. Sensing her gaze upon him, he opened a sleepy eye. The early morning sun cast through the thin, white curtains of the motel room, framing her face in a soft light. He spoke *good morning* through a long yawn so it came out, *Gaaamarneen*. She laughed, leaned over, and kissed him on the mouth, "Hi you sweet man!"

Rubbing his eyes into focus, he looked at her. "What are those beautiful eyes hiding?"

"I'm just thinking about how it's over. It's been quite a journey."

"We've still got six hours of driving before we get home, so it's *almost* over," he said to her with a laugh.

"You know what I mean. We got the justice he deserved."

"We did Anthony proud," he said.

"Listen, I know some people back home. They went through a similar experience. The punishment did not fit the crime. The system failed them too. They're beside themselves and don't know where to turn."

"What happened?" he asked.

"Some low-life raped and murdered their daughter, just a terrible crime. The guy was released after six and a half of a fifty-year sentence. He's on the street already and is still in the state. What do you think about getting them some justice? Either that or I might as well toss this red wig."

"I don't know, I kind of like it," he said to her with a smile.

They heard two car doors slam somewhere outside and not too far from their window. He rose from the bed and pushed a corner of the dusty motel curtain to one side.

"What is it?" she asked, holding her breath.

"Hmmm, I don't see a thing. Want me to go grab some coffee?"

Exhaling, she said, "No, I just want to go home."

"Let's pack up. I'm ready to leave," he said.

A loud banging on the door caused them both to jump.

A male voice yelled, "Open up!"

There was more pounding on the door. "Police!"

Tommy looked at Rita. She reached for her gun. He grabbed his, too.

Acknowledgements

Creating this book required several steps: researching, planning, writing, and rewriting. It took the work and patience of several people to get this idea of mine into your hands. At the top of the list, I must thank my beautiful wife, Constance. She encouraged me every step of the way and quietly dealt with countless nights waking up and finding me staring into my computer screen, trying to resolve a scene or reading the Chicago Manual of Style as I tried to figure out proper English. She was also one of my beta readers and provided her input as I designed the cover. She wears many hats, but I am most grateful for her love and companionship on this journey we share throughout life.

Also, many thanks to my aunt, Lois Johnson. Lois did extensive editing of the first two iterations of this novel, running out of sticky notes in the process! I think she's read the novel almost as much as I have. Her hard work is noted and her efforts made this work much, much better. My cousin, Pam Larson, also did a read-through and offered some valuable input on phrasing and she found some obscure errors. She, too, helped make this work better than it should have been.

I am a relative newcomer to guns and to that point, I have some friends I'd like to recognize here. Randy and Deb Cameron were very generous with their time, reading the manuscript, and answering firearms questions. Randy also provided the three .45 caliber bullets on the cover. The staff at *my* range, Crossroads Shooting Sports in Johnston, Iowa, friendly as ever, also answered my general gun questions, including, "How loud is a .45 when it is fired inside of a car?" The obvious answer? Deafening.

I have been fortunate to receive an abundance of positive encouragement and assistance with this project. That said, any errors that remain are mine, and mine alone.

Read a book, then read another one...

About The Author

Born in Des Moines, Iowa, Jeff spent his formative years chasing bugs, playing sports and riding his bike around the neighborhood. Once forced to grow up, he spent 42 years in the information technology field, before retiring in 2022.

His retirement freed up time to pursue writing, an avocation that has always interested him. Besides this novel, his first, he has had flash fiction published and dabbles in poetry. He is currently working on an encyclopedia of minor league baseball in Des Moines, a new detective series, as well as a work of dystopian fiction.

When not busy writing, he also enjoys bringing new life to old pieces of furniture, target shooting, and spending time with his German Shepherd Dogs, Jax, and Jaycie.

We're being reminded to mention the love of his life, Constance. So there.

www.ingramcontent.com/pod-product-compliance
Lightning Source LLC
Chambersburg PA
CBHW020131310726
48970CB00006B/1815